W9-BZO-968

# THE CELEBRATION

## IVAN ÂNGELO

Translated by Thomas Colchie

Dalkey Archive Press

*For my wife*
*Maria Angela*

Copyright © 1976 by Ivan Ângelo
English translation copyright © 1982 by Thomas Colchie

First Dalkey Archive edition, 2003
All rights reserved

Library of Congress Cataloging-in-Publication Data

Ângelo, Ivan, 1936–
   [Festa. English]
   The Celebration / Ivan Ângelo ; translated by Thomas Colchie.
     p. cm.
   ISBN 1-56478-290-5 (pbk. : alk. paper)
   I. Colchie, Thomas. II. Title.

PQ9698.1.N474F413 2003
869.3—dc21

2002041569

Partially funded by a grant from the Illinois Arts Council, a state agency.

Dalkey Archive Press books are published by the Center for Book Culture, a nonprofit organization.

www.centerforbookculture.org

Printed on permanent/durable acid-free paper and bound in the United States of America.

The appellation of cruel, however, should not matter to a prince striving to maintain the unity and faith of his subjects, because with rare exceptions it is he who is the more compassionate than those who for the sake of greater clemency allow disorders to occur, from which may arise assassinations and plunder.

—MACHIAVELLI, *The Prince*

I have tried everything. I have prohibited the sale of crystals and ouija-boards; I have slapped a heavy tax on playing cards; the courts are empowered to sentence alchemists to hard labour in the mines; it is a statutory offence to turn tables or feel bumps. But nothing is really effective. How can I expect the masses to be sensible when, for instance, to my certain knowledge, the captain of my own guard wears an amulet against the Evil Eye, and the richest merchant in the city consults a medium over every important transaction.

—W. H. AUDEN, "Herod"

The subject is time, present time, present life, present man.

—CARLOS DRUMMOND DE ANDRADE, "Hand in Hand"

This is the voice that's left me.
This is my head that's pounding.
This is the final drop, you see.
To end the celebration.

—CHICO BUARQUE DE HOLANDA, "Drop of Water"

# Table of Contents

# A SHORT
# DOCUMENTARY

Witnesses who happened to be at Plaza Station shortly after midnight this morning reported seeing a Northeasterner with dark complexion and about fifty years of age boarding the wooden train that was to carry him and some eight hundred other drought victims back to the Northeast. Several passersby stood to watch the railway guards, soldiers, and detectives forcibly, but not violently, herding the refugees into the waiting railroad cars. Witnesses asserted that roughly forty minutes later the entire eight hundred were under guard aboard the train, which awaited the order to leave the station.

Anyone not directly implicated in the matter would have been hard pressed to explain how a fire could break out in four cars at the same time, and could only have observed that the flames first erupted on the outside of the cars, burning intensely—certainly no accident.

The turmoil began at 1:45 A.M. with shouts of a fire. The refugees swarmed out of the burning cars in a panic, dragging the eldest, carrying children, crying for safety. The police, caught off guard, had no idea whether to apprehend the fleeing Northeasterners or attempt to put out the fire. Greatly outnumbered, they turned to both tasks at once, shouting, bumping into one another, pushing and clubbing their way through the general chaos. A riot truck that had been sent there to quell any disturbance, should that have been necessary, turned its hose instead upon the flames that were rapidly consuming the wooden freight cars. Police on horseback attempted to pursue isolated groups that were dispersing from the crowd.

Witnesses across the way at the Hotel Itatiaia reported suddenly noticing a highly organized group advancing from the station in the form of a wedge. At the front of the triangle was the fifty-year-old Northeasterner, identified later as Marcionílio de Mattos, together with the reporter Samuel Aparecido Fereszin, attached to a morning daily here in the capital. The elderly, together with the women and children, were all marching at the center of the triangle, thus protected on three flanks by the men of the group: some armed with clubs, some with fishing knives. De Mattos himself carried a machete; the vast majority however were without weapons of any kind.

3

Police who spotted the organized group in the midst of the general disorder tried to regroup in order to prevent the maneuver; but the surprise of the attack favored the Northeasterners, since the soldiers could only muster eight to ten of their number quickly enough to meet them. Nevertheless, they boldly attempted to halt the march (the refugees kept advancing): first with threats of force (the refugees kept advancing), then with warning shots (the refugees kept advancing), lastly by firing point blank and wielding truncheons until they were swallowed up by the multitude, beaten, trampled.

The Northeasterners continued to stream out of the station, dispersing into small bands of five or six persons on street corners. By the time police reinforcements were able to catch up with them, only a handful could still be found of the more than three hundred refugees that had formed the wedge—a dozen or so of the eldest, along with a few women, whom de Mattos was trying to lead away with him. The journalist Samuel Aparecido Fereszin was no longer on the scene.

The fire raged until four in the morning.

*(Excerpt of a story suppressed by* A Tarde *from its coverage of events at Plaza Station, in the March 31, 1970 edition of the paper, at the request of federal officials, who alleged reasons of national security.)*


## FLASHBACK

### (Before the birth of de Mattos)

I am convinced—absolutely convinced—that without the utilization of slave labor these vast sugarcane plantations under a single ownership cannot be adequately cultivated—absolutely convinced that freed labor can never be adapted to the present system of agricultural production. . . . However, the division of property into small lots owned by freed laborers could, in my opinion, overthrow slave labor and its capital, here in the province of Bahia, and erect upon the remains of an ignominious and deplorable black feudalism a new life of free villages and small, independent colonies.

*(Robert Avé-Lallemant, a German doctor, in* Travels throughout the North of Brazil in the Year of 1859.)

Inside the boundaries of properties of the great landowners there are no political rights, because freedom of opinion is nonexistent. For the peasants, the landowners *are* the police, the courts, the government itself—in a word, everything. And apart from whatever right or possibility they might have to leave the land, the lot of these unfortunates in no way differs from that of serfs in the Middle Ages.

(*An anonymous collaborator in the* Diário de Pernambuco, *a newspaper of the mid-nineteenth century.*)

The composition of our territorial properties, amassed in the hands of the privileged few to form vast landed estates, only infrequently permits ownership and dominion—of an occasional few feet of land—by the poor. As a rule, the poor are confined to being tenant farmers, domestic servants, ranch hands, and so forth. And their lot is more or less equivalent to that of the ancient serfs of the glebe.

(*Domingos Velho Cavalcânti de Albuquerque, president of Pernambuco in the 1870s, cited by Paulo Cavalcânti in* Eça de Queiroz: Agitator in Brazil.)

There has appeared in the northern backlands an individual who goes by the name of Antônio Conselheiro, and who exerts a great influence over the minds of the lower classes, making use of his mysterious trappings and ascetic habits to impose upon their ignorance and simplicity. He lets his beard and hair grow long, wears a cotton tunic, and eats sparingly, being almost a mummy in aspect. Accompanied by a couple of women followers, he lives by reciting beads and litanies, by preaching, and by giving counsel to the multitudes that come to hear him when the local church authorities permit it. Appealing to their religious sentiments, he draws them after him in throngs and moves them at his will. He gives evidence of being an intelligent man, but an uncultivated one.

(*Laemmert Almanac from 1877, published in Rio de Janeiro some twenty years before the Canudos campaign.*)

What calamity, my God, what barbarity in those backlands!
(*Teodoro Sampaio in* The São Francisco River and the Diamantina Plateau, *an account of his journey to the Northeast in 1879.*)

. . . backlanders, fanatical in their devotion, who betook themselves to him out of a belief in the communism so forcefully espoused by this

Conselheiro. . . . The number of estates seized by the Conselheirists throughout the region has risen to sixty.

(*Dispatch from Salvador, Bahia, published in the January 30, 1897 edition of* O País, *a Rio de Janeiro paper which described as its source "a respectable gentleman returning from the region of Canudos."*)

Canudos did not surrender. The only case of its kind in history, it held out to the last man. Conquered inch by inch, in the literal meaning of the words, it fell on October 5, 1897, toward dusk—when its last defenders fell, dying, every man of them. There were only four of them left: an old man, two other full-grown men, and a child, facing a furiously raging army of five thousand soldiers.

(*Euclides da Cunha in* Rebellion in the Backlands, *where he describes the massacre of Antônio Conselheiro's army of the poor, by the fourth government expedition sent against them in the Canudos campaign.*)

In 1900, more than forty thousand drought victims abandon the state of Ceará. Again, in 1915, of the roughly forty thousand more refugees embarking from the port of Fortaleza, only about eighty-five hundred actually head south, while the remaining thirty thousand or so choose the traditional route . . . farther northward.

(*Rui Facó,* Outlaws and Fanatics.)

And, in 1917, Virgulino Lampião joined the guerrilla movement to become, within a short time, the terror of the backlands.

(*Optato Gueiros*, Lampião—Memoirs of a Former Commandant in the Special Forces.)

## END OF FLASHBACK

This is to certify that on fol. 43, vol. 2, in the Official Registry of Births, the name has been registered of one Marcionílio de Mattos, born 6:00 A.M. on the ninth day of August, 1917, in the district of Traíras, of the present municipality, at the home of his parents on Rua das Secas, of masculine sex, of mulatto race, the legitimate son of Divino de Mattos and Maria Leontina Albuquerque de Mattos, having unknown paternal grandparents and Tenório Albuquerque de Mattos and Antoninha Leontina de Mattos as maternal grandparents.

So sworn by the father of the same.
Almas, September 19, 1917.

Francisco Gudin Velho, presiding civil registrar
(*Birth certificate recovered by police, at Plaza Station in the city of Belo Horizonte, shortly after events of the night of March 30, 1970, with the following phrase penciled in on the margin beside the registry date in a handwriting police ascertained was that of de Mattos himself: "Year Lampião become outlaw."*)

. . . that his father Divino de Mattos worked as a hired gun for Colonel Horácio Mattos, strongman of the republic from the backlands of Bahia and much respected by Lampião; that the father also took part in the war of the colonels against the Prestes Column in such places as Olho d'Agua, Riacho d'Areia, Roça de Dentro, Maxixe, and Pedrinhas; that the father always cursed the Prestes rebels because they set fire to Roça de Dentro, the county seat, after capturing same; that he himself was no admirer of Prestes either, a man who could put a torch to the whole city that way; that ever since he was knee-high the man he most admired was a gunslinger who rode at the head of Colonel Horácio's men, one João Duque by name; that this same João Duque fought with an ax against ten (10) rebels from the Prestes Column, all armed with rifles; that he had no idea if Prestes was already a communist in those days, but knew for damn sure he was one now; that precisely because Prestes is a communist, he (the deponent) don't like the communists; that he was nine (9) years old when Roça de Dentro was burned to the ground. . . .

(*From testimony by the refugee Marcionílio de Mattos, taken on April 1, 1970, at the headquarters of the Department of Political and Social Order [DOPS] in the city of Belo Horizonte, State of Minas Gerais, subsequent to the grave disturbances touched off at Plaza Station on the night of March 30 and continuing into the morning of March 31, 1970.*)

A solitary figure wielding an ax, he rushed headlong against the entire troop now advancing toward the trench, mercilessly endangering himself in a gesture of heroic proportion.

Then, with both hands, the outlaw swung that terrible ax above his head and hurled it violently at our soldiers, in a final effort of defiance.

The formidable missile whirled through the air, only to fall vainly to earth, a few feet from our lines, without achieving its purpose.

Another shot rang out and the hero tumbled, like some titan struck by a lightning bolt, stone-dead upon the ground.

*(Lourenço Moreira Lima, secretary to the Prestes Column, in* The Prestes Column: Marches and Combats, *from a section narrating the campaign of the rebels at Roça de Dentro, in the interior of the state of Bahia.)*

No episode looms larger in the mythology of modern Brazil than the march of the Prestes Column. A military, revolutionary movement was defeated in the civilized centers of Brazil in 1924, thus launching fifteen hundred rebel soldiers, like Aeneas's Trojans, across the frontiers of barbarism on a mission to reconstitute the nation. For more than two years they wandered over 25,000 kilometers, from the pampas of southern Brazil, through the forests of the Paraná valley, back and forth across the arid interior of the Northeast and the savannas of central Brazil, through the swamps of Mato Grosso to the borders of Bolivia and Paraguay. Resisted almost everywhere by bandits, hired gunmen, and all the forces the warlords of a benighted land could muster, they were forced by cruel necessity to despoil the already impoverished, to burn villages, and to cut the throat of at least one priest.

*(Neill Macaulay,* The Prestes Column: Revolution in Brazil.)

So I asked him why on earth he didn't fire at the rebels.

"Well, son," he answered, "you got to understand, it's a way of life. If I was to go and shoot at every monkey I come across, I'd a been six feet under by now, wouldn't I."

*(Virgulino Lampião, explaining to a scout named Miguel Francelino that he had refrained from attacking the Prestes Column because, to him, outlawing was "a way of life." Lampião had actually been hired by Floro Bartolomeu, a political boss, and Father Cícero Romão, his spiritual partner, to rid the backlands of the Column. For this purpose he received weapons, money, and a commission in the army reserve. Related by Optato Gueiros in* Lampião— Memoirs of a Former Commandant in the Special Forces.)

. . . that the family moved to the state of Alagoas, the result of a falling-out between his father and Colonel Horácio Mattos; that, in Alagoas, they started working for a Colonel Joaquim Resende, who owned the Pão de Açúcar Ranch; that this colonel was also close friends with the outlaw, Lampião; that, naturally, Lampião came by the ranch every so often; that his (the deponent's) friendship with the outlaw (Lampião) began around that time; that, to his way of thinking, Lampião wasn't just a bandit but a brave man as well, who set out to change the backlands; that he, the deponent Marcionílio de Mattos, was around fifteen (15) at the time and damn well old enough to know who Lampião was; that, in fact, if he had to choose between a Prestes and a Lampião, he'd choose Lampião any day, because at least Lampião wanted to fix the backlands, not go into politics; that he understood fixing the backlands to mean putting a stop to the power of the colonels and giving land to the poor, work to the poor, and justice to the poor . . .

*(From testimony given by Marcionílio de Mattos on April 1, 1970, while in the custody of the DOPS at Belo Horizonte, the capital of Minas Gerais, concerning disturbances in which four people died at Plaza Station.)*

More than a way of life, outlawing is a method of survival that tends to proliferate throughout the Northeast during the great droughts. During such periods small bands are formed—of generally three to ten men at most—the majority of which disappear once the disastrous climatic condition has passed.

*(Rui Facó, Outlaws and Fanatics.)*

. . . justice to the poor; that he understands justice to mean not having a person die of starvation, not having to sell your daughter, seeing to it that the rich are arrested as well as the poor for a crime, actually getting the help the government sends you during a drought instead of having it wind up in the pockets of thieving politicians; that if he (the deponent) had Lampião's savvy and half the guts of a João Duque he'd go and do exactly that: Give justice, land, and work to the poor; that this is what he was trying to do, very peaceably, bringing these poverty stricken people down here from the North; that it wasn't his fault if the peaceable got to be unpeaceable; that they hadn't come armed or looking for trouble; that yes, he had a fishing knife—what the hell, everybody carried a fishing knife, it's like having a bat or a handkerchief; that it was ridiculous to think they'd purposely picked the night before the anniversary of the revolution to arrive in Belo Horizonte; that they were fleeing from a damn drought; that it took them over twenty (20) days to get here, not to mention a lot of strain and heartache to bother about looking at some date on a calendar; that no, he had no previous connection with the student Carlos Bicalho, from the College of Economics and Social Science;

that he had no connection with the journalist Samuel Aparecido Fereszin either; that he couldn't say if the two . . .

(*From testimony by Marcionílio de Mattos, while at the DOPS in Belo Horizonte, during the inquiry regarding an incident at Plaza Station in which 4 persons died, 216 were arrested, and 17 were admitted to a nearby first aid station for treatment of flesh wounds, on the eve of the sixth anniversary of the so-called revolution which brought the military to power in 1964.*)

As I watched the white dove
Fly from the drought,
Though my heart was yours,
I fled to the South.

And now, miles away,
Feeling sad and alone,
I wait for the rains
To take me back home.

When the green of your eyes
Spreads over the land,
Then I swear, my Rosinha,
I'll find you again.

(*Luis Gonzaga and Humberto Teixeira,* White Dove, *a popular North-eastern ballad of 1952.*)

At present, news continues to arrive concerning the invasion of many parts of the interior by waves of beggars—sacks on their shoulders—pleading for food. For the moment, at least, these migrations are peaceful, but it will not be long before the communists begin to take advantage of the situation, to incite the people to violence.

(*Juvenal Lamartine, ex-governor of the state of Rio Grande do Norte, in a letter to the editor published in the* Tribuna da Imprensa, *Rio de Janeiro, March 12, 1953.*)

Of the three thousand peasants who invaded and sacked the marketplace at Arapiraca, a good two-thirds of them were "drought people" and virtually starving. The rest simply took advantage of the ensuing chaos, fomented by agitators and subversives hoping to utilize the worst phases of the drought in order to promote civil disturbance and acts of rebellion.

These refugees from the backlands, as far as police in Alagoas have been able to ascertain, were being led by a certain Marcionílio de Mattos, a former hired gunman from the Pão de Açúcar Ranch, owned by Colonel Joaquim Resende. De Mattos turns out to also be a fugitive, wanted for the murder of an overseer at the mentioned ranch, and has already been linked to remnants of the outlaw gangs once prevalent in the late 1930s. It was he who actually fomented the recent disorders and personally led the invasion of the marketplace. He is currently being held, under heavy guard, at the criminal penitentiary in Arapiraca.

(*From the March 15, 1958 edition of* O Palmeirense, *a daily published in Palmeira dos Indios, state of Alagoas.*)

### The Drought Victim

. . . wherever we traveled we found him starving, ragged, sad-eyed, and skeletal, in search of help that is not forthcoming. Already without hope, though his only ambition be the smallest provision of manioc flour, to ease the hunger which day by day devours his system, and a minimal amount of commiseration, due even the lowest of humans. . . . Here in Brazil, where we seem quite proud of ourselves, singing out with paeans of self-praise, expecting to be numbered among the great concert of nations, by virtue of such an elevated level of civilization—here, in Brazil among our population at this very moment, it is estimated that more than two million people live in the most abject state of malnutrition and poverty possible to human beings. . . . And still, the misery continues, a people persistently exploited by their fellow beings, with money being endlessly squandered through the negligence and/or complicity of the authorities. Meanwhile the drought itself is only remembered as a problem when its evils are omnipresent.

(*Colonel Orlando Gomes Ramagem, subordinate chief of staff to the armed forces of the republic and personal observer for President Juscelino Kubitschek of the drought of 1958. His report, however, was suppressed by the Kubitschek government and only made public by the following administration—that of Jânio Quadros—in 1961.*)

. . . that no, he had no previous connection with the student Carlos Bicalho, from the College of Economics and Social Science; that he had no connection with the journalist Samuel Aparecido Fereszin either; that he couldn't say if the two of them knew each other; that no, it was not true that he'd brought the refugees south with him at the express orders of either of the above; that neither had he received money from anyone for such a purpose . . .

*(From testimony by Marcionílio de Mattos, following the dramatic events at Plaza Station in Belo Horizonte where police seized 183 fishing knives, 31 penknives, 2 pistols, 5 clubs, and a military saber, all in the possession of the insurgents.)*

The first waves of refugees have already reached the major Northeastern capitals, with the same repetition of dismal facts that characterize every drought. On Sunday at the marketplace in João Pessoa a woman offered her children to anyone who would take them.

*(The newspaper* O Estado de São Paulo *on March 25, 1958.)*

All classes have an organization in this country—with the exception of the peasants. The laborer has his union; the student, his federation; the merchant, journalist, or civil servant each has his own association; the officer and industrialist have their clubs. Only the peasant still lacks a class organization capable of defending his interests. And this, his just yearning for representation, has continually been thwarted by violence. It is, quite simply, a crime to speak of a league for peasants.

*(Congressman Francisco Julião, as quoted by* O Estado de São Paulo, *December 15, 1959.)*

### Freedom for Marcionílio!

*People of the Northeast:*

For two years the government of the refinery bosses and the cattle barons has held our brother, the peasant leader Marcionílio de Mattos, imprisoned without a trial.

This man, whom the landowning press has portrayed as a bandit and assassin, is in fact an authentic revolutionary from out of the Northeast.

Yes, he was an outlaw, but that was at a time when to be an outlaw was the only means of survival in the drought-beleaguered lands of the Alagoan interior. And as an outlaw, he never took from the poor, but rather from those who had much to be taken.

The landowner-controlled press accuses him of murdering the overseer at a ranch whose owner had given him shelter. But the fact is that he struck in the legitimate defense of his honor and was subsequently forced to flee so as not to fall into the hands of a jury already sold to Colonel Joaquim Rezende. His case is not the first of its kind here in the backlands, nor will it be the last.

His other crime? Leading those victims of the drought—and of landed aristocracies—out of the state of destitution to which they were reduced; bringing them to Arapiraca, where he tried every means of obtaining assistance from the government; and only as a last resort, so as to be able to feed the twelve hundred souls for whom he felt himself personally responsible, ordering the assault on the central market in Arapiraca during which one shopkeeper was, unfortunately, killed.

This is the man the government of Alagoas holds a prisoner in Arapiraca. What is his crime? Trying to help the poor!

*People of the Northeast:*

Enough waiting for justice! March on the penitentiary at Arapiraca, on the first of February, and demand:

**Freedom for Marcionílio!**

— Peasant League of Southern Alagoas

(*Leaflet distributed throughout the principal cities of southern Alagoas, during the month of January 1960.*)

Commissioner Humberto Levita, of the DOPS in Belo Horizonte, estimates the full investigation into the disturbances that took place at Plaza Station on the thirty-first of last month will require another three months to complete. "Any disclosure prior to this," he stated, "would only prove premature." He also noted that some sixty-three depositions had already been obtained, including testimony from numerous refugees, from various relatives of the deceased parties, from those arrested, from a number of witnesses, from local police on the scene, and from at least two ministers of state.

The most serious problem confronting authorities at the moment is what to do about the more than four hundred refugees who were the source of the disturbances. About one hundred sixty of those detained on the morning of March 31 are said to be "drought people," many of them heads of families. Their dependents, naturally, have refused to return to the Northeast without them, while they themselves are prohibited from attempting to leave so long as the investigation is still in progress. As a consequence, over four hundred migrants—aside from an unspecified number who managed to escape on the night of the revolt—are to be seen wandering about the city, from house to house, begging for food. It is estimated that the number of new indigents thus entering the city has climbed to well above the eight hundred mark.

"What authorities tried to avoid here, on the morning of the thirty-first, has mushroomed into a far worse problem, and as a direct result of actions undertaken by the very same authorities. The ironies of fate," commented Commissioner Levita.

(*The newspaper* O Estado de Minas Gerais *on April 12, 1970.*)

Seventh day: Fifteen hundred armed peasants seize and occupy the Coqueiro Refinery, located in Vitória de Santo Antão and owned by Constâncio Maranhão. They commandeer supplies, kill oxen, and arm themselves with rifles. . . . The usurpers are divided into well-organized groups as they set up defenses, organize forays, and utilize tactics of guerrilla warfare.

(*From a report by the Sugar Refineries Association of the State of Pernambuco, presented to President João Goulart on October 22, 1963, and concerning the Peasant Leagues and their activities in the North.*)

. . . that neither had he received money from anyone for such a purpose; that he'd always tried to help those who suffered in times of drought because it's a terrible disgrace; that it's true they would take food if there was no money to buy any; that no, this was the first time he'd ever been south; that yes, he did belong to the Peasant League up in Pernambuco; that he'd left Alagoas back in 1960, after they got him out of the penitentiary at Arapiraca in Alagoas, before his trial; that he'd been forcibly set loose by the Peasant League—the one in Alagoas—so he had to flee to Pernambuco; that in 1963, the case against him was dropped just the same, for lack of any evidence to support his involvement in the death of a shopkeeper from Arapiraca during the invasion of the marketplace by refugees from the drought; that back in that same year, 1960, he'd returned to Alagoas, to the city of Pombal, to try to find his wife and daughter; that he found her all right (the wife), but living with another man, because she figured he (the deponent) was dead; that he returned by himself to Pernambuco without the wife or the daughter; that no, he had no idea where they were now; that once back in Pernambuco he started working in the cane fields; that no, he didn't personally know Congressman Francisco Julião, the founder of the Peasant Leagues; that this Julião was a communist and a politician; that from

1960 to 1964, yes he (the deponent) could find work, yes even during the droughts, because of the power of some of the leagues; that he (the deponent) took part in the seizure of the sugar refineries while up in Pernambuco; that he had no idea if this Julião, the congressman, was exploiting the ignorance of the masses; that he (the deponent) was, that's right, arrested along with other workers, interrogated, then released, back during the revolution of . . .

*(From testimony by the subversive known as Marcionílio de Mattos, detained under the statutes of the National Security Act—for inciting to riot—and accused of premeditated homicide, in the death of a policeman during the massive insurrection which occurred at Plaza Station on the morning of March 31, and which is currently under intensive investigation by the DOPS of Belo Horizonte.)*

A number of outlaws from out of the past converged yesterday at Congonhas Airport here in São Paulo and were welcomed by still others who met briefly with reporters. There was Marinheiro, who spent one year as an outlaw, then became a bureaucrat in the Office of the Treasury. With him was Pitombeira, who claims to have become a bandit for three years to avoid being murdered by the police, and is now a clerk at city hall. A certain Criança boasted seven years of outlawing, culminating in a spectacular two-hour shoot-out with a special forces patrol—which he held off single-handedly while his men made good their escape. Today, Criança sells tomatoes off a pushcart.

*(The newspaper O Estado de São Paulo of October 18, 1969, reporting the reunion in São Paulo of a group of ex-outlaws, to coincide with the publication of a new book:* Tactics of Warfare among Outlaws in the Backcountry.)

. . . according to Commissioner Humberto Levita, those primarily alleged to be responsible for the violence at Plaza Station are Marcionílio de Mattos, an ex-outlaw, and the journalist Samuel Aparecido Fereszin. It has already been established, for example, that de Mattos—currently being held incommunicado at the DOPS—was a known subversive who participated in the Peasant Leagues of ex-Congressman Francisco Julião. The journalist Samuel Fereszin, as has been noted, was working for this paper and . . .

(Correio de Minas Gerais, *April 13, 1970.*)

Gravatá, Cotuzumba, Avenca, Pajeú, Itapeti, São José do Egito, Saque, Quixadá, Brejo da Cruz, São Bento, Pedra Nova, Corunas, Jacaré dos

Homens, Cacimbinhas, Boqueirão, Crateús, Currais Novos, Novas Russas, Limoeiro do Norte, Jaguaruana, Crato, Mombaça, Senador Pompeu, Canindé, Granja, Sobral, São Luís do Curu, Tauá, Quixeramobim, Orós, Ipaumirim, Juazeiro do Norte, Asaré, Cedo, Jucas, Mauriti, Brejo Santo, Aracati, Maranguape, Copiara, Acarapé, Icó, Baturite, Cariré . . .

*(Names of towns hit by the drought of 1970 and asking for governmental assistance.)*

I came to look at the drought, this year, with my own eyes; and what I have witnessed is the total drama of the Northeast. I came to look at the drought of 1970; and what I have witnessed is the misery and suffering of always.

*(General Emilio Garrastazu Médici, president of the Republic of Brazil, in a speech delivered on June 6, 1970.)*

PEASANT LEADER KILLED IN ESCAPE ATTEMPT
*(Headline from a news item on page 8 in* O Estado de Minas Gerais, *June 7, 1970.)*

I saw the parched landscape, the lost plantations, the dead villages. I saw the dust, the sun, the heat—the mercilessness of man and of weather. I saw desolation.

*(General Emilio Garrastazu Médici, president of the Republic of Brazil, in a speech delivered on June 6, 1970.)*

According to information obtained from security officers, the peasant leader and ex-outlaw Marcionílio de Mattos was killed yesterday in a shoot-out with security agents, after having attempted a spectacular prison . . .

*(Item published in two columns at the foot of page 8 in* O Estado de Minas Gerais, *June 7, 1970.)*

What we looked upon are scenes we ought never to have witnessed, regardless of the inclemencies, misfortunes, or calamities of nature. It is imperative that none of us accede to such a state of reality.

*(General Emilio Garrastazu Médici, president of the Republic of Brazil, in a speech delivered on June 6, 1970.)*

. . . after having attempted a spectacular prison break from the headquarters of the DOPS here.

De Mattos, the frustrated peasant leader who, three months ago, attempted to extend his campaign of rural subversion to the city—by leading a veritable regiment of migrants closely aligned with extremists here in the capital—yesterday seized a police officer's gun, immobilized a guard, fled from the headquarters, and ran down Avenida Afonso Pena while firing back at his pursuers. A shot by one of the agents who was chasing him struck de Mattos in the head, whereupon he fell lifeless.

*(Item published in one column, on page 12 in* Correio de Minas Gerais, *June 7, 1970.)*

# THIRTIETH
# ANNIVERSARY
## . . . PEARLS

HUSBAND

—I have so much to do tomorrow.

It was some time ago that she began this business of making plans for tomorrow. But tomorrow she's going to die.

—Tomorrow, definitely.

and yet it was so extraordinary that first time, with our youth and a feeling of sinfulness (there was a god, back then), as we rested in each other's arms, completely dead, as if we really were dead, frightened in the face of such pleasure

i thought i must be dying and you
i did too
i could die this instant
so could i
i want to die when it's no longer like this
so do i
i want us to die at the same time
so do i
swear
i swear
before we become old and ugly
yes
or if one of us is ever incurably ill
that too
we must die together
mmm-hmm
in each other's arms
we will
i mean it
so do i
swear to god
i swear i swear to god
which one of us decides the day
we'll know it together

and during the first few years we lived under the spell of the magic of that pact, it was our protection, our superiority, our single greatest achievement in those years; born within us and yet so much greater than ourselves, like some divinity from whence we derived the inner strength that so scandalized the people around us

—Tomorrow.

The old whore thinks she's fooled me. She's already mentioned tomorrow six times so far today. And yet by tomorrow she'll look even less like the photograph, that lovely girl in the photograph. From so many other old bags she's finally learned how to bear glances of indifference, how to sit forgotten at a party with some semblance of dignity, how to slip into bed with a man but not be seen naked by him, how to remove blemishes, not to get too upset when someone who's chased her for so many years finally looks the other way, to have her orgasm once a month, to go in secret to the dentist, not to laugh at her husband's paunch every morning at eight o'clock, and to believe somehow that any of it can still be worth all of that.

—Tomorrow, now don't forget, okay?

I would make love to her slowly, timidly, with an excessive tenderness that she shared with me as well. I'd kiss her fingers (a sweet smell of freshly painted nail polish), kiss the palm of her hand, gently cupped like a seashell, slightly warm. Ah, if only . . . if only I could forget, just forget how it was. Her other hand would linger on the back of my neck, so timid about our caresses, as if resisting one another. I'd smile; and so would she, tentatively, her small hand gently stroking my neck, then: why did you just smile, nothing, tell me love, it's silly, but tell me, I was thinking about the first time I kissed you, what's funny about that, nothing, tell me, I'm remembering how you didn't like it, you felt that way, (she looked a little offended) I thought so then but not anymore (I kiss the tip of her nose), even so, but it's silly to get angry love; then I'd take her by the shoulders, firmly, powerfully, protectively; she'd surrender a little further. It was always like that, always that air of timidity which so inhibited us: an apprehension on her part, a scruple on mine. And so we remained caught in a tenderness with no intimacy, suffering the imminence of committing sin, while my right hand (not exactly my hand, more precisely my fingers), while my fingers would caress her neck as we continued to gaze upon each other, and to feel that tender yearning transform our gaze into something almost unbearable. Afraid of it, we clung to one another, cheeks touching, her hand sliding downward to linger on my shoulder, almost an embrace (we felt) as we leaned a bit closer, cheeks touching and my hand caressing her face like someone whispering I love you, which she understood and answered, gently rubbing my back, until I thanked her by softly brushing my lips over her earlobe; a kind of secret dialogue. Our two bodies could actually converse: I love you, my body uttered; yes, I know, hers would respond and hesitate a little before saying, and I love you. Then we'd smile together, leaning closer (but still she had to hold back slightly), our bodies so close, almost, touching, the slightest movement would make it so, by a shifting of weight, for example, from the right to the left foot, until hips softly pressed together. My right hand leaving her neck and sliding down her back to stop at her waist, for support, ah . . . for protection, so she could lean back a little, trustingly, obliging my support in a hand bracing the small of her back, a hand transmitting its beat through the thin cloth of her blouse. I was so tender and warm and young, and she would surrender a little further, drawing her body closer to mine, resting her head on my left shoulder, as I pressed my cheek to her forehead, where an artery pulsed: I love you, in Morse code. I love you too, my sweet girl, love you too, oh my sweet woman. Bodies speaking. Turning my head slightly to place a kiss on her temple, as I moved my lips downward in gentle caress. Bodies touching more confidently. She watching the dark pink of my mouth draw closer, her serious lips awaiting mine, until I'd gently touch them, so gently! Together slowly opening our lips to each other . . . she, taking my lower lip between her lips, while I, her upper lip between mine, both of us tasting with pleasure, our bodies pressed close together in gentle embrace. And then she, slowly sensing my erection, without fright, loving me for such desire. Bodies speaking of love and of youth. She tightening her embrace, I sliding my tongue into her mouth (in her eyes a quickening of apprehension to my intrusion), she opening to it, gently tasting, biting it, then sucking with pleasure, biting harder, until I withdrew my tongue in pain and nibbled the inner flesh of her lips. She began to breathe quickly, panting, surrendering herself to the arm that held her firmly, as she finally gave in, to the contact of her stomach against my desire; ah . . . what affliction, our virginity; what desperation. Yet we were frightened. My tongue would lick her cheek, slide into her ear, making her shiver and writhe, rubbing her loins against my sex. As I arched over her a little, she would arch back slightly, accommodating, opening her legs a little more, then wildly, our bodies shuddering, her sex encountering mine, desiring one another beneath the clothes, and still we were afraid. So painful and exciting, and she almost moaning, a torrent of sighs. So wild, that first day, as I could only give her my tongue, not to hear more, and she sucked it down with violence. That's how it was, always; before we had the courage. So painful and exciting, we'd thrust our sexes into each other and writhe, one against the other, nervously kissing, with mouths altogether open, hungrily. So painful and exciting, my God, how could it continue like that, such desperation, as our hands coarsely explored our bodies; I would squeeze her breast, her eyes would encourage me, I love you, it was so good! I was violent and tender, my God! Something came from so deep inside, a pain, a burning we felt, as we kept rubbing against each other that way, writhing more urgently, with almost a hatred, now: hating! No, no! A heat, palpitating in my groin, as she was engulfed by a desperation, without air, liquidly watering. Ahh, she was fainting . . . ahh, she was flooding, my sweet man . . . oh, my sweet man. She wrenched. Ahh . . . letting out a sigh from deep within her breast, a burning sigh, gasped, released, filled with love and gratitude.

— We have tickets tomorrow to a wonderful play.

First act: The Heroine Full of Sighs. She takes off her evening makeup, dressed in a yellow peignoir with lacy edging, while I take my milk of magnesia and get into bed. She finishes cleansing her skin with no sense of modesty, then applies a nightly facial cream, after which I switch off the lamp on the night table. She slips into bed beside me, attempts a little conversation about her day, to which I mutter something inaudible, pretending to be nearly asleep. She falls silent and begins to sigh, getting no practical result whatsoever. She then invents some pretext or other to turn the night table lamp back on, which hurts my eyes. She draws her legs out from under the covers, massaging them while pretending to look for something, again without practical result. So she sighs, turns off the light (at my request) and lies there, offering herself in the dark, with additional sighs, still without practical result. For a long time she continues to resort to said sighs without practical result, until I, half asleep, believe I hear a muffled sob, which brings the first act to a close.

Second act: The Woman Satisfied by Life. Awakening, I find her already seated in front of the mirror, removing night cream from a despondent face. When she finally realizes I've awakened, she smiles and resorts to musical forms of expression. I go into the bathroom and, upon my return, find her rubbing on some dry-skin cream. I await her (a good half hour) for morning coffee, while reading the papers. She arrives (finally), taking a deep breath of the fresh air, opening her arms to the sunrise—good morning sun!—like some actress in an operetta. During coffee, I get to listen to some dull happenings with regard to her friends, as she relates in detail that so-and-so now has a lover; I depart, to deliver my morning lecture at the college, and thereby close the second act.

Third act: Madame Goes Shopping. (This act is played without me, though with occasional encounters on her part.) She begins by applying facial cosmetics especially recommended for daylight hours. Having donned a suitable outfit, she leaves the house. In town, she looks in all the shop windows, merely asking about prices, given her want of exactly nothing; occasionally she exchanges greetings in the form of little kisses—with even more casual girlfriends; stares insinuatingly at men who fail to insinuate back, *helás;* enters a drugstore to look at cosmetics and buys a few jars of cream or perhaps a set complete with powder; runs into an old girlfriend and tries to seem youthful, saying her goodbye with a "Drop over the house sometime, promise?"; looks at fabrics in a department store, where the young man always waits on her with a refreshingly gracious air, but then she doesn't purchase anything; returns home feeling hungry, tired, a failure, and with a ridiculous little package in hand.

Fourth Act: Vacuousness *en Petit Comité.* It begins at dinner, during which she relates ad nauseam some sort of stimulating afternoon adventure. Afterward, she removes her daytime face with a cleansing cream and applies some heavier cosmetics for the evening. She dons a suitably appropriate outfit, should the program be social rather than televised. We receive at home or drop in, one way or another passing the time with those who have nothing to offer. She acts modestly superior, staring attentively at whoever happens to be talking, and with the slight smile of someone clearly in the know, to the point of repeatedly blinking her eyes out of so much attentiveness; and when asked for her opinion, she flusters: "I'm sorry, I wasn't paying attention." Then manages to shift over to talking with an old girlfriend, pleading for the sordid details of her latest affair while whispering: "But you're insane!" . . . confessing that she'd never have the courage to try a stunt like that with me. And finally, goes on to drink moderately, eat moderately, chat moderately, chide moderately, until we say goodbye or they say goodbye. In the bedroom again, she slips on her blue peignoir with lacy edging. I take my Phillips, while she proceeds to remove the evening's makeup with a cleansing cream, once more preparing for her part in the Heroine Full of Sighs . . .

— Shall we go to that celebration tomorrow?

One dies so terribly late in life, with not a shred of dignity; and all the while just aging, procrastinating, waiting. No! No one else is going to decide when I die—I can still choose, myself. This relic of a conscience still wields some power. The fact is, I should have been more mindful in the past: during the revolution, for instance, all that trying to keep out of sight; then taking care to cross the streets properly; and, who knows, refusing to eat cooked mussels if not entirely open but no more sliding into these instinctual traps!

The old whore still thinks (believes!) that pleasure could be the same (with those breasts!), still imagines I grow more and more accustomed . . . (to old age!) Doesn't bother to sneak out of bed and check the gas anymore. No longer lies awake nights to avoid my treachery. Not even afraid to eat whatever I bring to the table. Obviously, she feels secure now. As if liberated from the pact, somehow. That's why it's the perfect moment.

WIFE

—Tomorrow she said. —You really will? —I will, she promised, you needn't worry about that. —But what about the professor? We should be careful. —Oh, he doesn't care. I'll explain everything when I see you tomorrow. And she thought: Why do I always tell them that. —Where? the young man asked her, a hotel? —If you want. I'll go wherever you like. —Tomorrow afternoon? he asked. —That's right, it can only be in the afternoon. What's your name again? —Carlos, he told her. —Well, Carlos, why don't you give me your phone number.

When Juliana got back from shopping she checked the kitchen to see if everything was going smoothly, admonished the cook not to use too much salt, and went into the living room to relax until her husband arrived. She dozed off a bit, then woke up startled to find her husband seated in the other chair, staring at her. She realized that he had probably been watching her like that for some time, which brought a sudden flush of resentment to her cheeks. Calm yourself, calm yourself. She reassembled the bits of her dismantled heart, reanimated it, then sat up in her chair smiling and said:

—Imagine, I fell asleep. What time is it?

There was no answer. Juliana brushed away with a hand some particle of dust that wasn't on her dress, then rubbed her forehead while attempting a different approach:

—I went for a long walk, today. That's why I must have gotten sleepy all of a sudden. Why don't I just go up and take a quick bath?

It was not a question, though at the same time it was. She had grown so accustomed to this manner of conversing but not conversing that she went on:

—Oh well, it's probably too late to take a bath now anyway, dinner's almost ready. I'd be holding everything up . . .

He wasn't about to say: Why don't you, I'll wait. Nevertheless, she allowed the interval of a response to pass, as if rehearsing alone for the scene of a play, and then:

—I guess I had better see how things are in the kitchen. Dinner might not even be ready for a while.

Still, she didn't get up right then. She sat thinking: What if I stare right back at him and say, Listen, since tomorrow's our thirtieth anniversary, how would you feel about having a few friends over? She quickly dismissed the idea as absurd, then got up to go to the kitchen and—as if jumping ahead a couple of scenes at rehearsal (so the new lines bore no relationship to the old)—said (thinking of Carlos):

—I have so much to do tomorrow.


—Come here, the young man told her. —Not yet, she said, first I want to explain everything about Candinho. —You mean the professor? the young man asked. —Yes, she answered, nodding, my husband.

Today's our thirtieth anniversary. He hardly says a word to me anymore. For three years we've done nothing in bed together. No one can go so long like that, without—what do they say? Well, without anything. When it first began to happen, when he stopped wanting me or—that is, when he started just wanting me less—I didn't pay that much attention. I hardly remember when it was, actually, but it must have been about five years ago. And then one day I spoke to him about it. I asked him why he didn't seem to want me, why sometimes more than a month would go by, why I had to be the one to always pursue him, why all this was happening to us. So he said something very strange to me, I mean I thought it strange at the time. He said, "Don't you think the time's finally come?" It was something I ought to have understood, judging from the way he had said it, but I didn't understand—not at all. I didn't remember, you see? And I said nothing, because it might have been something I'd forgotten but shouldn't have. So without really knowing what it was, I said: "No, not yet"—just to put it off a while and try to remember what it was he was talking about. And he seemed satisfied, thinking I hadn't forgotten. We were all right for a while, I guess, till the day he tried to set our house on fire. And then suddenly I remembered what it was he must have meant when he had said that to me, and I cried out to him. I screamed, "Not yet, Candinho! Wait a little longer, please? I swear, Candinho! I swear I'll tell you, I haven't forgotten!" It was something we had decided to do together, so long ago. I was just a girl then. I must have been—I don't know— maybe sixteen years old. A childish oath, that's all it was. We agreed to die together, before getting old. The day of the fire, though, made me realize that Candinho wasn't well, that he was partly unbalanced. The doctors took him away, to treat him at a hospital. Since that day he's never again wanted me in bed. But you see, except for those periodic attacks he's normal enough, he's not a crazy man. But even so, there's nothing more between us, not in bed. And I never know exactly when a crisis is coming on, or when it's abating. I can only go to bed after he's asleep. Once, more recently, he turned on the gas jets, and I lay there smelling the odor until he fell asleep. I kept breathing through the sheet, hidden in the dark, and when he was finally asleep I got up and—half crazy, I think, from the gas—rushed in to turn it off. I opened the windows; he never saw. But now Candinho hardly says a word to me. I sit there, talking alone at dinnertime, trying to distract his mind a little. The doctor says it's good for him. I never know if one of his crises is coming on, or about to dissipate. All day long, I take various precautions. I make sure the knives are locked away; each day I look to see if he has another gun hidden in a drawer somewhere; and I check the gas. The doctor claims Candinho will never resort to direct physical violence against me; only these little traps of his on the sly, but how can I be sure? The doctor tells me it's those little traps I have to watch out for. I know it seems a bit crazy on my part to even stay with him there in the same house. He might kill me at any moment, but I still cling to the hope he'll go back someday to being what he once was. Dr. Santoro claims Candinho's problem could just disappear altogether. Some men get that way, at a certain age, and then it passes. For twenty-five years he was the closest, warmest friend and dearest lover a woman could ever wish for.

THE YOUNG MAN UNZIPPED THE BACK OF HER DRESS, UNHOOKED HER BRASSIERE, SLIPPED HIS HAND DOWN BETWEEN HER BREASTS. —DO I SEEM OLD? SHE ASKED HIM. —HOW CAN YOU SAY THAT, YOU'RE BEAUTIFUL. WITH HIS OTHER HAND HE LIFTED UP THE BACK OF HER SKIRT, AND SHE FELT HIS HARDNESS THROBBING AGAINST HER RIGHT THIGH. —I DON'T WANT TO DIE, SHE SAID SOFTLY.

so softly, on my hand, my face, my hair, a gentle caress, the nape of my neck, each of us gazing into the other's eyes. I became so aroused, my body so hot whenever he looked at me that way, and he'd hold me and say I love you, kissing the tip of my earlobe, as I drew closer, and he drew closer, and my body pressed to his. He kept kissing my face, ever so gently, until he reached my mouth; gently, and soon not gently anymore, harder, until I felt his erection, pushing against my belly. And I arched to feel it, even more, thrusting against my own sex, his embrace, so hard, my breasts ached . . . that thing, moving, against my legs, my loins . . . aahhhhhhhhh!

—I'M A WOMAN OF FORTY-SEVEN, SHE SAID, IT'S NOT RIGHT. —DON'T BE SILLY, THE YOUNG MAN TOLD HER, NOWADAYS EVERYBODY DOES IT. —I NEVER DID IT, SHE SAID. —IT WON'T HURT, THE YOUNG MAN TOLD HER.

An endurable pain, continuous, renewed; the anticipation of a pleasure. Then later, one substituting the other (pain or pleasure?); one diminishing, or one intensifying (pleasure or pain?). And finally, only one (pleasure? pain?), intensifying, intensifying . . .

—Aaaaaahh, Candinho! Aahhhhhhhhh . . .

—I thought I must be dying. And you?

—I did too.

—I could die this instant.

—So could I.

—I want us to die at the same time.

—So do I.

—Swear?

—I swear.

—Before we become old and ugly.

—I know.

—Or if one of us is ever incurably ill.

—That too.

—We must die together.

—We will.

—In one another's arms?

—Mmm-hmm.

—I mean it.

—So do I.

—Swear to God.

—I swear.

—Which one of us decides the day?

—We'll know, whenever it's time.

Something that was so beautiful to utter at that moment of first experience, like in a novel. He, serious; and I, so sincere, as if we were in a great love story.

I don't want to die.


—WE WERE MARRIED SO YOUNG, SHE SAID. I WAS SEVENTEEN, HE WAS TWENTY-ONE. —WHICH MEANS HE'S WHAT, NOW, FIFTY-ONE? —YES, SHE SAID. —GEE, HE SEEMS SO MUCH OLDER, I WOULD HAVE GUESSED HE WAS SIXTY. —IT'S TRUE,

SHE SAID, IT'S FROM HIS ILLNESS THOUGH, HIS DEPRESSIONS. —AND YOU, YOU
SEEM SO MUCH YOUNGER, THE YOUNG MAN SAID. —YES, EVERYBODY TELLS ME
THAT. —YOU COULD BE HIS DAUGHTER, THE YOUNG MAN SAID. —OH, NOW YOU'RE
GOING A LITTLE TOO FAR, AREN'T YOU? —IT'S TRUE, THE YOUNG MAN SAID, IF I
WERE YOU, I'D WANT TO DUMP HIM AND GET MARRIED AGAIN. —YOU SHUT THAT
FILTHY MOUTH! SHE SAID. DON'T YOU EVER SPEAK THAT WAY ABOUT MY HUSBAND
AGAIN! I'M WARNING YOU, EVER! —WHAT'S THE MATTER ALL OF A SUDDEN? THE
YOUNG MAN ASKED. BLOWING UP OVER SOME CRAZY COOT WHO WANTS TO KILL
YOU? —HE WAS THE FIRST MAN I EVER LOVED, SHE SAID. AND YOU, ALL OF YOU!
YOU'RE GARBAGE, GARBAGE!

Juliana got back from her shopping and went up to take a bath, to wash
from her body everything that was Carlos and return to being clean again,
married. On walking into her bedroom though, she let out a small, quick
scream: there, on the bed, a wrapped package. Her first thought was simply
to run, to flee that presentiment of danger. Calm yourself, calm yourself. On
top of the package, half slid into the wrapping, was a small envelope with
some writing on it. She thought: a present from mother; from our in-laws;
from a friend for our thirtieth anniversary, that's it. She picked up the envelope with a trembling hand, anticipating and deluding herself at the same
time: I recognize the handwriting. Deluding herself before she could read it
and be certain: Candinho's writing! Again that sensation of imminent peril.
She stood there, afraid to open the package, death inside, a bomb inside.
She picked it up with great care, gently shook it. Nothing suspicious, nothing
heavy, no noise. Then Candinho came into the room—with a different face
though, the face of so many years ago—and said smilingly:

—Open it, it's for you.

With a quick, suicidal gesture Juliana opened the package, a box. And
inside, a lovely, rare, incredible string of pearls. Stunned, confused, she began to cry, to gain some time, fingering the necklace.

—And what about me, no present for me?

She said nothing. The joy of having him back undermined the fear of
losing him all over again. Still insecure then, in that confidence she so desperately wished to maintain, she pleaded half in tears:

—I . . . I forgot. Let me give you yours later, Candinho. Will you forgive
me, please?

—Why don't you put on something special tonight. We can have a lovely
dinner, just the two of us. . . .

Juliana came into the living room to find Candinho standing there, waiting for her. She felt relieved to see that her dress matched the sobriety of his suit and tie. Candinho, though, was staring at her. It was as if he were posing a question, or perhaps searching for something, and she tried swiftly to surmise whatever was wrong. On the sideboard was a cake. The table was set for two.

—Didn't you like the necklace?

Suddenly, she grasped the meaning of the stare, and felt relieved; then guilty, mortified:

—Oh, no, I adore it, Candinho. It's that I just forgot, I . . . I'm so . . . let me run and get it.

—No, leave it.

—But I love it, it's so beautiful, really.

She went quickly to retrieve the necklace and return, to surrender herself to that confidence she so desperately wanted to have. They sat down, Juliana rang the bell, calling the maid in to serve dinner. At first she found it rather difficult to talk; she, who was normally the only one to say anything at dinner, was troubled now by a new sensation. Yet she sensed, coming from Candinho, an attempt to somehow rescue her:

—With a little effort we could have the perfect evening.

Juliana was hopeful too, and began to talk, although at first only about dinner: "Could you pass the rice please?" and "Isn't this a lovely wine?" but later on, about more personal things, like a certain film she'd seen several nights before. And little by little she embraced the joy of true conversation with her Candinho, of clear responses—phrase complementing phrase—of all she had languished for for so long; the pure joy of it returning as the warmth, the wine, and the food helped them on and on into their evening, and they were once again Juliana and Candinho versus the World. She even brought up the notion of a trip she had wanted to take, a voyage to one of those exotic places: "Japan fascinates me," she confided, and suddenly his hand, touching hers! Intensifying her joy. She felt an urge to telephone her mother and smilingly say: "Mother, don't I even get a call on my wedding anniversary?" but all that was unnecessary now, for now was the perfect, perfect day. And who was to say if tonight he might not put his arms around her, like so many years before, and all would be forgotten. She kept fingering the pearl necklace around her throat as they talked and talked, drinking the wine, until all of a sudden . . . there he was, across from her, staring at the cake; and she felt absolutely certain: the poison is in the cake.

—What's the matter, Juliana?

—I don't know, I . . . I don't know.

—You look so serious.

She hesitated to believe in her discovery:

—It's nothing, Candinho, it's nothing.

He took her hand again and said perhaps they might really take a trip like that, off to Japan. After all, they'd spent so little money over the past few years, their savings could easily cover the cost. And she was already doubtful of what she had surmised, preferring to cling to that other Candinho, the one from the past, who had come out of madness and could speak of a voyage.

—Let's cut the cake, she suggested, determined to put an end to her doubt, refusing to let it spoil the only perfect day in five whole years.

He answered her calmly, without urgency, not the slightest hesitation in his voice:

—So quickly? At least have a little more wine, first.

—No, I've had so much already.

—All right, she said, serving himself with what was left of the second bottle, then downing the glass at once. —This wine *is* a bit strong, isn't it.

—Yes, yes it is. She smiled, convinced of her mistake.

—No more left?

—You're too late, she said giddily, nearly breaking out with a laugh.

—What do you say we open another bottle, shall we?

—No, she said trustingly. —Let's cut the cake now.

—But not that way, he told her, interrupting her hand and the knife it held. —Not like that. Juliana stared uncomprehendingly, and he said: — Let's do it the old-fashioned way. You know, the two of us holding the knife together, the way we posed for our picture, remember?

They cut the cake, laughing contentedly; they served themselves, one at a time. Juliana took the first bite. She was already saying: Mmmn, it's delicious . . . when, looking up, she saw Candinho hesitate for the briefest second before biting into his piece. Then, noticing he was being watched, he offered a smile of contentment:

—It is delicious, isn't it.

So Juliana nodded yes, finished the rest of her slice, and braced herself for the onslaught of its poison.

# ANDREA

BIOGRAPHY: discovered by the author among papers belonging to one of the characters in the book, who should perhaps be identified at some point later on.

# 1.

She was stunning, all right. Perhaps the only truth about her, and the basis for all subsequent lies, was just that: Andrea's beauty. Overly attractive women too often tend to be thrust into the spotlight—of a family, of a first communion, of a classroom, of an office, of a party, of any milieu—and end up with the responsibility of always remaining so, in the spotlight, the rest of their lives; an illusion that grows tedious and causes much suffering. By adolescence, Andrea was already snared in the trap.

She wanted to be in love—not a little, but totally: like a heroine. By the age of fifteen she was already "violently" in love, because the first kiss is always a disturbing revelation. Her fear of committing sin—Catholic, middle-class, born and raised in Tijuca—prevented any further exploration of endearments in this period of her life. Henceforth, however, she was always to experience a disturbing mixture of frivolity and danger at the moment of any kiss.

Then one day Andrea's father discovered and read her diary, which spoke too much of kisses. Furious, he sent his daughter off to live with an aunt, where she attended normal school and acquired the uneasy ignorance that she was to cultivate all her life.

At seventeen, Andrea discovered her legs were provoking fistfights in the local pubs of Vassouras. One swarthy type actually cracked a fellow on the head with a pool cue because of those very legs. Then, on the run from the police, he wrote her a note in terrible Portuguese, which she had the delicacy to overlook—acknowledging he had fought because of her. Long afterward, though never having once laid eyes on him, she still clung to her passion for that bloodthirsty fugitive, fully capable of murder! In dreams she was repeatedly violated by him. She held onto the letter.

When her schooling was over, Andrea returned to Tijuca. They talked of how beautiful she was, in that summer of '51. And whenever anyone fell in love with her she was appropriately moved. She found it understandable to be drawn to so lovely a person as herself, and she treated young men with compassion. Older men followed her; boys masturbated. And in that summer of her eighteenth year, Andrea fell in love with a young man who was about to start a career in plastic utensils. They even talked of marriage, until her father was suddenly forced to "accept" a transfer to another state. Andrea romantically wished to elope, but the young entrepreneur confessed, regretfully, that he was in no position to do so. She held onto a three-by-four photograph of him.

## 2.

Now begins Andrea's Minas Gerais phase. Her cousins from Belo Horizonte, capital of the state, had quickly introduced the girl to the good families of Minas: genteel people; sensitive, relaxed, solicitous, captivating, mythic, petty, malicious people. Andrea now entered a circle much too rich for her, a milieu much too spoiled, and was totally unprepared. These people knew themselves well enough not to be trusting, and their contacts were always cautious, tactful, prudent. After all, what did she offer them? Two nearly forgotten beaus, her own self-centeredness, beauty, a three-by-four photograph, a few kisses, one (dreadfully-composed) letter, and a family in difficulties. Not very much to set against such comfortable people. And her first mistake was to let herself become fascinated.

She never realized—to realize immediately, in Minas, is already too late; better to have anticipated entirely—never realized that, because of a basic defect in her perception, she was reversing roles. She believed herself to be the center of much attention, society seemed fascinated by her; truthfully, she was being exploited. They were taking from her what they themselves no longer possessed: beauty, and a certain innocence. There was no cunning involved, of course. Nothing was deliberate.

One of the first things she picked up from her newfound milieu was the need to color, to embroider. That first beau of hers and the subsequent departure for Vassouras, she presented as a variation on the theme of original sin, complete with expulsion from paradise. The uncouth admirer on the run from the police was gradually shaped into an outlaw of insatiable lustings. And the young entrepreneur? Why, hadn't he ruined himself on her account? Her social life: a madness! The provincials sat there, listening (and commenting), willing accomplices to that life of adventure as they engulfed her a little further.

Soon her picture began to appear in the local papers, the society pages were often taken up with her (she saved the clippings). She was invited to dances, admitted to private clubs; she troubled the Sunday swimming pools. She dated, yes, but was much too lost in her own fascination to have the time or the patience to fall in love. Sufficient unto herself; friendly. One of her admirers, however, achieved a partial victory when he managed to slip a hand up her dress and keep it there for a while. Afterward, he bragged about it to whoever wanted to listen and forgot about her.

She was enmeshed, very carefully, in a net of sympathy: he's not worth a second thought, everybody knows that; a sleazy operator, if ever there was one; always boasting about what he does with each little conquest. Thus forcing her to go on the defensive: there's nothing he could possibly have to tell about me; I was already quite tired of his boorishness; as far as I'm concerned it's just as well, let him invent whatever he likes. Then relaying her defense back to him and listening, in turn, to his rebuttal: if anyone was "quite tired" of anyone, it was me of her; never met a person so dense upstairs in all my life; didn't bang her though, couldn't be bothered. Then back and forth all over again: to her, to him, and to others; recounting each reaction. In a few months' time they had managed to draw her in completely; with her compliance. Nothing was intentional.

(But why? For no reason: to feel united, powerful, capable of imposing the rules of the game. To have something to talk about, pass the time, keep in shape. To be up to date, stimulating, stimulated. To engulf a living thing, participate, be part of the scene, forget their own meaninglessness. And feed upon—like so many amoebas—whatever was closest: to survive. Why not?)

## 3.

So, around 1953, they began Andrea's trial. She was no longer the fascinating girl from Rio, but someone about whom they could cite a goodly number of compromising details. Testimony, of course, was rendered in whispers, not to offend the accused; that Minas Geraisean sense of delicacy.

To counter the first accusation (of availability), Andrea presented to one and all an insistently celibate body. A troubling game on both sides. She became restive, nervous, and took to daydreaming over her fugitive, that swarthy brute who liked to take his pleasures out on her, repeatedly. She began to experience states of hyper-excitability that made no sense to her. Things that had previously held no attraction for her (a movie-star Tarzan in a loincloth, an ambiguous word like pleasure, a leg touching hers on the bus) suddenly became disturbing phenomena. She masturbated often during this period.

As part of her defensive strategy she set out to create still another illusion: that of her competence. She began working in a bank as a receptionist, at a time when this was rather chic and society girls could think of nothing else. Her dedication provided her with her first witnesses: Andrea is a very efficient girl. The accusation of being "dense upstairs" had caused her untold anxiety, so she put in appearances at concerts, gallery openings, and plays; she read the papers; she devoured whatever novels were in vogue (aaah, the perturbation of Lady Chatterley's epic orgasm); she memorized lines from the poet in vogue, entire passages from whatever book was in vogue. The results were at least sufficient to make the issue polemical: Andrea is quite intelligent; you think so? I don't think so; Oh, I think so.

When it was no longer so much of a problem to defend the terrain she had mastered—a young woman of twenty-two basking in illusions of independence, the principal topic of a number of society pages and even a few literary ones, the occasional victim of a poem or two—Andrea experienced what was to prove the deepest, truest, and most abiding (carnal) love of her life.

## 4.

It's just possible (I won't swear to it) that the beginning of Andrea's affair with the young playboy may have had something to do with her trial, although neither of them may have been at all conscious of the fact: he, undertaking the conquest of the girl everyone talked about; she, a conqueress in her own right, netting the difficult catch, breaking another record. Nothing was deliberate.

Their love was the result of a complementary resistance, a competitive challenge, as it were; both with a desire to maintain their own position and reputation. They needed that competition, without which their affair would have ended immediately—needed it so much that they wooed around the clock. Often with absolutely nothing to say; merely that peculiar opposition, uniting them. And once the period of resistance had been exhausted, they withdrew.

About a month later everybody was certain: they love each other. Slowly and submissively, the one sought out the other; receptive now, softened by love. After all, they would have time, wouldn't they? Until, finally, she would love like a heroine.

There followed two years of a diffuse happiness called "courtship." When eventually he began to neglect her, it troubled her. She felt that she was profoundly unhappy and, somehow, had always been so, even as a child. In a final attempt to hold onto him (and judging it to complete the image of independent woman which had so obviously attracted him), she allowed him to make love to her, in 1956. Yet not to have been able to do so in a more lucid fashion—it was in the backseat of a car, they were a little too drunk— left her with feelings of frustration, disillusionment, guilt. (Over the car radio, the voice of Nat "King" Cole with: "Mona Lisa, Mona Lisa, men have named you . . .")

They quarreled and he disappeared for several weeks, which went by miserably for her. And when he returned she tried to avoid sex—without knowing why, without succeeding. Insecure, from having ceased to have the spotlight focused upon her; unhappy, because without it, what sex there was proved unsatisfactory. Above all hovered a troubling sense of sin.

He went out with other girls; she knew that. Whenever he disappeared, it was to go out with other women. As for her, she was too distraught to be circumspect. She let herself be drawn in: accepted commiseration, cried on people's shoulders; she admitted her unhappiness. After all, this was the great love. When he did show up, she laughed again; if he disappeared, she cried— all quite simple. And at the soirees, swimming pools, beauty salons, and bars, she was now officially the beautiful girl who suffered from pangs of love. In this, at least, she managed appearances.

They never really ended their affair, and for years afterward she would have occasional visits from him. There were always the same old conversations, the same idle sensuality, coupled now and then with a certain nostalgia toward her body.

## 5.

From time to time Andrea would view her situation with a degree of desperation: twenty-five, brought up in a land where a woman's virginity is still a necessary virtue, trying guiltily to guard her secret (if the family ever found out!), yet treated indifferently by the very man she loved. There were fits of uncontrollable weeping, shored up with occasional sips of brandy. She took sleeping pills (obviously: everyone knows how easily distress can lead to insomnia); then stimulants, Alka-Seltzers, tranquilizers (the pharmaceutical props of her drama). And each of the labels on such remedies elucidated the genuine state of her sorrow.

It would not be incorrect to date from this epoch—with a certain flexibility, of course—her inclination to confide in people, her tendency to drink too much, her pleasure at bestowing gifts. She confessed to numerous little personal problems, fabricating whole melodramas out of a need to be listened to. (It became known at this time, for instance, that there had actually been a case of embezzlement involving a member of her family; presumably the father.)

She gave presents to people—she liked to—with brief dedications written out on the cards she enclosed, which invariably began: "For my dear friend . . ." (if male); or "For my lovely friend . . ." (if female). Generally speaking, the offerings betokened minor, unconscious bribes in the form of trivial little keepsakes: rings, scarves, key rings, combs, earrings, lighters, pens. Throughout this whole period of adjusting to unhappiness (and still rather unaccustomed to it all) she continually relied on such mementos, to counter the fear of being abandoned. And she bolstered the illusion of staying in the spotlight by crediting her unhappiness with the power to move people.

In an attempt to escape matters, she quit her job—to relax—and avoided alcohol, pills, get-togethers. She also began psychotherapy sessions (they were just becoming fashionable). For the next five months not much was heard of her. She traveled, apparently to Vassouras; she came back, apparently feeling better, certainly looking tan and well rested. A few kisses to her credit, a few gifts to her debit. The playboy, she treated coldly. In some manner the spell had finally broken.

Andrea hinted that she was looking for a job, and awaited an offer. The former impulses that had been felt toward her were still operative, so they offered her a variety of positions; she accepted one in journalism. The position of social columnist gave her ascendancy over the very circle that had once judged her—yet, innocently, she failed to take advantage of this. Instead, she flattered them. Not out of generosity, mind you, but from a desire to hear them say: Andrea is a sweet girl, isn't she?

Through the magic of the kind of thinking she would always resort to, she managed to dispel from her mind the thought that the invitations to more and more prestigious gatherings were simply the result of her new profession. For the first six years, they had taken her for one of those irrelevant courtesans their sons played with for a time before going on to choose a wife. Now, however, they had to send her invitations; they needed her. And she failed to perceive that she was being used by the parents, after having been used by the sons. Thus, her happiness and her confidence actually returned. Among her fellow journalists she was likewise a center of attention, as a pleasant novelty.

Oh, and one more error: letting herself become fascinated all over again.

## 6.

The force of attraction she exerted now on the journalists around her bore something of the aloofness, glamour, and sex appeal of the film star. What she felt for them, in turn, had more to do with the spectacular array of facts they obviously had at their fingertips. It seemed incredible to her that any one person could say not only what had just occurred in some incomprehensible kingdom called Laos, but simultaneously whatever happened to be going on in the back rooms of the capital, the names and political parties of countless congressional leaders, and even confidential matters pertaining to the president—not to mention all the art news and society gossip of the day. And all of it treated with the same cynical irony, peals of laughter, beer, maliciousness, and vulgarity.

In this period ('58, it was) she developed a habit of putting on airs, bragging about herself, inventing stories, feigning friendships with important people ("Oh, so-and-so? We're very good friends; you didn't know?"), showing off, posturing, presuming herself to be generally indispensable to society. She was often indiscreet about things like: who's mad about whom; who's up to no good with you-know-who; who in fact adores what, when, and how; where so-and-so's money really comes from; what they say about etc. Oh, so-and-so? We're very good friends. . . .

At the paper, though, they still seemed to think she was a little dense upstairs—Andrea, in fact, suspected what they were saying. The signs were almost physical: she felt embarrassed, somehow, the moment she stepped into the office. She compensated for her own insecurity by falling in love with the editor in chief of the paper, who referred to her as "the vestal." (Otherwise, how to explain her passion for an ugly-looking married man who constantly ridiculed her?)

So she went to bed with her second lover, wanting him to see that she wasn't what he thought she was (what's a vestal, anyway?), but once again she failed to discover in sex that satisfaction ascribed to the great paramours of literature. In her attempts to flush out Constance Chatterley's crushing orgasm, she took to giving herself in strange places: the roof of the Acaiaca Building, a vacant lot (the sound of passing footsteps!), even the back of a pickup truck early one morning. Bit by bit, her passion finally spent itself at a variety of barroom beer tables.

At twenty-seven, jaded-looking, dependent on pills and liquor, Andrea finished out the decade of her youthful, formative years—that of the fifties, which had forever left their mark upon her.

# 7.

She also quit the newspaper crowd, wounded by the sort of contest that revolved around her, in which she was the prize in a game of now-let's-see-who-has-her-next. She devoted more time to her column, managing to publish a few items under her own byline and—with the resulting praise—to forget to a degree, her newfound unhappiness. She turned to promoting young artists, to judging beauty contests for *Glamour* and *Miss,* to giving occasional parties. With so much to do, there was little time left for beaus. She went out with her friends, danced, worked hard, shunned intimacies. The latter at small expense, since she had yet to "expire" from an orgasm. True, it did feel pleasurable to have a man inside her, but she got no further than that. During the more than two years that followed (before deciding to quit Minas for a time), she would attempt her great orgasm only once more—this time with a total stranger picked up at a nightclub. A dismal failure. . . .

Through work, Andrea became involved with the younger intellectuals, and they with her. She found it agreeable to have a discreet coterie gathered about her that was so timidly respectful of her presence. She grew especially fond of a particular young author who often collaborated on the literary supplement of the paper. And finally she told him everything about herself—in hopes, perhaps, of becoming a character.

She understood very little of what they talked about. Alarmingly incomprehensible words shot across café tables, ricocheting against bottles, glasses, and Andrea: infrastructure, pop art, phenomenology, bilateral patterns of decasyllabic verse, ontological, transcendental, structuralism, immanence. They spoke of ending the parliamentary regime "engineered by the military"; of forcing a plebiscite to restore Goulart's presidential authority and permit him to carry out "the needed social reforms"; of exploring more popular forms of culture, popular theater, country music, oral poetry—while Andrea tried to understand why this or that business couldn't go on much longer. A few members of Radical Action relayed plans across the barroom prattle. Yet she felt a confused contentment (what's Radac?) to be in the eye of the impending political storm. So when someone made a comment and her young author objected, calling it ridiculous, she (who was unable to figure out what exactly was ridiculous) would agree. Andrea also picked up certain phrases like: "Women must no longer accept marginal status." In '62, this was one of her favorite phrases.

She was always relying on his help, his discernment. When they went to a play, for example: he would quietly point out what he found laudable or inadequate so that by the time the last act was over she would already have her opinion prepared; she was saved; she felt confident enough to discuss the ramifications of the drama while they exited, tranquilly, from the theater. A subtly unacknowledged give-and-take: knowing themselves to be master and pupil with not the slightest outward sign of this awareness.

The Young Author is one of the ephemeral myths of Belo Horizonte. Principally, he represents Hope. Ex-Young Authors of the municipal variety, the ones who have failed to achieve a national reputation, are naturally envious, but keep the Faith. After all, he might be the new Carlos Drummond de Andrade, the new João Guimarães Rosa, and they themselves could hardly afford, later on, to be listed among the Pharisees—those who had failed to Believe. Following some three years of such Faith, however, the City begins to hunger for a Miracle—water transformed into wine—the natural consequence of that first book of Annunciations. One, two, three years of careful hedging—intimations of an Illumination in several literary quarterlies—but no Miracle. The decline of the Faith sets in. Old and even middle-aged authors begin to regard him more and more affectionately, and gradually welcome him to the Fold.

The particular young author on duty at the time, 1963, preferred to flee the city before their Embrace. (One more literary generation of Minas Gerais torn asunder and scattered to the wind.)

Two months later, in the wake of his departure, Andrea went back to Rio. For the next six years, very little was to be heard about her. Only rumors.

## 8.

Then, she returned. Ah, how the city welcomes (with an irresistible fawning) those who do return. Diminutive were Andrea's actual triumphs in the world. Only there, in such a place, among all those prisoners of the mountain (as windmills who would be giants), did her adventures have the power to fascinate. Andrea and the city were suited to each other.

There wasn't that much to hear about, not really . . . a story involving some effeminate count who was madly in love with her . . . then some victim of amnesia who wanted to marry her . . . Vinicius, who wrote a samba for her . . . Playboy, imagine, offered her two thousand dollars to . . . if only the military hadn't taken over, she would have had a post in Rome by now . . . that's right, he was just saying goodbye to her, there at the door, when these three tough-looking men wearing trenchcoats arrived . . . half-owner of a boutique in Copacabana . . . they say she really came back to Minas because she'd been having an affair with one of the ten most fashionable women in Rio, exactly, when the husband caught them in. . . .

Galloping along with her on her adventures, those people of the mountain soon reconquered her . . . by being enchanted—in Minas, it was merely a subtler form of domination.

And so the fascinating adventuress, already taken to be the consecrated muse of the literary generation just prior to '64, now mixed with an even younger group of intellectuals and recouped (in the year of her return, 1969) her old position on the staff of the paper. A woman brought up in the true Carioca style, in dress, speech, and demeanor; physically well rested but sexually underused, Andrea tried to be the youthful woman at thirty-seven. And told everyone she was thirty.

She started going out with the latest young painter of the city: winner of a prize at the last São Paulo biennial; set and costume designer for an avant-garde theater group, wealthy heir to some tremendous import-export firm, and as lost as she was in his own game of appearances. Obsessed with mannerisms that he struggled to conceal (or to reveal with a studiedly relaxed air of naturalness). Sensually, transmitting insecurity and hope to both sexes; but socially, only to women. Some men use women as an amulet, to ward off the evil eye. Homosexual?—she refused to believe it.

## 9.

Andrea held his attention, all right. He wasn't about to miss any part of what he termed "the masterly performance of the mediocre prima donna." What he waited for was the final collapse, the climax to the drama, the insupportable (to Andrea) moment when she would have to finally interrupt her own playacting.

There were those who imagined she performed for the sake of the audience, but this was only partially the truth, and the young painter penetrated the matter more deeply: Andrea, early on, had recognized herself as mediocre and had therefore created a woman for her own self to admire; a woman who was variously fabulous, beautiful, a heroine, a free spirit, intelligent, loved, unhappy, pure, dramatic, unobtainable, a fascinating creature, sensuality itself, competent, desired, young, wanton, decadent, wonderful. In her prolonged egocentrical delirium, however, Andrea had become incapable of recognizing at what point her interpretation either began or ended.

After five months of discoveries, masturbation, and mutual frustration they believed themselves suitably marriageable. The idea was actually his, which she proceeded to accept in the surprised, nubile, maidenly, bride-to-be fashion of the 1950s. Carelessly self-assured, Andrea felt protected by the notion of his being so much like herself (as always, hiding from herself the fact that this was merely another defense), believing herself to be in love with him for that very reason—"at last, I've found my spiritual likeness"— and guarding deep within herself a terrible misconception: that he could never wound her without somehow wounding himself. Blinded by her own love for a woman she had invented, she now imagined she was rewarding him with the gift of her. She could never conceive of her (only of herself) as a rejectable offering. What was worse: she would never herself come out of her long enough to get to know him, and thus was unaware of his cruelty, of the assassin-of-women who lurked within him.

Ah, Andrea, Andrea. . . . They could have spared you, spared you the truth, had they not wanted to watch you truly suffer. For if someone should ever penetrate your armor, Andrea, and feel no compassion, the result must be fatal. Your young painter, so beautiful, false, and insecure, wanted one day to destroy whatever there was of beauty, falseness, and insecurity, in you! And when that day came, he attacked you with all the pleasure in destruction and annihilation of which the strength of an artist is made.

At a party full of close acquaintances (including her old journalist flame) (who remembered her as one of the saddest episodes of his life) (the communist author, over there, she had also known) (it was a birthday celebration for her betrothed, intimate of all the young intelligentsia) (the same day that Belo Horizonte was invaded by a trainload of Northeasterners) (after this party, Andrea could never again pretend to be someone else, yet she failed to reassemble her only self) he massacred her in a woefully self-destructive scene which revolved around a game of To Tell the Truth. Originally put forth as a bit of playful nostalgia for the '60s, the game turned into the knife that immolated Andrea. The betrothed and his audience feasted upon her with a voluptuousness of complete destruction. Through him, they ended up knowing about things that she even hid from herself:

—A perfect couple: she's frigid and I'm impotent.

—Of course not. We masturbate.

—She has a fear of penetration. So do I.

—Her greatest wish is to have a real orgasm. She even tried it once in a vacant lot, to see if that would help. It didn't.

— A dowry, are you kidding? All I got from her were her debts.

— You must be kidding. The one who always redoes her column for her is J. J. I should actually say "does" . . . everything. With that many errors, it's better just to start over.

— Thirty? Hell, thirty-seven. I've seen the birth certificate.

—Oh, she's made love, all right. To another woman, but I can't recall her name.

—A real pill-popper, I'm telling you . . .

—I prefer men.

So Andrea got totally drunk and proceeded to offer herself to all the men at the party, provocatively aggressive (she actually scratched a few with her fingernails!), eliciting an atmosphere of uncontrollable desire (a few studs offered to break her of her frigidity; one of them grabbed her hand and put it you-know-where, so she could feel it!), until at some point a lesbian walked into the bathroom on her (and started kissing her wildly, on the mouth!). Yet it was all this madness that ultimately saved her. It thrust her, triumphant now, into the spotlight of their desires.

## 10.

In the days of drunkenness and solitude that followed, throughout that long April of 1970, Andrea reread—at times, crying—the old letters, the clippings out of newspapers; looked back over all the photographs (from that simple three-by-four), presents, poems, dedications, and souvenirs. Like an old army general reminiscing over his medals—the proof that all had taken place.

Society reopened its case against her, this time with evidence. Witnesses testified behind closed doors; intimacies were disclosed. There were even rumors of an obscene diary, written by a subversive journalist, quietly being sold in mimeographed copies. Apparently it recounted, in incredible detail, his secret affair with Andrea. They reviewed all that had been said by the young painter at that infamous birthday party, with modifications to suit the tastes of the narrator or listener. It was a way of seeming to be better informed, as if the whole thing were a competition and some didn't mind cheating.

Finally, the sons and daughters of outward appearance, in the face of so much evidence, could hardly be seen with Andrea; her readers, moreover, refused to be subjected to the taint of her transgressions. Summarily condemned, incapable of rising from the ashes, Andrea left their city without a backward glance.

The prisoners of the mountain expressed a sigh of relief. Yet, in the years that followed, they were gradually overtaken by an inexpressible longing.

# CORRUPTION

## FATHER. 1941.

He looked at his wife's belly: genitals, laboratory, nest; capable of delivering, expeditiously, a tiny crying baby. My little son, though, is to have everything I never had: affection, a father in the house, toys, comfort, security. An insecure male, asserting himself through paternity.

## MOTHER. 1941.

The worst is at night, when I'm so tired: to have to get up in order to breast-feed. Ah, Lord, what's the point of having my own anyway? Better to adopt one that's already grown up a little.

## SON. 1941.

(Like this:) *whann whann whannn* (tears) *shap-shap-shap* (someone coming) *mhnn-mhnn-mhnn* (mama).

## FATHER. 1942.

One year, now. Already a person about whom one can have no doubts: a man with a son. Upon this small defenseless creature he could openly exert the enormous ill/good effect of wielding an influence, escaping that woman who always surrounded him with a dubious protection. Brazilian ships were being torpedoed off the coast; people ran through the streets, hurling rocks; President Getúlio Vargas seemed to hesitate; the homes of Germans were set afire, businesses wrecked, Italians were left without flour—they were the "real culprits" of the war. It hardly disturbed the father though, licensed to strut down the street, attaché case in hand, smoking an Adelphos: after all, the man is working to guarantee his son's future. Still, there were those in government who believed that the real criminals of the war lay elsewhere: speeches by Franklin Roosevelt were censured, Soviet defeats were applauded. Of course, if his son needed applause for learning a new word or for the unsteady effort to toddle across the room without stumbling, he was there to provide it at the right moment. Not Lenice though, she hardly paid attention. What a mother; it's like she's rejected him! Thirty-seven Brazilian ships sunk, nearly a thousand dead. Impossible to avoid war, to go against the people. Góis Monteiro and the Greenshirts still resisted; the fifth column engaged in continual espionage; Lenice paid no attention; and, finally, Vargas was forced to declare war on the Germans. Thus ended the dream of a fascist Brazilian state. And he learned to compensate for Lenice's inadequacy by intervening in favor of the boy—a creature who could be led astray—and out of pure good/ill will he became the barrier between the toddler and his mother.

## MOTHER. 1942.

I'm losing him, I've already lost him. I knew it would end up like this, I knew he'd come between us. I, who cherish him more dearly than anyone could cherish a son, who protected him from all danger, who gave him all the love he needed for survival, I'm actually losing him. I've already lost him. He doesn't even miss me, doesn't have a desire to come back into my body, receives my affections coldly. It was so good before. To have him inside me, mine alone, my boy whom I protected and cared for. So fragile, so beautiful. Now there's this baby who's come between my Cléber and me.

## SON. 1942.

—Give it back.
(He gave it.)
—Gi't ba'.
(They gave it to him.)
(He learned.)
Mama get angry. Dadda not get angry. (Therefore:) Mama ugly. Dadda not ugly.

Mama give appa' sauce. (Therefore:) Mama good.
Dadda play. (Therefore:) Dadda mine.
(He learned.)

## FATHER. 1943.

An outing. He was watching how his son's hair reflected the morning light. A few people walked by and remarked: what a beautiful boy! Father and son, there in the park together rolling on the grass, running along the pathways that circled the greens, or simply talking—while the son played the grown-up and Daddy played the child—small talk about intimate things, like where to make pee-pee, which the father resolved in the simplest fashion: do it right over there. He stared at the mouth and chin which reduplicated his own. Spends the whole day with me and never gets tired. With Lenice, he gets bored right away. Anyway I never saw a mother like her, always exhausted, nothing but ill will toward her own child. He patted the boy's blond curls, an impulse of protectiveness, rewarded with a smile. Even if Robby needed her, she couldn't stand to be with him for more than half an hour at a time. The son ran along unsteadily, the father watching him attentively. He observed the brutishness of the boy, plunging ahead without equilibrium or direction. He'll be a tough one when he grows up, all right. I never had this kind of freedom, the security of having a real father around, that crazy bastard. The son now asked for attention, now for a popsicle, now for a pony ride, now for a balloon, now for an orange, but not with the skin on it. And to go down the slide, and carry me, and wanna get down, and wanna drink of water—while the father took satisfaction in the act of providing, in being on hand, in forming the only certainty in that blond head full of whimsical desire. Always, on such mornings, they came home dirty, ruddy-faced accomplices.

## MOTHER. 1943.

He doesn't like me anymore, I can tell. It doesn't matter, I tell myself, it just doesn't matter. I act as if I don't notice. I keep telling myself I'm not going to be tortured I'm not suffering, see? You can't torture me! . . . But each day I get more and more discouraged, until finally it begins to creep up on me again, and I suffer, me of all people, so terribly tired. It's funny, I guess I've always been alone. . . . Not in that first year of marriage though, only after this child was born. It's so long since he's come to bed with me, and I tell myself: it just doesn't matter, I can do without that. But can I? And it's Cléber who drives him from me.

## SON. 1943.

The table hides (behind) the chair (he learned).

(By experimenting, raising and lowering his head on the back of the chair, he learned, surprised that) the chair hides (but does not eliminate) the table.

(Some objects actually served to hide others, like) the toy chest covers the toys.

So Robby hid his little truck (elsewhere) to play with (whenever).

Robby can (also) hide (himself).

(On the first try, soon followed by others:) she didn't see Robby.

(It failed, however, when) he hid Cléber to play with (later:) Cléber vanished (didn't stay there).

(Therefore, the anxiety was born in him that) Cléber goes away, Mommy goes away. Cló go 'way (people don't stay)!

My truck mine (he consoled himself, finding it in the same place: objects merited confidence).

(Some objects provoked happy surprises:) Robby made a choo-choo, Daddy. Found it here, Daddy (behind things were happy surprises too).

(He looked, didn't find and cried, abandoned:) Daddy go'way from Robby.

(One day he opened a door and saw) Cléber squeezing her tightly. (Fighting?) Daddy go 'way to Mommy (he suspected whenever he didn't see him).

Daddy, don't go sleep with Mommy (he pleaded jealously and deceived, before bedtime), no!

## FATHER. 1944.

He became rich. With the urgency of a man who has already let too much time slip by, he assumed full control of the import-export firm of Miranda, Oliveira, Martins and Co., which his own father had led to bankruptcy six years before. The Russians—a *real* surprise!—liberated Leningrad from the German siege which had lasted for two years, and they were shifting to the offensive in the Baltic and the Ukraine. England and the United States, caught by surprise, accelerated their plans for the European counteroffensive. Except for work, he dedicated himself totally to his son, although occasionally at nighttime Lenice would lock him between her avid legs. Brazil finally entered the war: with a waving of white handkerchiefs, a V for victory, and many a mother's tears. The cobra's off to sea: "Our final victory / the glory of my rifle / the ration in my sack / if God be willing / I'll be back / from whatever lands / I travel by / to see home again / before I die." The war ate up sugar, coffee, meat, cotton. And he, he bought his first car, a '41 Chevrolet convertible: stops on a dime!

She has no feelings whatsoever for Robby, I'm sure of that now. And she wants to separate me from him, to go back to the way it was before. But he would refuse to, and take pains to be a good father in his own eyes, remotely wishing *his* father could see him now, to learn something about the state of the art. He was rehabilitating fatherhood, ironing out the flaws.


## MOTHER. 1944.

Both of them act so deviously toward me. Now, they walk in and out of the house without so much as blinking at me. Easy to guess what they're thinking: I'll walk right by and not even look at her. One's corrupted the other. Cléber used to be so affectionate; he was my little boy. How could I have ever wanted another child? This one: so distant with me, so devious in his behavior. Whenever his father isn't around he goes off and hides somewhere in a corner with his toys—I've already told that boy he's not to play with scissors—hiding from me! Doing nothing, totally silent till Cléber comes home. As if I didn't exist!

And I'm the one who gets them ready for their outings. Each wearing himself out over the other; while me, me they give nothing! Robby during the day, Cléber at night. Everyone tells me I'm even more beautiful than when I was single, like Maria Montez; they say it. Well, I think I'm more the Dorothy Lamour type, but a lot of them insist I could pass for Maria Montez's sister. But after making me this son, Cléber thinks he has no more obligation to me. Every time one of them has to acknowledge me a little, I can tell how furious it makes them, as if one were betraying the other.

## SON. 1944.

The tiger's hidden behind the hill. The little boy's running away with his father, fleeing the mother who won't let the father take a walk with the little boy. The little boy doesn't want to go any farther, no, because he's scared of the big tiger, but his father promises to kill the tiger. No, the boy doesn't want him to kill the big tiger, no, because the mother's coming after them, so let the tiger eat her. The little boy's father tells him to come and hide in the big forest because the mother and the tiger are getting closer. The mother's getting closer; closer and closer, and calling: Oh, little boy! Oh, Cléber! Come on out of there because I already see where you are. But the big tiger hears her calling and comes running out and *rhaaaaaaa-ruaaahhhh-uhnnnnn-raaaahhuummmmmmmm.*

—Give me those scissors, Robby.

Mother (always) spoils everything. (Suddenly) no more tiger, or father, or boy, or thicket, because mother said scissors and the tiger was the scissors and (therefore) the father was the box of matches the little boy was a match the thicket was the button box the mother was a scrap of cloth.

(Later, he put on his father's slippers and took a pipe in his mouth and was saying:)

—Now, now, Lenice, what's wrong with the boy having a little fun with some scissors?

(Until mother came and spoiled everything:)

—Go put that pipe right back where it belongs, Robby. You'll break it.

(Lots of things he couldn't do, the hard thing was to know exactly what, or when. Therefore:) he liked it better whenever he could hide somewhere, do whatever he wanted, but no noise, no, or she'll come.

## FATHER. 1945.

The National Democratic Union was organized in Minas Gerais, and he was right there, on the side of the liberals. The city praised him. He was thirty-two years of age, five of them married, with one child of four. He had earned the right to show his face, offer opinions, exert power. Victory in the war was certain, President Vargas was still uncertain, political prisoners were granted amnesty (Vargas hoping to adjust to the shifting currents). New parties surfaced: the Brazilian Workers Party, the Social Democratic Party, (power slipping through Vargas's fingers; and he, still failing to recognize the times, or recognizing them only too well and therefore legitimizing) the Communist Party. More and more sure of himself, the father would argue the strategy of the German defeat, (perhaps) the sense of continuity in the Vargas-backed candidacy of Marshal Dutra, (but more importantly) the interests of his own class. Of course, hadn't he done just that for the Association for Commerce, when confidently rising to his feet (flanked by several women who obviously desired him), to urge the right-wing candidacy of Brigadier General Eduardo Gomes, he asserted: either we put him in the presidential palace right now, or we inherit a worse mess later on. . . . In the streets they were shouting *Vargas! Vargas!*, threatening the elections. Then the bomb exploded; Japan surrendered; and Vargas was deposed.

Roberto's games with objects and with people left the father astounded. He pretended to understand most of it, cautiously accompanying the magic of his son's inventions—you could never be sure a box was just a box. He marveled, and told his friends: someday that boy's going to be quite an artist; no, really. And he considered himself privileged to have a son who would hide until his father's return, as Lenice had so often complained. I wish I'd had a father like me.

### MOTHER. 1945.

One. Two. Four. Five. Six. Six o'clock. Cléber ought to be leaving work by now. Not one call today—is this the way it's to be? Every day, longer and longer—and this awful heat! When was it, not even five years ago: oh, how I loved to wait for my Cléber—think of nothing else the whole afternoon. First I'd plan our dinner. Then I'd have my bath, perfume my body—all for Cléber. Finally, I'd start his bath running, set out his bottle of Atkinson's cologne. What did it matter if he was still at work; he kept me company just the same. Seems like only yesterday. Now I sit here waiting for someone to phone, all alone in this house—I could have a man here, nobody would ever know—waiting for afternoon to arrive, waiting for evening to arrive, waiting for morning to arrive, watching the moon go by, who cares for starlit skies, when you're alone the magic moonlight dies. . . . What was it I did? When did I lose that little boy who married me, even more a virgin than I was? This isn't my husband, a man who thinks he knows everything, then discusses politics all day long—what do I care what some crazy Carlos Prestes and his communists are up to? Robby isn't the one to blame, it's too late now. It's all Cléber's fault, with that head of his. I'll never feel about anyone else the way I felt about him—not even for Cléber, supposing now things magically change and he needs me again. That's what's so horribly sad. And who can ever feel the way he used to feel about me? No one. . . . My Roberto? Always such a strange little boy; almost never smiles! Just willful, strange, always silent— my God, how am I to blame for all this? Give me time, dear God! Time enough and presence of mind to see that Robby grows up a happy boy!

## SON. 1945.

(So complicated.) He would look at a grown-up person, his father, then his mother who was smaller, then himself who was even smaller, then a little baby who was still smaller, then (he imagined) a little tiny baby no bigger than an ant—but he couldn't understand: when does a person begin to grow, how does it happen? (The easiest thing would be to ask, but he deceived himself by pretending to know lots of things and only ventured asking once in a while.) (To know, for him, was the means of astounding and at the same time imitating his father: Daddy always knows everything.)

—Mommy, how do people start growing?

—Oh, Robby, what a question.

She almost never knew right away. (You couldn't always like her.) He'd ask her some other time. (Once you fell into difficulty, you had to be very careful, so as not to stumble over the same mystery again, but it was easy to lose track.)

—Well, Robby, after people are born they grow and grow until finally they become all grown up.

—Well, how do people get born? (A new problem, which he was keeping to himself—with the responsibility of solving it at some point later on—until driven to ask out of curiosity.) How do people get born?

—Mother asks God up in heaven, and then God sends a stork that carries the little infant in his beak and delivers it right to mother's door.

The father laughed and told it a different way.

—The mother has an egg almost like a chicken egg only much smaller, but she doesn't lay it, it sits inside her stomach. But instead of a little chick hatching from inside the egg, a little baby gets born, which later on comes out of the mother at the hospital, and then grows and grows till he's all grown up.

(Mistrustful, he avoided asking his mother other questions. Her certainties only caused added insecurity.)

### FATHER. 1946.

After he turned off the light, Lenice's legs wrapped tenaciously around him, and what he heard seemed like a snarl. He tried deftly to disengage himself, but her legs gripped him all the more inescapably. He relaxed himself, to seem lazy, trying still another means of escape, but felt her groping with one hand for his penis. Continuing to relax that way, he persisted in flight until he heard her snarl again, muffled in the pillow: "At least be a man." Struck, exposed, and exposing himself, but now to a question of pride, he rearranged himself to attend to her. His body, however, refused to respond to the obligation she imposed. He'd let himself be drawn in—that challenge to prove himself a man—and become totally ensnared by it. Yet what was fundamental was still lacking: any attraction to her, any desire. "It's no use, it's no use,"—he heard once again, in that same muted snarl; now with a hatred for her, a desire to run her through with a prick-knife, to finish her! Then he discovered, furiously, how quickly the will to crush her worked to disinhibit him, his penis suddenly hardening. Here, here!

### MOTHER. 1946.

There's nothing left for me in this house. What is there if no one wants me? I was a fool to put up with it all this time. Now it's gotten to a point where, when I want him, he gives me his hatred: I won't be defiled like that. And Roberto's just the same. Could anyone have made more of an effort than I did this past year, to try and get him to pay me just the slightest bit of attention! Even helping him with his scrapbook on the war. Just the picture of General Patton was missing. No use, though. Each caress only drives him further from me. Neither one of them wants me, I might as well face the fact. There's something so unhealthy about all this, but I don't even want to think about it; God help me. What is there about me that they find so awful?—as a mother, or even as a woman. I was a fool to think all this time that I was the one at fault. It's them! They're the ones who act so peculiar with that intimacy of theirs, God forgive me. Well, I've taken all I can stand. It's no use, they don't want me, and that's the end of it. I'm leaving this house.


## SON. 1946.

Some things God never manages to prevent: that he should see them in bed, for example. God sees everything that we do in secret, his mother had warned him. He knew that God was watching and wasn't pleased by what he saw; that it was risky to get out of bed and go see Daddy and Mommy sleeping. The danger was strangely enough the best part. Nothing happened, day after day, simply the expectation that something might actually happen. (In his memory, something had already happened yet he still didn't manage to figure out what it was, or where.) He waited, hidden—God watching him there in the darkness—until the certainty came that they were sleeping, and that only when they were awake could what might one day happen really happen. Through the slightly open doorway he listened to the breathing of their sleep, fading-fading-fading, falling asleep.

Then one day it happened.

After his father shut off the light the darkness seemed the same, as if nothing were going to happen, and then suddenly he heard her voice, furious:

—At least be a man!

He awaited the reaction of his father, but heard nothing—no slap, no smack; nothing—only that silence. No, it wasn't silence: they were fighting! He heard (fleeting memory) that wordless struggle, only exertion and breathing and squeezing. Knowing it was no fight and wondering: why are they fighting? Then he heard the muffled voice of his suffocating mother, smothered in the pillow:

—It's no use! It's no use!

Was his father winning? (What? If it wasn't a fight.) His own eyes couldn't adjust to the darkness; he could barely make out a black shadow on the sheets.

—Here! Here!

Was he getting furious too! Hitting her? He didn't hear any slap, only the exertion of the struggle. He listened, distraught now, to that increasing and

diminishing exertion (incomprehensible), and when he finally did see something it seemed like his father was squeezing her, tightly! (This had already
happened once—when? Cléber was breaking his promise—but what had he
promised? Not remembering clearly, Roberto did what he could, not to catch
his father in the wrong.) He began to feel afraid of all the darkness, God,
silence. He delayed calling out: Father! (expecting his fear to become finally
intolerable).

—I'm leaving this house, Cléber.

His mother's voice, in that tone that meant it was really going to happen.
His fear subsided and Cléber was once more his and God didn't matter.
Shrunken in the darkness, he listened to Cléber's mute approbation. He
thought about a house without his mother in it and and imagined a blank
space where he could have everything: toys, Cléber, house—everything!
Outside it was beginning to turn from black to gray, he heard a rooster crow-
ing in the distance, father and mother were asleep, and he went back to his
bed thinking that tomorrow, at last, he'd sleep in his mother's place.

# SANCTUARY . . .

. . . OF ONE JORGE PAULO DE FERNANDES, AGE THIRTY-ONE, SUCCESSFUL YOUNG LAWYER, FORMER BUDDING AUTHOR UNTIL AGE TWENTY-FIVE, WHEREUPON THE DEFECT WAS WHOLLY CORRECTED SOCIALLY AND REASONABLY WELL TOLERATED BY INTELLECTUALS, AUTHOR OF ONE REALLY FIRST-RATE SHORT STORY, PUBLISHED BY A REPUTABLE QUARTERLY IN 1961. SINGLE, RICH, STRONG CONTENDER FOR A TOP SLOT AMONG THE TEN BEST-DRESSED BACHELORS OF THE CITY OF BELO HORIZONTE IN 1970.

He stepped out of the elevator and headed toward number 306, a little too hastily, a little too anxiously, on the run. Produced the right key, opened the door, entered quickly, and closed the door behind him.

Safe. Dark in here.

He locked the door.

Not quite dark, yet.

He put on a light.

Doesn't help.

Shut off the light.

—Damn.

Put on the light.

Well, it's better on.

Looked at his watch.

Five after six. Plenty of time.

Went to the table. Found a letter and a note.

Maria's handwriting.

Read the note.

"Dr. Jorge: Mr. Roberto Miranda called to remind you about the party over at his house tonight." Second time I got this message today.

Threw the letter onto the table without opening it.

Bank statement. Long time since anyone wrote me a letter.

Left his attaché case on the table. Went into the bedroom. Took off his jacket. Placed it on the bed. Took off his tie, without undoing the knot. Placed it on the bed. Sat on the bed.

Have a rest later.

Took off his shoes. Stretched, wriggling his fingers, yawned. Took off his socks. Looked down at the floor.

Damn. How many times have I told Maria not to keep putting my slippers under the bed.

Leaned on the bed with his right arm and, with his left hand, tried to reach his slippers.

—Shit!

Stood up and looked around, searching.

A broom. —That stupid Maria again.

Left the bedroom. Crossed the living room, into the kitchen.

Floor's goddamn cold.

Got a broom from the pantry. Crossed the kitchen, into the living room. Entered the bedroom. Put on the light. Crouched in front of the bed and swept the slippers out with the broom. Left the broom there.

Fuck Maria.

Put on his slippers. Paused.

Now what? Have to piss. Wonder if Maria left dinner ready for me? What time should I go to the party? What'll I do till then? Should have bought a magazine. Ah, *O Globo,* in my briefcase.

Left the bedroom. Went to the table. Opened the attaché case and took out the paper. Sat in the easy chair. Read the back page.

Forgot to piss.

Read the funnies. Read the editorial on the front page.

Damn straight: nothing but fucking commies. Aah, have to take a wicked piss.

Got up, leaving the paper on the chair. Left the living room. Went into the bathroom. Took a look at himself passing by the mirror.

So fine.

Stopped in front of the toilet. Urinated, watching the bubbles foam in the bowl.

Ah, that's better—Hmmmmmm.

Stopped urinating and shook his penis a few times. Looked at it. Pulled back the foreskin, exposing the glans.

Eh, pecker.

Smiled. Covered his penis, wiggling his hips a little. Smelled his hand. Flushed the toilet with the other hand. Went back to the mirror. Took his hand from his nose as soon as he saw himself.

Pig.

Looked at himself, rubbing his face with the other hand. Put on the light. Lifted his chin, scratched his chest, his cheeks.

Stubble already. Christ, did it this morning.

Turned a little to the left, catching the profile. Then the same for the right side. Looked at his hairline.

Getting old. Better get married.

Lifted his face closer to the mirror. Pulled the skin under the eyes. Stretched the skin on the temples.

No. Still got a way to go.

Smiled. Tightened his smile and examined the teeth.

Yellow. Cigarettes.

Left the mirror. Carefully washed his hands. Dried them. Checked that they were clean, carefully examining them and rubbing the fingertips. Had one more look at himself passing the mirror. Left the bathroom.

Take off these clothes.

Saw the paper. Hesitated a second. Entered the bedroom. Took off his pants and left them on the bed. Once seated, examined the front of his undershorts.

Always a few drops left, no matter how you shake it. What should I wear? Aah, nothing. Too hot.

Checked his watch.

Ten to seven. Still pretty early. Read some more and then give myself a shave.

Left the bedroom. Sat in the easy chair.

Jesus, forgot about dinner.

Made a move to get up. Changed his mind.

Still plenty of time.

Opened the paper. Read about the nation. Scratched his nose. Considered a statement by retired Senator Filinto Müller. Scratched his nose. Slid the index finger up one nostril. Kept reading. The finger explored in a gradual, semicircular motion. Kept reading. With the thumb, removed the material from under the nail collected from his nose. Kept reading. Let his arm dangle over the side of the easy chair, with two fingers already hard at work, circularly drying out the little ball. Kept reading. Raised his eyes momentarily from the paper, looked around, searching for the right place, then flicking the little ball under the other chair. Went back to reading. Rubbed his nose with the back of his finger. Snorted, to test the nostril. Turned to other news.

Christ, six years since the revolution. Seems like yesterday.

Read about the droughts up in the Northeast.

Fifty thousand refugees? Agh, damn papers are always exaggerating. That's half of Maracanã Stadium, for Christ's sake.

—No way.

Turned the page. Read everything on Vietnam. Shifted position: lifting his right leg onto the arm of the easy chair and switching the paper into the right hand. Began reading the society page. Massaged his leg a bit with his left hand, then reached into the fly of his undershorts to touch his privates. Scratched his privates. Read the society page about elegant Verinha Nabuco. The hand lingering in the opening of the fly. Verinha Nabuco was currently caught up in a flurry of activity over preparations for her charity benefit. His hand scratching around the scrotum, the penis, playing with it. But Verinha Nabuco's annual bash, this year, for the benefit of unwed mothers, is bound to be a success. Raised the hand to his nose. Finished the column. Sniffed. Opened the paper fully with both hands and scanned the day's crime reports. Closed the paper and tossed it onto the coffee table.

Now what? Dinner.

Shifted his position again: taking his right leg off the arm of the easy chair, stretching both legs until they touched the coffee table, placing both elbows on the arms of the easy chair, slouching back and relaxing.

Who needs undershorts.

Looked down at himself, naked now.

Keep on dieting, got it? Doesn't cost you anything.

Looked at his fingernails.

Perfect.

Held his hands up at a distance, to see better.

Beautiful.

Looked at his feet.

Better cut the toenails. Later.

Shifted his weight a little to one side and farted.

Smell?

Nothing. Besides, with this diet. You eliminate the gas and the stomach shrinks.

Farted again. Yawned.

Better take a nap. Won't be in shape for the party.

Closed his eyes.

Should leave here about nine-thirty . . . ought to be right. Damn Maria, naturally forgets to write down the time, shit. Bet everybody'll be there. Better think up a few intelligent remarks, couple of jokes too. Make a list in a while. Rodolfo and that crippled son-of-a-bitching queerbait of his like to play games with me. Better get a neat little list together, real juicy stuff, shut their little mouths up good and tight. Elêusis ought to be there too, incredible tits, never any bra. Boy, what I could do with a woman like that.

Smiled, enjoying the thought.

Be the envy of everyone . . . gets 'em all, all right. Mônica.

Stopped smiling.

No comparison. Who wants to fuck brains? The body's what counts, nice, tight receptacle. Mônica acts more like a prude. To see her behave you'd think she didn't even like me. But she does, all right, crazy about me. Hides it though, all caught up in this modern-woman crap. Put a few choice bits down for her, too. Here in the apartment, no problem: me on top, her on the bottom, strictly old fashioned. Outside comes all this modern bullshit, and suddenly it's the woman who's got to be the one on top. Should teach her a lesson. Make her behave like Maria: my slave, and doesn't hide it from anybody. Obviously a creole's got to be different, but Christ, that has to be one beautiful creole. You'd take her for a movie star. In here, though, a slave to me.

Opened his eyes.

Grovels on the floor, not enough courage to be even jealous of Mônica. Serves coffee to her and me in bed the next morning and doesn't bat an eye. Scared I'll decide to get rid of her. Come home and she's waiting right here by the chair, ready to take my shoes off, my jacket, my shirt, my trousers, carries it all inside for me, gets my bath ready, comes over and kneels down in front of me, on the floor right at my feet, waiting to see if I'll give her my prick. Slave.

Fixed his eyes on the ashtray, which was reflecting his face in irregular outline.

Tonight at the party, have to make Mônica confess right in front of everyone: crazy about me.

Smiled to himself.

I'll do it.

Looked at his watch.

After eight. Better eat something. Wonder if they'll have any food at the party?

Got up. Went into the kitchen. Put on the light. Checked the table. Opened the refrigerator.

Hmm, hungry.

Took out a plate.

Ham, boiled egg, salad. Crazy about me.

Put the plate down on the place mat, the table already set for him. Sat down. Checked his hands. Smelled them. Got up. Went into the bathroom. Washed his hands. Returned to the kitchen. Sat down.

Mônica. Hmph. Hesitates to back me up even when I say something. Not a question of disagreeing with me either. Afraid all they'll think is she's backing me up because she's in love with me. Always cautious. But I'm sick and tired of all her cautiousness—yeah, fed up—stupid pretensions. That day when—who was it? can't remember who it was said my cuff links were gross, must have been that crippled little faggot. Think she'd speak up to tell him they were a present from her? No way, just sat there, deaf and dumb, till finally I had to tell them: Mônica gave them to me, so they wouldn't think I'd buy crap like that. Can never count on her; only here.

Started chewing.

Ashamed of liking me, can you believe it? Must be sick. Egotistical, that's all. Incapable of saying love, honey, sweetheart to me like she does here. Not in front of anybody else. Christ, you'd think it was on purpose.

Stopped chewing, alarmed.

Wonder if anybody thinks that? No, too subtle for that crowd.

Started chewing again.

Afraid of them; might make fun of her. Come to think of it, pretty rotten on her part. Like to have somebody hide in the bedroom sometime, just to see the way she performs in private.

Stopped chewing. Smiled, enjoying the idea. Started chewing again.

Like to see the expression on her face when she realized somebody was in there, watching.

Smiled, chewing.

Wow, she'd hate my guts.

Stopped chewing.

Come on, you think I'm about to pull something like that on her?

Started chewing again.

Stupid nonsense. Just get her to stop pretending in front of other people, that's all.

Ate the rest of the meal. Got up from the table. Looked at his watch.

Eight-thirty. Better shave.

Left the kitchen. Entered the bathroom. Looked at himself in the mirror. Raised a hand to his chin, rubbing the stubble with his fingers.

Five o'clock shadow. Better use a new blade.

Opened the medicine cabinet. Took out the shaving cream. Wet his face. Applied the cream with his right hand, watching himself in the mirror. Smiled.

—You handsome devil.

Chuckled to himself.

—You sap.

Rinsed off his hands. Opened the cabinet. Took out his razor. Took out a new blade. Switched the blades in the razor. Started shaving.

Have to teach Mônica a lesson tonight. Don't know how exactly, but somehow. Obvious you can't just ask her, in front of everyone: Mônica, you love me? No . . . maybe you can.

Stopped shaving.

—Mônica, you love me?

Made a face of total revulsion,

No way.

Shaking his head to himself. Started shaving again.

No good like that. Need just the right touch, or they'll do a number on me. I shouldn't even be the one to ask her . . . Ruiter, maybe. Have to talk to him. No. Got a better idea: somebody who doesn't even like me. Rodolfo! Yeah, that's it. Manipulate the guy. Without his even knowing; make *him* do it. That's it!

Stopped shaving.

That's why I can't stand that guy: thinks Mônica doesn't even like me. That's it exactly. Yeah, that son of a bitch be just the one to ask her. To give me the business: Mônica, you mean to tell me you actually like Jorge? And her: of course!

Smiled again, enjoying himself. Started shaving again. Paused. Laughed.

—Kill two birds with one stone.

Started shaving again.

Has to start out casually, just fooling around. A game, maybe—but a game everybody takes seriously.

Stopped shaving.

What about To Tell the Truth? No, they'll think I'm a square, that goes back to the '60s. If only . . . shit: nostalgia! That's it. We'll play with the '60s. That's perfect. Ingenious, matter of fact.

—In-*ge*-nious!

Better make a note of it.

Set the razor on the sink. Went into the bedroom, found a pen and pad. Returned to the bathroom. Put the seat down on the toilet, crouched, placed the pad on the seat and noted: "1960" as a heading. Under the heading wrote: "Music, jokes, events, films."

Who was at Roberto's party in 1960?

On another line: "Who was at the party in '60."

Who got married? Who died? Who mov—

On a another line: "Who married, died, moved, etc."

What else? Finish shaving or I'll be late.

Stood up. Wet his face and applied another layer of foam. Shaved the right side a second time.

Rodolfo and Luis are about to get themselves fucked over tonight, by yours truly. No one could hatch a more ingenious plan.

Leaned his chin out and began to shave his throat a second time.

Have to lead into it slowly. Remember a few jokes from 1960. That fag ass won't even be able to complain. Everyone used to tell jokes in the '60s. What was that one about the guy who went to get laid in the park? And when the woman's already spread-eagled, behind some bushes, and the guy's got his meat out, this cop arrives and arrests him. But the guy says: what the hell am I doing wrong? Then the cop: fucking in the bushes, that's what. The guy says: fucking who? The cop points to the ground and says: well suppose you tell me why that woman's lying right there. And the guy: woman? Christ, officer, if you hadn't warned me I'd have pissed all over her.

Began laughing. Stopped shaving. Bent down and noted: "Joke pissed all over her."

Stood up. Shaved the left side a second time. Paused and lifted his face closer to the mirror, twisting his mouth and chin to the right.

Goddamn, a pimple? Just my luck, shit! Wanted to look perfect tonight. Squeezed it.

Not a pimple. Ingrown hair.

Examined the leakage, wiped it.

Whew, just a tiny hole. All I need is for them to start kidding around with me about masturbation and pimples.

Began shaving again.

Always have to be careful with that crowd, everybody out to fuck you over. But today it's my turn. Before bringing up To Tell the Truth though better I start with some other game. Important people who died, maybe:

Camus, Kennedy, de Gaulle, Hemingway, that sort of thing. Whole shitload. Make up a couple of teams, see who winds up with the most points. Or maybe: first team says some important name, say from Brazilian politics, in the '60s; then somebody on the other team has to tell something about him. Brochado da Rocha. Auro Moura Andrade. Tancredo Neves. Ranieri Mazzilli. Márcio Moreira Alves. Abelardo Jurema. Everyone'll fall for it.

Smiled. Stopped shaving. Bent over and noted: "Test Your Memory—names of Braz. politicians." Stood up. Began to shave around the lips a second time.

Afterwards, easy enough to shift naturally from a game like that to the idea of playing To Tell the Truth. A question of nostalgia, pure '60s. Perfect. And Rodolfo won't miss the opportunity, you can bet, when Mônica's there in the middle.

Smiled again. Became serious.

What if Mônica says no? Even as a joke?

Stopped shaving, the razor poised in space.

Might not want to say; in front of the others. I wonder.

Became very serious: apprehensive.

Would she chicken out? No, Mônica's not like that.

Relaxed again.

Takes things like that seriously. Believes in speaking the truth. No way she'd do that.

Smiled again. Finished shaving. Rubbed his face with his hand.

That's better.

Looked at himself carefully in the mirror.

Now I'm looking good. Best one at the party.

Laughed out loud. Checked the tiny hole from the ingrown hair. Fixed his brow, intently. Rubbed his cheeks with both hands.

Perfect. Now for a quick shower.

Turned on the shower. Adjusted the temperature. Took off his slippers.

Leave 'em for Maria. Likes to pick up after me.

Took off his watch. Tested the temperature of the water. Got into the stall. Scrubbed his face a while, under the shower.

What should I wear, a suit? The charcoal gray one, yeah: look fantastic in it. Soaped himself.

Pale blue shirt. Tie? The Pierre Cardin, pumpkin color. Black socks, black shoes. If Maria didn't shine my shoes for me I'll tan her black ass, tomorrow. Cuff links . . . the black leather ones, should do the trick. Perfect.

Washed his privates, amorously.

—This is what she likes, that hungry little pussy.

Laughed to himself. Scrubbed his penis until he had an erection.

—So what do you want, you hungry little fucker? Nothing for you right now. Back to sleep; that's right, that's right; that's better.

Patted his penis. Laughed.

—Hungry little . . .

Rinsed it with care. Smiled.

—Think you're hot stuff, don't you.

Soaped his legs.

Should have cut my toenails. Aah, tomorrow. No one can see.

Rinsed himself. Dried himself. Got out of the stall. Checked himself in the mirror.

Healthy tan. Perfect.

Checked his teeth.

Yellow. Cigarettes; what can you do.

Brushed them with toothpaste. Rinsed his mouth. Spit. Looked in the mirror.

Cigarettes.

Checked his face.

Perfect. —Looking good.

Laughed. Picked up the watch, put it on his wrist. Picked up the note pad and the pen. Put on his slippers. Left the bathroom. Entered the bedroom.

Can't wait to see the look on Rodolfo's face.

Wrote on the pad: "To Tell the Truth." Combed his hair. Slapped his cheeks with aftershave lotion. Took a charcoal gray suit from the closet.

Boy, I'll look fantastic.

Put on undershorts, pants. Switched his wallet from the other pants to the ones he was wearing. Put socks on. Got shoes out.

Ah, she did polish them. Perfect.

Telephone rang.

—Fuck!

Answered it.

—Hello? . . . Yes, it is. . . . Carlos who? . . . Yes, I know him. What's the problem? . . . Arrested for what? . . . Friend, nothing. Look, you want to know something? It's just as well, it'll get rid of him for a while. The guy's a pain in the ass. . . . Oh, do you think I have time to fool around with stuff like that? No way. I'm busy now, understand? I'll look into it tomorrow. . . . To-morrow, my friend, forget about it till tomorrow. Good night now, ciao.

Hung up.

Aah, communists. —They make a mess of things and then come crying. They can go to hell.

Sat on the bed. Put on his shoes.

She loves polishing them.

Rubbed some cologne on his neck, chest, arms. Got into his shirt. Put the cuff links on. Checked how he looked.

Perfect.

Put his tie on. Looked at his watch.

Nine thirty-five.

Slipped into the jacket. Took his keys. Checked out his whole appearance in the closet-door mirror.

—Splendid, George.

Combed his hair a bit more. Turned from one side to the other before the mirror. Brushed some lint off his suit. Checked himself again. Smiled.

—Best damn one at the whole party.

Tore off the top page from the note pad.

—My artillery.

Slipped the piece of paper into his pocket. Looked at the pile of clothes strewn all over the bedroom.

What a mess.

Shoes, socks, jacket, shirt, broom, slippers, pants.

So, Maria cleans it up. No one can see.

Saluted goodbye to himself in the mirror. Left the bedroom. Paused by the door in the living room. Took hold of the doorknob.

Forget anything?

Patted his pockets. Stared at the apartment.

My things. Home sweet home.

Became serious, a little apprehensive at the thought of imminent departure from his sanctuary.

God protect me defend me and keep me.

Crossed himself, opened the door, and exited from the sanctuary.

A short time later, an admiring glance from the doorman acknowledged Mr. de Fernandes pulling out from the garage, looking suave as always and giving off an agreeable scent of cologne.

# CLASS STRUGGLE

Ataíde left the house at seven in the morning and worried about the bus being late.

Fernando left at eleven-thirty, angry with life because some notes were falling due.

Ataíde had given a warm kiss to his wife, Cremilda so-and-so, promising to come home directly after work.

Fernando didn't always remember to kiss his wife. He was too preoccupied.

Ataíde managed to scrape together three ridiculous minimum wages but was hoping for better times.

Fernando usually slept until ten and then threatened his employer: either I get the raise or it's ciao, baby.

Ataíde every now and then had a terrible toothache, and on those days it was better to stay out of his way.

Fernando was always telling his wife not to talk so much—with no hope; with no results.

Ataíde had no children as yet, but was planning to.

Fernando had two children, despite all the planning.

Ataíde was a bit younger.

Fernando was thirty-something.

Ataíde liked to strum a little samba once in a while.

Fernando, without a good soccer game on Sunday, was unbearable by Monday.

Ataíde made love to his lovely Cremilda at least every other day.

Fernando was on tap once a week: Saturday night, or Sunday morning.

Ataíde—how many times!—because he was quite a boxer, wouldn't put up with insults, even though his Cremilda always warned him a man shouldn't be so proud, especially if he's poor, because someday he might have to beg for something, and that would come as a hard day. But he always answered her by saying I promise you, baby, I'll think about that, but not right now, okay?

Fernando generally tended to shy away from a showdown.

Ataíde had rather dark skin and black, kinky hair.

Fernando was already showing a bit of a potbelly.

Ataíde, around eleven at night, usually tried to get in a little soccer with a big ball of socks. It helped him digest those poorer cuts of meat, always a little tough despite the efforts of his Cremilda.

Fernando was muttering to himself in his Volkswagen and decided: today, I want to get good and bombed.

Ataíde considered himself something of an artist: he backed away slightly from the wall he was painting—one foot behind the other, his head cocked a little to one side, right hand on his waist—admiring the work he was finishing and telling himself: man, you sure are one hell of a house painter.

Fernando—whenever Inês brought another check over for him to approve would try out a different approach, because Inês had a pair of cover-girl legs, and he liked temporary girls a lot: typists, stenographers, secretaries.

Ataíde had plans to take his Cremilda out to the Palladium Cinema next Sunday, to see the latest James Bond thriller—that is, if he still had some money.

Fernando read cloudy weather with possible showers for the weekend forecast in the papers, and calculated with fury that it would probably spoil the soccer match on Sunday.

Ataíde stopped work at 6:00 p.m. and walked to Plaza Station to buy a coconut chocolate for his lovely Cremilda. While he was there he took the opportunity to have a couple quick shots of rum.

Fernando had left the office at 5:30, and was already drinking by twenty minutes of six—he was good at that sort of thing—when he got into a scuffle with a mulatto who knocked his glass over while buying a coconut chocolate there at the counter: hey, watch what you're doing, faggot.

Ataíde didn't hesitate, and slammed him.

# PREOCCUPATIONS

## . . . 1968.

a) of the mother of a college student

lead him not into temptation but deliver him from all evil amen.

My Carlos, every day he says: I've got an ad hoc committee meeting tonight. Every day: I won't be home for dinner, Mom, got another ad hoc session tonight. Where? Over at the Student Union. My God, what's all this ad hoc business? I keep meaning to ask Carlos. I know they're up to something, with all those girls in their miniskirts.

A mother's work is never done. . . .

Ay, dear God, lead him not into temptation, deliver him from all those girls on the streets, including the daughter of that Nonato. Better he marries that girl from school. Even with her legs showing all the time, at least she's a decent child—you'd think she hadn't a mother to look after her, out on the streets every night—but better with her.

Imagine the nerve of that Nonato, even before he left Ponte Nova: I don't want your son hanging around with my Cristina. One day God will punish him; then I'll be the one to say: tell your daughter to stop following my son around, the little tramp. My poor Carlos crying every night in his room like that, but you can't let on you know and try to comfort them, they get so angry. But one day God will punish that Nonato.

A daughter would have been so much easier to keep up with. What can I do, just a poor widow. . . .

You never know what condition they'll come home in—picked up by the police, shot, a leg broken—with all that running around. Never know *if* they'll even come home. I can't stand to think about it: arrested, dead! Deliver him from evil. Amen, amen!

The Lord only knows what's gotten into these kids. A thing so dangerous, without rhyme or reason. Every time he goes out of the house he leaves me in this state. And these tear-gas bombs they make, they can blow off an arm— it's not just gas anymore. And then in the stampede, the Lord only knows: he might get clubbed over the head, trampled by a horse. Dear God, save me, save my Carlos. But can I say *anything* anymore? Nothing helps, they never listen to you. They treat you like dirt, always too busy doing something—no time, running and running. My Lord, what's so important to make them run around like that?

I tell him: look at those clothes, just look at them! Shirt torn, pants faded—
if you're not poor, that's another matter, but poor people can't afford to go
around looking like that. And I don't dare ask him to get a haircut, I've given
up on that. And the beard? "You're so out of it, Mom." Out of it? I hope so.

How am I to tell if he's brushed his teeth or not before he goes to bed?
He comes in so late. . . . Just noises in the bathroom, at least then I know he's
home. But after he's been out with God only knows what kind of woman.
Lead him not into temptation. . . .

Don't forget to brush those teeth before you get into bed, you hear me!

Walking around with bare feet on a cold floor. Go ahead, wind up with
rheumatism. It's no use putting his slippers by his bed every day. Next morning, there he is in the kitchen: barefoot for his coffee.

Of course, the worst thing you can do to put a strain on your eyes is to
read without the proper lighting. I'm sick to death of telling him.

You shouldn't go out into a draft after a shower.

Smoking causes cancer, it says right on the package.

Cross at the corner, not in the middle of the block.

You're supposed to chew your food.

Try to respect your elders.

Italian ice with a sore throat—have you ever in your life. . . ?

Don't step on the grass.

At least try not to smoke in the elevator.

Honor thy father and mother.

A few little things . . .

I hope the day comes when somebody will finally put a stop to all this—
this mayhem by students—so a mother can get a night's sleep for a change,
knowing her son is safe and sound.

Long hair and miniskirts! If we'd only forbidden that sort of thing to
begin with, if mothers all over the world had only put a stop to that kind of
thing before it got started, nipped it in the bud, saved our sons. . . . If we'd
only prevented them from learning all those wild dances a few years ago,
they wouldn't act the way they do now, so totally crazy. If we'd simply prohibited the Pill, once and for all, outlawed even the mention of it in the
newspapers. My Lord, if I had a daughter in this day and age I think I'd go
insane, or die of worry: checking her purse all the time, reading her letters
somehow without her knowing, eavesdropping on conversations, taking away
those books they read. That's where the problem lies, if only they couldn't

publish all that stuff about sex, forbid them from undressing on the stage and in the films and on the beaches, those disgusting hippies smoking their marijuana and flaunting their filth in front of all the news cameras—they shouldn't be allowed to show things like that. It's up to us to protect the minds of our children, the eyes and ears of our sons and daughters. Made them get a haircut, that's what we should have done, but now it's too late. They're all over the streets that way, yelling and screaming—it's just playing with fire, allowing them to smoke marijuana. Not my Carlos, thank God. It made him angry that I even suggested such a thing: "You're so completely out of it, Mom. It's not my bag anyway." My bag? What kind of language is that, orangutan? Tell me, really, what do you kids want out of life? "Everything," he says to me, "we want it all." Crazy! That's what they are. As if the power were out walking the streets somewhere. *Youth* power? My Lord, just imagine them deciding what should or shouldn't be done, and the parents can go jump in the lake—no more laws, not a shred of decency left in anyone: unwed mothers, hippies with long hair and no jobs, that disgusting music, filthy magazines. That's all they want: smut—but it's got to stop! The governments should band together—from France, from Brazil, from the United States, Mexico, Germany, everywhere—band together and put a stop to all this. Because a mother can only put up with so much anguish—hardly any money coming in, a widow's pension, the little extra I make with typing, and that's supposed to pay for a son's education? A son who tells me to bug off—that's right, to get lost. His own mother. What do we have our presidents for if they won't take care of such problems. But the governments tell them to go right ahead. Look at France! They let women sit on the beach without a halter. They let students take over schools and throw out the professors. Who's supposed to give the classes? How do you teach without professors? But they think everything is in a book; all you have to do is copy it out on a piece of paper. But they're only kidding themselves. They're no different from the rest of us: if they still have all their teeth, thank God, it's because we made them brush after meals. If they're in college now, it's because we taught them how to read and write, to honor thy father and mother, to respect the rights of others. But they want to pretend that none of that counts anymore. Doesn't count? I'd like to know why? It's time someone came along with the power to help us, to truly comprehend the depth of our affliction, just as we forgive those who trespass against us and lead us not into temptation but deliver us from evil, amen.

I only hope Nonato has to pay, someday, for what he's done. My poor Carlos only got this way in the first place because of that Cristina girl. He used to be over there all the time, poor thing. But at least I knew where he was: every night, all hours. At least there was none of this ad hoc nonsense; singing protest songs, marching at rallies.

Now even the priests are in on it, you can't go to them for help. Instead of calming the kids down, they throw more and more wood on the fire. And we, the mothers, have to sit at home nursing our affliction, with none but God to help us.

A mother's work is never done. . . .

You can't bring up any of this with Carlos, though. It doesn't matter if you want to help them—they take it as a mortal sin.

Stay away from bad company; that's all I ask.

Only the rich can afford to take handouts on the street. If you're poor and accept a handout, they think you have nothing to eat at home.

Don't listen to just anybody on the street.

It even says so in the papers. There are lots of people who try to take advantage of you that way: handing out fliers, getting you to sign something, right in the street. The paper says you shouldn't sign *anything* in the street.

If you have to eat calzone when you go out, at least get the plain cheese, you never know what they put in that sausage.

And don't buy Italian ices off those pushcarts. Your grandma always swore to me they hire lepers to make the syrup and one day her own mama got a little piece of finger in one!

There's nothing wrong with *reading* poetry but why do you want to write it? The world already has enough poetry. You like it, you enjoy it, fine! Read what's already been written—I do, don't I? I always did. You can spend your whole life reading poetry, and still not finish what's already been written.

You put your life in their hands when you drink out of those glasses at lunch counters; they never sterilize them.

Look at how dangerous it is out on the street; but kids nowadays think they know everything.

Where is this mayhem going to lead us? Where is it all going to end? What do these kids want? It's time for someone to come along who can truly appreciate a mother's affliction and put a stop to all this, once and for all. Someone who can make our sons come home to their mothers and their sweethearts, who can give us back the old certainty of things and reassure us that our only children are safe and warm and properly fed, but deliver us, oh Lord, from this evil, amen.

b) of a police commissioner from the DOPS

Day by day the prayers multiply, I hear them, the lamentations. I am cognizant of the fact that, in the outlying slums, carefully attired chauffeurs driving limousines are delivering jewel-bedecked, proper ladies to the doorsteps of fortune tellers, witch doctors, and other purveyors of the black arts. Already there are those who hold more faith in horoscopes than in brokers or physicians. The festival of the sea goddess Yemanja actually rivals New Year's Eve in cities like Rio and Bahia. Reason, once again, is threatened by the Miraculous. The sale of playing cards has risen sharply, with no corresponding increase in the popularity of poker, and there is reason to suspect that cartomancy itself is back in vogue at middle-class cocktail parties.

At a time like this, the people must not be abandoned to their own self-indulgence, after so much effort has been made to lift them from the superstitious world in which they once floundered. At least their leaders are no longer chosen on the basis of their personal magnetism, for the charisma of a mustache, a grandfatherly smile, or delicate hands. Instruction in mathematics has ceased to be simple guesswork and multiplication tables, while teachers are now required to master such difficult subjects as set theory. In the field of literature, words are shedding their former barbaric arrogance, as we come to appreciate the limpidity of the syllable, the phoneme, the white space. The "nest egg" has finally given way to the stock exchange, and the church—in its efforts to demystify a number of so-called "saints"—has caused the people to wisely mistrust the whole intangible hierarchy. The farmer, at least, puts more faith now in his nitrates than in *ave marias*. And we are well on the way to replacing spurious "numbers" games with a lottery run by the state and controlled by computer. This will spell the end of superstition and dream interpretation—both of which will be substituted by weekly computerized drawings.

After all these accomplishments are we to allow the people to lapse once again into mystical invocation? Progress must not fall back upon the hands of improvised talent. Not after we have at last set the nation on a truly scientific course, with a corps of technocrats competent to guide the ship of state up the steep slopes of production graphs. This professional elite—now that it has fully replaced the old coffee and cattle barons, the phony labor leaders, the provincial political bosses both fanatical and corrupt—this elite corps of technocrats must not have their work suddenly spoiled by the onset of a new illusionism. I cannot permit that to happen.

I have banned the immigration of gypsies. Films dealing with supernatural topics are rigorously state-controlled. Fireside incantations are subject to immediate investigation. The performances of circus magicians are now preceded by public announcements to the effect that each show consists merely of a number of obvious tricks, total illusions, everything quite explicable. After all, a respectable public has a right to an explanation, whenever they so desire. "But this spells the end of the great bond of secrecy among all magicians," some have protested ingenuously, ignorant of the fact that this was precisely my intention. The people themselves, however, are grateful to me, lining up after every performance, awaiting explanations. Because the people themselves, as has been overwhelmingly demonstrated, are ever avid for clarity, fascinated with the truth, and anxious to exchange their ignorance for knowledge. In the circus, therefore, artifice has given way to enlightenment, to self-improvement. In his every action, therefore, must a prince spare no effort to attain the reputation of greatness.

No one can accuse me of partiality, venality, disorderedness, or vulgarity. I have always sought to treat every man to equal justice or force. For men hesitate less to offend those who make them love than those who make them fear—the master of all princes has taught me. I permit no bribes. There is not a single dishonest policeman under my command. I demand that fingernails be cut. Tie clasps are forbidden. There are strict penalties for those who indulge in scratching their private parts in public, who pick their noses, who use brilliantine. The veto on public demonstrations applies equally to all fanatics, be they Christian, Marxist, or voodoo; miracle workers, political activists, marijuana smokers, or Buddhist monks. I may have been accused of being despotic, but never biased or unjust. It is my responsibility to watch over everyone impartially, protecting each from the other and all from themselves. A wise prince, loving men as they wish to be loved, and feared by them as he wills to be feared, need only avoid their hatred.

From the very heart of my people I can sense a growing cry: protect us; for our own sakes do what must be done to dispel this mounting anguish, this new fanaticism, this mystic madness among the younger generations. We were so at peace with the old order of things, secure in our labors, confident of our predictions: a drop in inflation, the rise in the stock market, victory in the soccer cup, an increase in per capita income, the irrigation of the Northeast—then along comes this carefully organized conspiracy of fanatics, to perturb our every certainty. As it is, we can no longer wake up at six in the morning with the same sense of optimism about falling peacefully back to sleep following the ten o'clock soap opera. We can no longer watch the news without spotting our own children running through the streets with senseless placards in their hands; or with glazed eyes, playing acid-rock music. We can no longer rely on the church, when the voice from the pulpit no longer speaks to us and the priests themselves prefer to pursue the new fanaticism of the latest golden calf. Yet we cannot appeal to the law, because there is nothing in the law to protect us from this exceptional menace. Only absolute authority can save us, cry the people. Save us, oh prince!

The consequences are all too clear: following the protesting of students and priests, the inundation of hippies, the resurgence of native dancing on nights of the full moon, barbarism will foster acts of flagrant disobedience. A lack of objectivity will characterize endless sterile discussions in the meetings of lofty executives. The politicians who worship at the altar of modern myths will judge themselves right to question the authority of Congress, as has already begun to happen. Acts of false heroism—bombings and kidnappings—will grow more and more commonplace, thus relieving the boredom of a new generation of fanatics. And in the arts, servile mimics will juggle about a number of such disorders, trying to lend them a system and thereby revive some dead ideology. Newspapers will take advantage of the prevailing weakness to demand a return to that older democracy of rights, while performing lurid autopsies on long-extinct corruptions. Then, leaders will arise and with them, chaos. A prince should always live among the people, avoiding a need for the powerful and thereby at liberty to reward or deprive the latter of influence of any kind. Yet he must never put his trust in any leaders arising from the people. Indeed, the people themselves fear such leaders who would straddle the chasm of death and perdition. Nor can the prince wholly confide in the law or its judges or entrust to them the matters of his people, lest his citizens too easily grow accustomed to obeying magistrates and—in a crisis, a question of national security—refuse to obey their prince alone.

My people are justified in their complaints. A growing fear looms over the hearth, where there are not enough doctors to attend to childbirths, where many are still reluctant to believe that man has circled the moon, where a certain herbal tea is held to be the cure for kidney ailments, where a special root at the front door of a house is thought to be the sentinel against the evil eye, and a rue leaf in the tub brings the bather good fortune. Who is there to defend them if not that authority which was itself entrusted with the power to do so? I cannot forsake this responsibility. I would that I could, but I cannot. . . .

Today I must make my decision. My own people plead no less of me. Help us finally to sleep without these explosions every night. Let our sons be educated, but without this indoctrination of hatred against us. We want politicians who care for the nation as a whole, not for islands of special interest. It is war they demand of me, with all its inherent cruelty. I would rather they spared me—after all, an intellectual. Yet how am I to refuse them, when the time is at hand. If only time itself could cure these times. . . . My staff informs me they can no longer act without special powers. My clerks complain that those who are now detained actually laugh with impunity and lodge formal complaints, demanding rights, alleging immunities. Officers are stoned in the streets! Witch doctors prowl about the houses of law-enforcement officials in the middle of the night. And the cross, a permissible sign, is suddenly presented as an amulet to ward off undercover agents at the gates of suspect monasteries. The time has come to unleash the means of crushing all disorder, though the future may judge me cruel. For I have learned: the appellation of "cruel" should not trouble a prince striving to maintain unity and order. On the contrary, he is more compassionate than those who would allow disorders, assassinations, and plunder to occur. Because the latter compromise an entire people, whereas the executions wrought by the prince offend only individuals.

And yet, why me? After all, I am an intellectual. I prefer to spend time reading Cicero in the original. Certain treatises and grammars bring me such pleasures as colleagues, less rigorous than I, derive from detective novels. I have even drawn up a prospective monograph on the backwardness of the sciences due to pressures brought to bear upon Greek rationalism by a Christian idealism. Why me, then, in this unprincipled century? Why not myself from the very beginning, prince?

# PRIOR TO THE CELEBRATION

*(Author's note:*

*What am I supposed to write about in this shithole of a country? Any-thing I write seems like a joke, as if I were totally avoiding the subject. What subject? Shit, that's all. And anyway, whoever said it was my responsibility? Why not write detective stories, or one-act plays for children?)*

### Editorial office of the *Correio de Minas Gerais*
### 8:07 P.M.

Samuel hears the click-click of Andrea's heels coming up the stairway and immediately has to stop working at the typewriter. What follows is the same scenario he has witnessed over and over for the past eight months: she enters with her eyes already trained on the managing editor's desk (probably feeling it's safer to look in that direction); walks straight toward the desk while busily opening her purse and taking out the four typewritten pages; exchanges a few pleasantries with her editor (remarks no one can decipher), as they laugh together. The rest of the office takes this opportunity to have a look at her legs and desire her a little. (Everyone knows she will turn around and—without acknowledging any of them, only nodding to whoever happens to step directly in her path—walk straight out of the room and back down the stairs.) She turns around and (something new!) stares defiantly back at the entire office. Samuel lowers his eyes, rather intimidated. And by the time he looks up again to overpower her with an even handsome glance, she has already passed by him on her way out the door.

### New Moon Bar and Restaurant
### 7:00 P.M.

—What has one got to do with the other? Do them both.

—The problem is time. A writer who doesn't work full-time at it ends up like this bunch around here.

—Then shit, decide. One thing or the other.

—That's exactly what the problem is, you see?

Flávio comes over:

—Leave something for the government to handle, you two.

## In front of the Rex Bookshop
**6:00 P.M.**

—You're gonna like this crowd, Samuel, lots of artists, writers, gorgeous women, queers, left-wingers, right-wingers, you name it. Look, it's got to be one fucking hell of a celebration.

*(Author's note:*

*Each one of the stories should have a date, either explicit or implied. The date of the party is 1970. Roberto, the one who is giving it, was born in 1941. So he's twenty-nine and the oldest of the younger artists in the city, most of them, say, between twenty-two and twenty-six, back in 1970.)*

## Alpine Restaurant
**9:10 P.M.**

The woman, beautiful-looking:

—Do you like me?

The man is handsome, in a kind of ugly-looking way:

—Of course. You know that.

—Ah, you don't seem to understand. Or maybe you're acting like you don't.

—That's right, the techniques of a not altogether orthodox analyst who sometimes runs into problems as a result.

—You have kind of a great advantage that way, you know.

—Analysts always have a great advantage.

Silence. Thoughts, probably. Then she:

—You don't feel bored?

—No, why? It's nice being here.

—I'm not talking about that. Well? Not even occasionally?

—No. I manage okay.

—And when everything goes haywire with someone?

—A little patience . . .

—There *are* happy people, aren't there?

—They're difficult to find in my profession, but they exist. So then you think: why are so many people happy, and not me, etc. etc.? Right?

—Sometimes I get the idea that . . .

—What?

—That maybe you do like me.

—That's all in your head.

—You mean you don't?

—Nope.

—I think I must be suffering from a deep lack of affection.

He smiled, somewhat embarrassed, because she really was incredibly beautiful.

—Let's go over and pick up Carlos. It's nearly time for the party.

### Editorial office of the *Correio de Minas Gerais*
### 8:35 P.M.

Samuel hands in the two news items.

—Is this all?

He tries to explain why the other stories hadn't worked out, and the managing editor sticks both his index fingers into his ears, looking at Samuel as if he were Samuel the Insufferable. The telephone rings; the editor doesn't hear it. The telephone keeps ringing; he still doesn't hear it. Samuel picks up the receiver. The managing editor laughs, answers the call, makes a note of it, hangs up the phone and:

—Well, since you've come up with nothing but a wash today, you can go look into this business about some student being arrested. A Carlos somebody-or-other from the School of Economics. Go over to his house first, have a talk with his wife. Here's the address. Then find out what the story is.

### Editorial office of the *Correio de Minas Gerais*
### 8:07 P.M.

Andrea handed in her column to the managing editor, then turned around and faced the whole office. The editors and reporters continued busily working, seemingly indifferent to her presence. Since her return to Belo Horizonte she had avoided the newspaper crowd. Old scars. Yet oddly, it appeared that the crowd had somehow anticipated this by rejecting her first; subtly, she became tempted once again to try to be accepted; but they conquered her by shutting her out. Nothing was deliberate. Belo Horizontean mysteries. . . .

What Andrea tried to say with that look was how little their rejection mattered to her now: she was going to marry Roberto. The two of them had made up their minds: tonight, at the birthday party, we'll announce our engagement. She felt highly prized as she walked out of the office; she even smiled slightly. Small victory, and none of them knew.

*(Author's note:*
*A play.*
*A man all by himself. Tape recorders, voices, slides, projections, record-*
*ings, newspapers, TV monitors. He plays opposite all the means of communi-*
*cation. It's he who builds skyscrapers, has a seat on the stock exchange, starves*
*in the streets, protests what's-happening-over-here, applauds what's-going-*
*on-over-there, denounces friends to the authorities, creates art, hates art,*
*governs the world, works as a notary public, falls secretly in love with TV*
*and movie stars. He looks like a little squirt (a role for a midget?) in compari-*
*son with the material he enacts. Obliged to make choices every moment, based*
*upon facts provided by the various means of communication, but the infor-*
*mation is never totally reliable, at times even contradictory.*

*Work on it until 1/30/69 and then send it in to the National Theater*
*Endowment's annual competition.)*

### New Moon Bar and Restaurant
### 7:45 P.M.

—Look, I'm very serious: with a theme like this I can undertake a critical dissection of Brazilian life for the past thirty years.

—Critical dissection, hmmn. Sounds good to me.

—Listen: the guy wakes up thirty years later, I mean, he's spent the last thirty years having suffered from amnesia, living as if he were somebody else entirely. Then, when he snaps out of it, he goes back to being who he was thirty years ago. And the novel incorporates his unending surprise at the turn of events around him, you see? It's actually more or less symbolic. The guy really stands for every Brazilian. Amnesia is the alienation. Hell, I've even thought of all the chapters: The Dead. The guy can't believe it when they tell him Vargas is dead. Vargas, Góis Monteiro, Osvaldo Aranha, Heleno de Freitas, José Lins do Rego. Well, I can analyze all that, make some sense out of those deaths, within the context of the novel. Another chapter: Language. The guy can hardly make out what the hell people are saying nowadays, and he keeps coming out with things like: don't flip your wig, hot as a match, keeping my head above water, solid as the rock of Gibraltar, you see? Then you have all the new inventions—television, imagine the guy's amazement at just television!—then all the progress in technology, the new writers, the military coups. Its a heavy idea, don't you think? Could be a wayout book, you know? Something Huxley might have dreamed up.

—Why not write it?

106

## 174 rua Grão Mogol, apartment 11
**8:52 P.M.**

Samuel, listening to the pregnant girl:

—They turned the whole house upside down. I don't know what they were looking for. He never even came home for supper, I imagine he's still hungry. I can't leave here, I've got to stay and look after my little girl—she's sick today, don't know what it is. Besides, I can't go very far in this condition, the baby's due anytime now. I never understand why Carlos has to get involved in these situations. It's like I said: he wouldn't hurt a fly, but he's very excitable, you know? He's got this mania for debating things with everybody. Always worried about other people's problems.

—How did you first hear about his arrest?

—Well, didn't I just tell you the cops were here turning the place upside down? They never tell you anything straight. They just *suggested* he might be incommunicado for a while. Apparently, something happened at Plaza Station, some business about a couple of refugees arriving from up north and causing problems for the police. Carlos works for the Department of Labor, you know? And that Mr. Ernâni, he's the one who got Carlos the job. So Carlos went over there to check out this business about the refugees; I already called his department and that's what they told me. Once he got there—I don't know why—apparently they arrested him. Do you think you could do me a favor and find out what's going on, and then call Mr. Ernâni—Otávio Ernâni—and tell him?

## New Moon Bar and Restaurant
**8:05 P.M.**

"When you see beauty, look for a long time," quotes the venerable poet, staring at the film critic seated at a table of young intellectuals where Esdras, the Hermetic, intellectual of the middle generation, has just sat down. Esdras's eyes, redoubled by a pair of very thick lenses, seem like those of a very frightened man. Esdras always wins his debates because of those eyes, not to mention a few other tricks he keeps up his sleeve. (Here you have a brief summary of what he said to his young listeners that evening:

"Have you noticed how nobody sings in the shower anymore? Know anyone who sings in the shower? Think about it. I've tried to find somebody who does: there isn't. Nobody sings in the shower anymore, not in Brazil.

"Literature isn't economics. You can't go and establish national priorities for literary investment, draw up five-year plans and decide what should be written in the next half decade.

"To debate the social responsibility of the writer is the same as debating the social responsibility of the scientist. In the end, the bomb explodes the same way, regardless.

"Our formalists claim their literary objective to be the purity of the Chinese ideogram, and they tell us that history, ideology, and semantics are irrelevant to literature. Now I ask you: what can serve as a similar model for Chinese writers? And even more curious: What would be the aim of the Chinese formalist?

"In Pirapora, a truck driver discovered his wife was cheating on him with a magician from the circus. He informed her he had to be away a couple of days on a long haul, perfectly natural for a truck driver, but he returned early the next morning and caught the two of them naked in bed together. They awoke to his curses, completely terror-stricken. Beside himself with rage, because a man's honor is cleansed by blood alone, he picked up the magician's revolver, which was over on the chair, and fired point blank. Out from the barrel of the revolver popped two brightly colored flags. The husband sat down on the floor and cried like a baby.

"Careful about how you go around shooting off your mouths. Remember those two little flags.

"Literary life never creates friends; only accomplices. That's Carlos Drummond.

"Well, I better be on my way.")

*(Author's note:*
*I think of happiness as the dynamic satisfaction of a person's needs. It takes an effort. It's only by working at love that one actually loves, and is happy in the process. Love, money, ideology, privacy, religion—whatever one wants to fight for. Still, I don't have the slightest chance, as long as I'm so caught up in contradictions.)*

## Our Lady of Carmo drugstore, rua Grão Mogol
**9:03 P.M.**
Samuel, talking on the phone to Mr. Ernâni:
—The wife claims he didn't do anything.

—Who arrested him?

—I think it was probably the DOPS, she doesn't seem to know for certain. The wife—I forget her name—she's actually the one who asked me to phone you. She thinks you might convince the police he has no dealings with any subversives.

—Well, at least I don't know of any.

—She's expecting a baby. Says she has no money in the house and doesn't know how she's going to manage. Quite a mess.

—With that, it's no problem. I can see to it that she gets proper care, tell her not to worry.

—And about his arrest? Isn't there something you can do about that as well?

—Not really. What can I do? That's something Security has to handle. But tell the wife that she can relax—hospital, we can take care of. No problem.

—But he was arrested as an employee of your department . . . over that business of the refugees over at the station.

—What!

—You haven't heard?

—No, what happened?

—Seems there was some fighting going on between the refugees and police and Carlos got arrested. That's all I know.

—Listen! I have to hang up because I have to get hold of Ernâni.

—But isn't that who I'm talking to?

—No, listen, I'm sorry, I'm his assistant. You'll have to excuse all this, but it's par for the course. You see I'm stuck here at the moment for other reasons—behind in my work, plus I'd hate to tell you what else. Hello?

—Yeah?

—Anyway, look, I'm sorry. It's the usual thing; you know how it is. Listen, let me do you one favor. Ernâni's going to be at a party later on this evening, let me give you the number. You ready?

—Go ahead.

—532-3747. I know he's expecting to go there. Try calling him a little later and he'll probably be there. In the meantime, I'll see if I can get hold of him.

(Author's note:
Research on Roberto as a child.
At one year of age—He repeats actions that have worked successfully (A. Gesell). The mother becomes bored with such repetitions, but the father

*continues to applaud them. The child is very attentive to the reactions of his parents; he learns words, repeats them, then grasps their meaning. Give me, and the mother does. Piaget: "To the extent that this change begins to take place—a shifting away from the total but unconscious egocentricism of the first stages to a situating of one's own body in the outer world—objects begin to take shape."*

*At two years—Curiosity to discover new objects and environments. (He goes into his parents' room and finds them embracing each other, a scene he will want to reexperience at five or six years of age and which should bring the story itself to a close.) Piaget: "The constructing of sets of relationships between objects, such as the notions of behind, upon, inside, outside, in front of." Piaget: "In the child, the acquisition of language, meaning, of a system of collective signs, coincides with the formation of symbols—that is, of a system of individual signifiers."*

*At three years—Things he can or cannot do. The problem is to know which, when, and how to decipher the parents' codes. He has recourse then to simulation (M. y Lopez), to rebellion, to acting in secret. The mother begins to see him as insincere. The father thinks he has a good imagination.*

*At four years—Objects have become more docile, permitting a greater variety of games and inventions, more readily adapting themselves to his imagination. People, however, resist magical thinking (Gesell, M. y L.).*

*In italics or parentheses, place concepts that cannot as yet be grasped by his intellective sphere; by the end of the story, the italicized words are reduced to a minimum, because by then he has mastered language.)*

**488 rua Tupis, 14th floor**
**2:59 P.M.**
—Yes?
—Hi, ice delivery.
—What ice?
—You're kidding. You mean you didn't order any ice?
—No.
—Roberto J. Miranda, that's not you?
—No. That's one flight up, the penthouse.
—Oh, Sorry. Didn't mean to bother you, okay? Thanks a lot.
—No problem. *(Shit! Another party upstairs again!)*

### New Moon Bar and Restaurant
### 7:49 P.M.

—Why not write it?

—It's no use. Not right now, anyway. Too depressed about everything . . . agh, I don't know. Is this what our generation is supposed to do? Write novels?

—Then shit, stop fucking around with the damn novel.

The other was surprised. They were habituated to that game, the game of what is or is not possible to do in a country like this. The game provided them the illusion of being, at one and the same time, activists-with-respect-to-the-social-problems-of-Brazil and/or writers-kept-from-writing-because-Brazil-had-no-need-of-that-sort-of-thing-right-now. The two remained quiet for a while because one of them had erred at the game, and so it became necessary to readjust to each other all over again, to await the demise of that major faux pas. At such a moment, you normally turn to another swallow of beer, swirling the contents thoughtfully in the glass, pausing to reflect. Then the conversation can be resumed:

—And how about that Luis, eh? Quite a weird business that relationship with the father, isn't it? Don't you think?

—Shit, do I think? Did you see him yesterday?

—Yeah, enough is enough—what a pisser, eh?

—I don't know. . . . Nuts, all right. End up killing each other.

### New Moon Bar and Restaurant
### 10:32 P.M.

—The 1980s, they'll be the ones to judge us! And what have any of you done? We'll have to answer to the '80s! But where are our books, our revolutions? What has this generation accomplished? Here we are, passing judgment on Fernando Sabino, Paulo Mendes Campos, on the whole Complemento generation; but the '80s will judge *us*, not them!

—Right, Flávio, only pay your share of the check and let's get going. We want to get to the party.

### New Moon Bar and Restaurant
### 8:12 P.M.

—A novel?

—Maybe, or could be a novella. The idea, I think, is a good one. It just needs developing. It's really a kind of satire on racism. The title—and not because it's mine, you understand—anyway, I think it's fucking great.

—What is it?

*(Author's note:*

The Refractory Jew. *Write it as if it were a report prepared by the commandant of a concentration camp, relating the attempts to exterminate one of the prisoners. He tries the gas chamber, the oven, but nothing works. He throws the Jew, still alive, into the crematorium, along with the others, all of them dead, but the Jew walks out again with that same fixed, blank stare. But he doesn't say a word, doesn't protest. They try shooting him: he bleeds a little, for a couple of days, bleeds until the wounds scar—including those over the heart—but he doesn't die. With a bayonet, the same thing. A depiction of Nazism, torture, oppression, physical violence. The Nazism thus operates as a symbol, and the refractory Jew represents what no amount of repression can destroy in mankind.)*

## Our Lady of Carmo drugstore, rua Grão Mogol
## 9:27 P.M.

—Is this Mr. de Fernandes?

—Yes, it is.

—Oh. You don't know me. Carlos's wife actually asked me to call you.

—Carlos who?

—Bicalho. His wife says you know him.

—Yes, I know him. What's the problem?

—It's that he's been arrested and the only lawyer . . .

—Arrested for what?

—Some trouble over at the station, something about a bunch of Northeasterners who arrived on the train. He was arrested as an agitator, seems like he's in a bit of a tight spot at the moment. His wife thought of you, since you're a friend of his, to see if . . .

—Friend nothing. Look, you want to know something? It's just as well, it'll get rid of him for a while. The guy's a pain in the ass.

—Well, he may be a pain in the ass, but he didn't do anything wrong, and since you're a lawyer . . .

—Oh, do you think I have time to fool around with stuff like that? No way. I'm busy now, understand? I'll look into it tomorrow.

—It's just that his wife . . .

—Tomorrow, my friend, forget about it till tomorrow. Good night now, ciao.

## Bed
### 4:00 P.M.
Marília looks at the clock and muses: mmmn, almost time for my honey to call.

## 174 rua Grão Mogol, apartment 11
### 9:16 P.M.
Samuel, again at the pregnant girl's house, and talking with a couple who have come by to pick up Carlos. The woman is quite beautiful-looking, while the man has a number of theories:

—It's undeniable, at least in the administrative realm, that they have accomplished certain things. Look, I think it may justify itself in the end. What can't be justified is all this euphoria among . . .

—Don't you think it's a better idea right now to see if you can get your friend out of jail?

The man smiled, almost apologetically, but the woman took an immediate disliking to Samuel. Then, her idea:

—There's a professor of his who's friends with the head of Security. He's half off his rocker, but maybe he can do something.

## 840 rua Itapeva, Vila Concórdia
### 8:33 P.M.
—What kind of party?

—Somebody's birthday party.

—Whose?

—I don't know. Some friend of Marcelo's.

—I don't like that Marcelo boy.

—Aaah, mama!

—Aaah, what? I don't like him and that's that.

—Well I like him.

—Aurélia, Aurélia . . .

— Yes, I do like him, and I don't have to answer to anybody!

— Listen to that mouth, listen to that mouth!

**Office of Dantas & Reis, Stockbrokers, Inc.**
**4:19 P.M.**
—Roberto? Marcelo, here. I'm fine. Of course I'm coming. Listen, can I ball someone at your apartment later on tonight? Obviously after the party. Mmm-hmm. We'll work out arrangements when I get there, okay? Ciao.

**Our Lady of Carmo drugstore, rua Grão Mogol**
**9:26 P.M.**
Samuel takes the receiver from the guy who tells him:
—Didn't I tell you?: the old bird's crazy. He says to me this isn't the time to disturb an old man, just because some student or other's gotten himself arrested. Anyway, he said he won't have anything to do with it and told me to enjoy life while there was still time.

The beautiful-looking woman smiled, but felt a definite antipathy toward Samuel.
—It's true. He's completely off his rocker.
Samuel saying nothing, dials another number and waits.
—Is this Mr. de Fernandes? . . . Oh. You don't know me. Carlos's wife actually asked me to call you. . . . Bicalho. His wife says you know him . . . it's that he's been arrested and the only lawyer . . . Some trouble over at the station, something about a bunch of Northeasterners who arrived on the train. He was arrested as an agitator, seems like he's in a bit of a tight spot at the moment. His wife thought of you, since you're a friend of his, to see if . . . Well, he may be a pain in the ass, but he didn't do anything wrong, and since you're a lawyer . . . It's just that his wife . . . Aah, fuck you.

**1717 rua Pernambuco, apartment 306**
**8:30 P.M.**
Tonight at the party, have to make Mônica confess right in front of everyone: crazy about me.
He smiled to himself.
I'll do it.

**36 Plaza Negrão de Lima**
**1:05 P.M.**
Son of a bitch. End of the month again. Where do I come up with some fucking money? Of course, fucking Roberto could have helped me out, wouldn't cost him anything. Little faggot. But I'll nail him tonight.

*(Author's note:*
*Include in "Prior to the Celebration" various "author's notes" (including*
*this one). Projects, phrases, ideas for stories, literary problems, quick sketches,*
*preoccupations. In that way, the author would become, together with Samuel,*
*the other main protagonist of the story he's writing. An involuntary protago-*
*nist, because he's the "other author"—he himself, or the man he would come*
*to be, artificially coexisting in time and space with the man he had been—*
*he's that "other author" who joins together the disconnected fragments of his*
*annotations.)*

### Our Lady of Carmo drugstore, rua Grão Mogol
### 9:30 P.M.

Samuel, realizing that the fellow just wants to escape with that beautiful-looking woman he has with him, puts the burden on him anyway:

—Look, I don't even know the kid, and I have to go look into this refugee business for my paper. You're his friend, you do what you think best. I have to get over to the station.

—But what can I do?

Hey, I don't know. You'll have to figure that one out for yourself. Look, a Mr. Otávio Ernâni will be at this number later on tonight. You see what he can do. So long now. Sorry, but . . .

Samuel walks away with a shrug. The fellow looks at the piece of paper, and:

—Hey, this is Roberto's number! So the guy'll be right there. Now, how's that for a coincidence?

The beautiful-looking woman squeezes his arm, smiling:

—Perfect. . . . Well, let's get over there.

*(Author's note:*
*In Samuel's actions and observations, the verb should always be put in*
*the present tense.)*

### Plaza Station
### 9:46 P.M.

Samuel, spotting four radio patrol cars, takes down the license plate numbers. He counts roughly forty MP's and also makes a note of that figure. Several light trucks with false license plates. Police in civilian dress. A team of observers from the armed forces, five members. The MP's, arms outstretched, form a human chain, and behind it, Samuel calculates, there must be about seven hundred or more people. Children are crying, others sleeping; the hum of prayers can be heard; a woman is weeping aloud; the men are crouching, standing, or stretched out relaxing. The smell is rather overpowering. Talking with various people, Samuel slowly puts together the facts: it was all more or less peaceful, but a great deal of confusion prevailed. The moment the refugees arrived, the police appeared; their orders were not to allow any of these victims from the drought to wander from the station; when some of the people began protesting, the police simply called in reinforcements; this chain of soldiers was thrown up around the refugees and none of them are allowed out, even for a drink of water; at a certain point there was a brief scuffle. It ended, and they took a few of them away.

*(Author's note:*
*What do I do with all this: a novel? a story? a pastiche? nothing?*
*A silent film in the science-fiction genre, vintage 1931, is being kept under lock and key in Washington by the FBI. At the same time, investigators are trying to discover anyone possibly connected with the making of the film: actors, cameramen, producers, director, screenwriter, set designer, etc. The reels, found in the basement of some North American theater that had been forced to close down—for lack of a public—in the town of El Dorado, Arkansas, have turned out to be one of the more disturbing legacies of the Johnson administration to his successor, Richard Nixon. An odd coincidence: El Dorado is just two hundred sixty-five miles from Dallas, Texas.*
*The title of the film was probably* The Assassination of the President, *a conclusion drawn by investigators from the notation—"Assas. of the Pres."— on the outside of the top canister among the lot (the first reel, which would have contained the complete title of the film, and probably the names of those who actually participated in the production, was unfortunately never recovered). The present owner of the theater, who had himself only recently acquired the premises, knew nothing about the film and simply informed the authorities of his rather odd discovery. The previous owner—an old, blind Texan by the name of Jerome Prescott—vaguely remembers having put aside a couple of reels of film shot by a group of independent producers who likewise handled their own distribution. It was a motley enterprise, badly organized, and not infrequently occasional reels and sometimes entire films would be left rotting in the basement of a theater for months on end, awaiting col-*

*lection by some representative of the company. That particular film—this much he clearly recollected—had been "one of the biggest flops in the history of that old theater. Let me see, it was back in 1931, or maybe '32. 'Course, any film without a Valentino or some pretty gal like Lillian Gish or Jean Harlow—just a lot of political hogwash, with a unpatriotic plot like that, and the dang thing takes place in the future, to boot—why it's bound to be a flop!"*

*The plot of the film relates, in such minute detail as to make it impossible to speak of coincidence, the assassination by bullets of a certain K., the president of the United States, in Dallas, Texas, in the hypothetical year of 1963. Obviously, that much alone would be enough to prompt a thorough investigation, but there happens to be a good deal more: the scene of the crime coincides almost point for point with reality, thirty-two years later! Of course, certain details—the chrome stripping on the cars, the fabrics used in the costumes, the names of commercial establishments—are not entirely accurate, only fair approximations. There also appear to be a number of major departures from the known sequence of events; but as to these, at least for the present, only the broadest supposition is possible. Only a few highly placed officials have actually seen the film—and they refuse to comment. According to certain sources, an additional assassin figures in the film and—they claim— he turns out to be a member of a secret branch of the FBI. A search of FBI archives, however, proves fruitless: the name under which he operates, in the film at least, has never figured in the rosters of official secret agents. But none of this is really so important.*

*Up until now, in spite of almost ten months of investigative effort, it has not been possible to locate even a single actor from the film. Copies of their photographs have been distributed to all federal agents, and the FBI is attempting to interview as many old actors as they can from back in the '20s, '30s, and '40s. Yet no one seems to remember those faces; not in Hollywood, not in New York. The investigation has now been expanded to include Canada and Great Britain: "Do you recognize this star? Can you remember the mystery-face in this photograph from 1930? Write or call in a name and, if your guess is right, win a brand-new electric range, refrigerator, or air conditioner!" So announces the television commercials of three great nations, disguising the manhunt as a quiz contest. Critics have justifiably raised the point that such a film could just as easily have been made anywhere. What is to prevent the introduction of English subtitles in, say, an Argentine production, for example? Extraterrestrial hypotheses have, at least for the moment, been eliminated.*

*The latest suggestion—this from the head of the FBI's special cinema division—is to actually distribute the film, with a huge promotional ad campaign. The authors, he says, will sooner or later present themselves, driven by their own vanity—because the film will undoubtedly hold tremendous box-office appeal.*

*Nixon, however, continues to vacillate. If presented to the public, The Assassination of the President will cease to be merely another mystery for the FBI; a world already festering with anguish will be forced to look upon a wholly insoluble— perhaps intolerable—engima.)*

### Department of Labor and Social Services
**6:16 P.M.**

—Hello, Marília?

—Yes?

—It's Otávio.

—Oh, hi. How are you?

—Fine. And you?

—Good.

—Listen, I'm in a bit of a rush. About Roberto's party . . . we going?

—Sure, no? What time?

—What time do you want?

—You'll come by?

—Sure.

—What time?

—Whenever you like.

—It's up to you, I'll be ready whenever you want.

—Around nine, then, okay? I just have one problem I have to take care of, some business about transit passes for some refugees. I'm leaving the whole thing to Bicalho, though. So just give me the time to get home, take a bath, have a quick nap, and I'll be over. Okay?

—I'll be waiting. Kiss for you . . . Bye.

### Department of Labor and Social Services
**7:01 P.M.**

—Is Otávio Ernâni there?

—This is he.

The voice said nothing further, a voice unexpectedly familiar. He insisted:

—Hello. Hello?

—It's Lena.

He had expected such a call for over a year now, and had always felt certain how difficult it would be. The voice spoke again, before he could recover his composure:

—I thought you would call me yesterday.

—I didn't even know you were back.

It seemed as though they had nothing to say to each other, phrases separated by long pauses. He had always known it would be a difficult call.

*(Author's note:*

*How did he "always know" it would be a phone call? Why not a letter, a chance encounter? This is beginning to stink of literature.)*

She:

—You didn't receive my letter?

—Letter? No, I didn't get any letter.

The old, complicated love he felt for her, once again, returning. He:

—Have you come back to stay?

(Not the right moment to ask that.)

She, again, a little surprised by his courage:

—I don't know. I still haven't decided things.

(See that you don't botch it this time. It's been hard enough, the past year.)

He:

—When will we see each other?

—I don't know,

she began, then suddenly remembering:

—Aren't you going to Roberto's birthday party? If you're not, I won't.

He recognized, with a sense of nostalgia, the same old Helena: so relaxed and at ease. She:

—Are you?

—Yes.

—Then come by and pick me up. Is your old "bug" still running?

—Still running. What time will you be ready?

—Anytime after nine, okay?

—Okay.

They remained silent for a moment, not wanting to hang up, awaiting some token of affection—a word, a sigh, "missed you," something. She:

—Well, bye-bye.

—Okay, ciao.

Love you love you my welcome home welcome back feel you feel you so close so close to he thought as he hung up and suddenly remembered:

—Holy shit, what about Marília!

## New Moon Bar and Restaurant
### 8:12 P.M.

—The idea I think is a good one, it just needs developing. It's really a kind of satire on racism. The title—and not because it's mine, you understand—anyway, I think it's fucking great.

—What is it?

—*The Refractory Jew.*

—Not bad.

—But there's one problem: I can't seem to write the thing, Esdras. Maybe it just doesn't make sense nowadays to be writing about a Jew. Like, who's writing about our own problems? Look at the Russian dissidents: Siniavski, Sakharov, Amalrik, Medvedev, and the others; right in the thick of it, struggling with their own real problems. The Americans, the French, the Peruvians—the same way. But here? Think about it: who's talking about us, about *our* problems?

—Literature isn't economics. You can't go and establish national priorities for literary investment, draw up five-year plans and decide what should be written in the next half decade.

—I'm not saying this is the norm. What the hell, I'm the one who can't write; it's my problem. So many people watching their step, afraid to say certain things. So many people just giving up, refusing to write, and now the ones with nothing to say are having their day. Or am I the only one who seems to feel this way?

—Well, if you have a book, write it.

—Fucked you there, didn't he. Nice going, Esdras.

—Fucked, hell! What do you mean fucked! And you want to know something? This is a private conversation, so fuck off. The point is, Esdras, it could be that some subjects just don't work nowadays. I mean right now, today, in 1970 I mean, suppose a writer's actually fed up because he's got other things on his mind, more personal maybe, but maybe deeper for that very reason. So maybe the thing to do is to set aside the other project, the one about the Jew. You know? Besides, this whole business with a Jew sounds like second-rate Sartre.

—Other Latin Americans write about anything they damn well please, at least they're sophisticated writers, and you people here, the left end of nowhere, you want to explain the Brazilian condition. . . . Bullshit.

## Plaza Station
### 9:45 P.M.

Samuel, interviewing an investigator nicknamed Hopalong Cassidy who assisted in the arrest of Carlos Bicalho, hears the following story:

—Listen, that kid's up to his ass in trouble, see? Our people were already on the scene and had the situation in hand, when this Carlos character shows up and starts to agitate everybody. Our orders were to round up these Northeasterners and send them back on the first available train. They didn't argue any; they're a decent sort. Then this guy shows up, this Bicalho fellow, and tells them we ain't got the right to do that, says his department is trying to see what they can do to countermand the order, and of course these poor beggars started swarming around him like flies, you know how it is. Plus after all that, it winds up that his precious secretary from the Department of Labor doesn't do a fucking thing—as far as I'm concerned, the guy isn't even from the Department of Labor. Anyway, like I said, he starts agitating the refugees against us, inciting to riot, stirring up trouble. Obviously, the whole thing is communist-instigated. Well, things started getting hot at that point, so we grabbed the kid—him and five or six other communists. He plotted the whole damn thing, you can write that down there.

*(Author's note:*

*This sheet of paper has been sitting in the typewriter, blank, for the last hour and a half, until I began to write this open letter to anyone who's interested—fuck, fuck, FUCK!!—I was putting the paper in the typewriter to start working some more on* The Refractory Jew, *but nothing comes out. Only F— U—C—K. I'd like to just give my fucking superego a fucking good kick in the ass. I need to figure out what the hell's blocking me this way. First hypothesis: Fear of criticism, which I camouflage with scruples about writing a useless book. Second hypothesis: the too-rarified atmosphere of freedom tends to inhibit me, to inhibit anyone, and writing has turned into some sort of trivial nonsense. Third hypothesis: I'm caught between* deus e o diabo na terra do sol, between writing to exercise my own individual freedom and writing to express my relation to the collective anguish; I imagine stories which I'm ashamed to write because they're so alienated, and I'm equally afraid to write committed stories because they seem totally circumstantial. Fourth hypothesis: I'm conscious of living through an obscurantist moment in literature, one of those sterile periods out of which history preserves nothing at all, and I know it's absolutely useless to write anything, committed or not, because it all comes out pure bullshit and will be lost in a wink of history, so the truth is it's better not to even waste my time. Fifth hypothesis: there's enough sterile crap being pumped out around here already, and I have no desire to become just another jerk-off.

So what do I do with my fucking crap? First hypothesis, I sell it to some North American author of worst-sellers. Second hypothesis, I write a book called If I Had Wanted to Write a Book. Because at some point or another, all this fucking bullshit has got to explode. People on the street look at me like I was some kind of a degenerate about to fucking jack off in public. I have to get some release, so it's either "nocturnal pollutions" or open letters to anyone who wants to listen. Ergo my special, unlimited offer of a few ideas, free of charge to all and sundry, because the author himself is unable to resolve a few personal problems. Suggestion one for Senhor Glauber Rocha: idea for a super-cinemascopic, allegorical screen epic in which you have the following characters: a gladiator, Christ, Billy the Kid, an astronaut, Lampião the Outlaw, a samurai, and Pharaoh Tutmes the Warrior-King. Sounds good, huh? Now, how about you, Señor García Márquez?: a certain trapezist from the circus leaped into the air and remained suspended for some five seconds while the trapeze bar swung first away and back and then away again, until the trapezist finally reached for it as it returned a second time, the way one latches onto a passing trolley. And that's only one of the many astonishing feats he managed to carry off while there in the town, the last of them being the virginity of the daughter of a local photographer, after which he vanished without a trace (the girl herself swears he actually disappeared zap! before he even rounded the corner) and, of course, was never seen again, although eventually a fourteen-month-old baby was born, who by the middle of his second week in the crib had already learned to talk! And what about this one— who'll take number three? Some character's walking along with a little fetus under his arm, aborted into a shoe box by the fellow's wife, but while he's taking it to be buried, he leaves it at the bakery shop, forgetting it there on the counter, and then—ah, el gran Borges, who knows if number four might not *have just the right touch of magic realism: a mortician is summoned to a house; he arrives; a woman answers the door and says there must be some mistake—no one there has called him; he returns to his funeral parlor and someone calls again; he goes back again to the same address; the same women answers the door and assures him that no one could have called him from that address; he goes back to the office, very pissed off by this time, and someone calls him again; at this point, of course, he says no way, no more wild goose chase, what do they take him for, a clown?; then the person making all the phone calls decides to go to the office personally, to clear the matter up; when he arrives, the mortician recounts how he went to the house, twice already, and they confirm it's the right address, no mistake; so the fellow who's been calling asks the mortician to describe the lady who had met him at the door; the agent describes her in sufficient detail (a very observant mortician), and the other person suddenly stands up, very slowly, turning completely pale, and runs out into the street—horrified: that's her! The deceased! She met the mortician at the door! Holy shit; gives me the willies just thinking about it. And this one, a cryptic concoction for a Mr. Hitchcock, maybe: the title should be something like* The Dare. *Or perhaps* The Duel. *A very elegant character, very aristocratic, puts a letter in the mail. Cut. Titles; music; the letter travel- ing through the bureaucracy of the postal system, until it arrives in the hands of the addressee: the local chief of police. This coincides, naturally, with the end of the opening credits. The letter, evidently anonymous, warns the chief that so-and-so is about to be killed and challenges the police to prevent the crime. He offers the constabulary a two-day head start, "not to take unfair advantage of you chaps," a jolly good sport. I also have something else here, let me see, something that might eventually prove useful to Monsieur Robbe- Grillet, why not?: the same scene is described repeatedly, with a few minor modifications. Such modifications, however, will provide both subject and action for the work—will constitute "ce que se conte," etc., etc. As if someone, ruminating on an event in his mind, were trying to remember its exact con- figuration; but while he remembers certain details, he forgets others: the to- tality always escapes him. It might also be structured as if it were the same event witnessed from differing angles. Begin with a very simple sentence, like "The body fell from the sixty-third floor." The other paragraphs, each one standing on its own as a complete text, would tell exactly what happened, but—for the protagonist—the event would forever remain a mystery, because he can never grasp it in its entirety: POW! SHAZAM!!)*

### New Moon Bar and Restaurant
**8:58 P.M.**

Luis, who lived on the street just behind the station, delivered the news to the crowd from the literary supplement of the paper.

—I didn't go too close because I began to hear some shots, and I don't have the legs for that sort of thing. From what I gather, the government was planning to utilize this trainload of migrant refugees for harvesting cane and beans somewhere out in western Minas Gerais State. I don't know why, but they decided instead to try to send them back North, and that's when the whole thing came to a head. And with the Northeasterners there was this one fellow who they say actually rode with Lampião, a genuine outlaw! At least that's what they told me.

So the crowd from the supplement went over to have a look.

### Plaza Station, Plaza Luncheonette
**9:56 P.M.**

Samuel phones the editor in chief of the paper, to let him know what's been going on. Then remembers:

—Look, you should send one of our photographers over, I forgot to tell Ênio. Everybody's got a photographer here except us. *O Estado* still has two of its reporters on the scene. The worst of it seems to be over though.

—What's the situation right now?

—It's quiet. But it could start up again, you never know.

—Have you got the whole story?

—Not all of it, but most of it. I've got the police version of it: now I plan to hear what the Northeasterners have to say. I mean I plan to try.

—Okay. Keep in contact with me though. And watch your time, you hear me? That stuff has to be in here by eleven or I'll boil your ass.

### 488 rua Tupis
**11:46 P.M.**

The two young men step into the elevator after politely allowing the young couple asking the doorman for Roberto J. Miranda's apartment to precede them: she, very lovely—looking down the front of her dress; he quite proud and happy there beside her. Then she and one of the two young men both reach out to press the button for the right floor and their hands almost (not quite!) touch en route to button 15, the penthouse. One of those unpredictable, pleasurably embarrassing moments. She yields; the young man hesitates, then pushes the button, and smiles at the couple: the couple smiles back. This is going to be such fun, she muses to herself.

### Plaza Station
### 9:57 P.M.

Samuel turns to the man who is trying to get his attention with taps on the shoulder. The man, a mulatto, takes a careful look around in every direction, then beckons Samuel over to one side with a few quick waves of his hand.

—You a reporter, right? I saw you talking with that fuzz over there, so I come over.

—You witness the disturbances?

—You kidding me, man? Been here the whole time, ever since about eleven o'clock. Let me show you: I got some identification—I'm a house painter, see? Look it there, that's my name: Ataíde Pimenta.

—Right, right. So what's the story?

—I seen everything. I been hanging around here the whole time. You know the Rua Januária? Sure you do, just up that way. Well, that's where I live. My wife, she home, must already be wondering, but hell, I want to hang around and see. And don't pay attention to what that badge been telling you.

He takes another careful look around, then continues:

—Cops showed up here acting stupid from the start. Me, I'm just passing by like every other day, coming back from work, when they come on the scene real heavy, pushing all them refugees into a corner, not giving a damn how they did it either. I'm telling you, you have to have seen the faces on some of them pitiful bastards, not knowing what the hell's going on. Police telling them they can't stay here, had to go back home where they come from. With the refugees trying to explain how they got no money to go back home, asking why can't they stay right here. So this lieutenant says he got his orders: like it or not, they had to go. That's when this kid, must have been that Carlos you was talking about with your cop over there. . . . Well, at some point he shows up and starts talking to the lieutenant, then goes to get hold of some secretary—somebody by phone to ask for help, but no dice. So then he just give up and started trying to make them refugees understand they really had to go back. He didn't seem like a bad kid, you know what I mean? But there he was, surrounded by all that damn misery, so he asks the people to help out the refugees a little. You see, by then you had a heavy crowd of people hanging around—they's coming home from work, or leaving from the station, or heading outta town. So this Carlos—must be the one you was talking about—he's explaining to the people how these pitiful bastards is goddamn hungry and nobody's letting them out to even find some food. And he was telling the truth, all right. I saw everything. Then the lieutenant, he told him to just shut his mouth. What the hell for? So the kid says no pig of a cop is telling him to shut up, and well, that's when his time run out. The cops wanted to bust his ass right on the spot, but they had the whole damn crowd in the way. Then the kid tells the crowd that he has his own authority because he works for the government too, so he starts authorizing the people to help out the refugees, and that's when the lieutenant ordered his men to grab the kid. Well, the kid, he reacted, the soldiers moved in, and the shit hit the fan. Then more cops and more cops start pouring in, to put the lid on things. By the time it was over—you should put it in the papers—the kid got hauled out of here, feet first. Anyway, the last hour or so they been keeping the whole place sealed off. You can see for yourself, it ain't right. What's a man supposed to do? I got my wife sitting at home, probably wondering what in hell happen. I'm not about to play the fool with my ass. But man, it's hard to take. That's for damn straight.

**28 rua Januária, rear**
**10:05 P.M.**
Dear God, dear God, why is my Ataíde so late—so late!

**488 rua Tupis, 15th floor**
**9:06 P.M.**
*it's ringing* It's ringing. *lúcio* Come on Lúcio, answer, answer, answer. *he's not there he's not there I bet he isn't why so long* Why is he taking so long? *somebody somebody somebody's there with no! nobody's home* Nobody's home? *somebody must be there with him! no! no!* Not even the maid? *somebody has to be there* Maybe? *with him!* Maybe he's got somebody there with him, *no!* so he doesn't want to answer. *oh God* No, not that. Oh God *I'd die* I'd die if that were to happen on the day of my birthday. Come on Lúcio, answer! Answer! *wrong number wrong number!* Did I dial the wrong number? *that's it* That's it, that must be it! Dial again. *the number now the number now ah* Two two four seven four seven six. *ringing* It's ringing. Has to be

right this time. *that business about the money who knows if it wasn't that business about the money the money* No one's home, that's it. *money* Oh, Lúcio, why did you have to ask me for money? Money spoils everything, Lúcio, and it's been so wonderful, so beautiful, *love* not the time to *they picked up!* Hello. *mother sister maid*

—Hello? What number is this?

Two two four seven four seven six. *sister bitch voice* Must be his sister. *is lúcio there?*

—Please, is Lúcio there? *he is one moment*

Who wants to speak to him? *aah, who wants to bitch speak to him*

—This is Roberto Miranda. *you dumb bitch*

Oh, he said he was going to your house, *here!* that there was a party. *oh God where did he stop* off? Hasn't he arrived yet? *apparently not you dumb*

—Well, apparently he hasn't. That's why I'm calling. *what time!* What time did he leave? *just now just a little while ago hardly ten minutes ago you just missed him*

Let me think. More or less . . . just a minute. Mom? *dumb* Ma-a-a! What time was it when Lúcio went out? *just now please just now* Hello, Roberto.

—Yes?

Mother says he left about *ten* twenty minutes *oh no!* ago. And he was going over to your house. *then what happened what happened what happened nothing oh God nothing happened lúcio lúcio's going to screw me* He's going to screw me, today of all days? Somewhere first, *yes that must be it* he went somewhere first, that's all, he'll be coming.

—Did he say he was going to stop somewhere else first? *ah that's it he said so himself*

No. He didn't. But he should be there any minute, right?

—Right. He should be. *cigarettes* Probably stopped to buy cigarettes, *of course something like that. *thanks* Thanks, okay? Good night now.

Good night. Click. *dumb bitch no sweet actually sweet* She was actually sweet, she didn't have to go call her mother like that or anything, obviously wanted to help. *ah he is coming he is* Obviously, he's coming. Went to buy cigarettes, *did he?* wants to talk a while with those friends of his that hang out on the corner. Talk about me? *no!* saying horrible things about me? *no!* I'm fucking this faggot over there *no no no no* just to scratch up some bread. *lies lies he liked me he likes me likes me something else quick some bread no something else god god antônio* He's coming, though, of course he's coming.

I just get so nervous whenever I give a party. *antônio* Stop thinking about it or you'll absolutely end up totally depressed. *antônio* Wonder if everything's in order in the kitchen? *antônio*

—Antônio.

—Sir.

—Everything in order in the kitchen?

—Yes, sir.

*excellent excellent*—Nothing we've overlooked now, is there?

—No, sir.

*perfect what beautiful eyes wonder if his cock jesus!* Fine. But remind Joaquim to be certain there's enough mixers and ice for the guests. Any problem, you speak to me at once, okay? *those eyes*

—Yes, sir.

—You can go.

Hmm . . . if he weren't a waiter. *no! lúcio* Forgive me, Lúcio, it was automatic, the flesh *alas* is weak. Think about something else, enough nonsense. *the party yes the party what about the party?* It's going to be a lovely *that's it* party *lovely.* Wonder if Andréa *that crazy* forgot to invite anyone? *oh no oh no that crazy bitch* I don't think she'd forget someone. *forget no* She's a crazy bitch, but on that level at least she still can function, she wouldn't forget anyone. Can you imagine? *I'd die* It's so disagreeable to have to explain any sort of faux pas *engagement* like that. *no andréa eeeh god the engagement* She took it so seriously, all that fuss about marriage. I *was the one I was the one no! no! something else please something else* Just don't think about that right now. *she's coming here soon* You have to. *she's coming here now how? how? how?* How shall I do it? We agreed to announce our *no!* marriage today. What an idea, my God, what an insane idea of Andrea's *mine. and now now now?* I can't, what's this madness all about, getting married, me? Doesn't she realize *doesn't she realize* I'm a *doesn't know she doesn't know don't say it!* homosexual? *talk to her* Marry her!? Talk to her, explain, that I met a boy the other day *lúcio* where's Lúcio, why is he taking so long? *come quickly lúcio come quickly and help me get out of this* Who's going to help me get out of this? *lúcio I met a boy how does it go now?* Ah, I met a boy the other day, a marvelous person, and I'm completely *is that it? do I say?* mad about him. Oh God, am I going to have the courage? *poor little poor little* Andrea, poor little thing. *what do I do? what do I do?* Andrea, darling, I have to tell you what's happened: I met *right* a boy *go on go on* the other day *right right go on* and I don't think I can *go on! go on!* marry you anymore. Poor thing, a marvelous girl, delightful, crazy, but I *my birthday*—I just hope this doesn't spoil the fun, for tonight's celebration.

### Plaza Station
### 10:10 P.M.

Samuel ascertains: the order (it seems) came directly from the head of Security, after direct consultation with the Governor's Palace and the Department of the Interior because, already a week ago, trains and trucks had emptied some five thousand drought people all over the state of Minas Gerais, most of them sick, all of them jobless and hungry. This measure, therefore, is aimed to prevent the situation from worsening. There are no jobs in the cities for this type of unskilled labor. Better they return to the backlands up north where they can tell the rest not to come here either. Little by little the word could spread, and the exodus would be halted. Certain sectors of the government feel that this is the only means of avoiding this wave of human misery in a state that, after all, has nothing to do with the problem. The department will grant whatever transit passes are needed to facilitate the return north. (Such is the information provided to Samuel Fereszin by Mr. Otávio Ernâni's assistant from the Department of Labor, at the moment representing his office there at the plaza.)

### Plaza Station
### 9:40 P.M.

The refugee Viriato is recounting his journey to the crowd from the literary supplement:

—They came from Curralinho, up in the state of Alagoas, but were soon joined by many others from Iguatu, Crato, Barbalho, and Nazarezinho, over in the state of Ceará; plus many more from states like Paraiba and Rio Grande do Norte, all across Pernambuco and Bahia; dry everywhere, all dry; what they had, they sold; the money, they used up along the way—for food; no one among them had any more land in the North, and what land was left the devil roasted and swallowed up; and now, here in the South, they couldn't even leave the station; but go back to what, what for—and what with?

The crowd from the supplement wanted to meet the man who had ridden with Lampião.

*(Author's note:*

*Epigraph?* "Statistics show that 1 percent of Brazil's population figures in the national average with a total gross income greater than the entire sum of income from 80 percent of the Brazilian population; which is to say, nearly nine hundred thousand Brazilians, in 1970, earned a sum greater than what was amassed by seventy-two million Brazilians; or put still another way, the income of the top 1 percent exceeds the sum of all income from the bottom 80 percent.")

### Plaza Station
### 10:34 P.M.

Samuel, listening to the answer from his editor in chief:

—Let them worry about that, you hear? The government can figure that one out for themselves tomorrow morning.

—Tomorrow will be too late. The police are shipping them all back tonight, by train. The paper could call the governor, though, and get him to intervene. He probably has no idea what's going on here.

—Don't be naive, Samuel. Of course he does! You just get that material over here. It's getting late.

—So the paper's not going to do anything?

—The paper's going to do exactly what the paper's supposed to: print the story. Listen, how about the photographer, did he show up?

—I haven't seen anybody. Who did you send?

—Messias. Wait a minute. Messias, right Ênio? Right. Yeah, Messias. He didn't get there yet?

—Well, I haven't seen him.

—He's around there somewhere. You get back here and write your damn story.

—Okay.

Samuel hangs up the phone, discouraged. He thinks about the student, Carlos Bicalho, and sympathizes with him. Would the guy with the beautiful-looking broad—or maybe that Ernâni character—look out for the kid, or at least try to?

### Itacolmi Television Studio
### 12:10 P.M.

—I'm a little bit afraid they'll ask me to sing something. I never get a minute's relaxation.

—If you don't want to sing, don't sing. No one's going to force you.

—I guess you're right. Well, bring the guitar anyway, and we'll leave it in the car. It might be a nice crowd there, you never know.

## 52 avenida Olegário Maciel, apartment 26
### 9:03 P.M.

Engulfed in a bathtubful of hot water, whose surface cuts her small breasts in half just at the nipples—two bobbing buttons, brownish and rigid—Andrea is aroused by the thought of what is to come in just a few more hours, feels the pleasurable insistence of the water gently possessing her. The complicated machinations of her inner certainties—she, that irresistible offering, that prize, that wonder—have already detailed to her the role she was about to play: bride! She, a fascinating, unattainable creature of the '50s, was about to bequeath to the man of her choice the ultimate privilege of possessing her: with its every intimacy, with her innermost fears, after thirty-seven disdainful years of age.

Andrea trusted in a certain similarity between them, in his own sexual timidity, in the attempts they were making to overcome each of their problems together. She felt, in his touches, the final maturing of her great orgasm, and had a presentiment that it would come to pass the moment she could maintain his erection long enough to be penetrated.

It was very little to change a life, but some lives change like the wind. Andrea in her engagement bath softly rocks beneath the tempest.

## Plaza Station
### 10:54 P.M.

Samuel, hearing the monotonous wail of a child rip through the wall of soldiers, cannot account for his own irritability or why it should connect to the wailing of a child. Meanwhile, the child's father quiets him with a slap.

Samuel walks over to the luncheonette, buys a liter of milk, some bread, some biscuits, and hurries back to the wall of soldiers, calls to the father, the child, the mother, and hands it to them. Others were in need, and beg him— for the love of God, please mister—he goes back, buys more, hands it out. Onlookers begin to imitate his behavior, happily discovering why they are actually there themselves. The man at the luncheonette is pleasantly shocked by the unprecedented commotion: a Christian and brotherly revolt which no one can restrain, everyone is suddenly alive with a flurry of effort to be good, communing in solidarity, saved perhaps; for whoever gives to the poor touches the hand of God; Faith, Hope, and Charity; God grant you, twofold, all you would bestow upon me.

*(Author's note:*

*We broke through the cordon of isolation. The soldiers didn't even notice, because Pena Forte and Valdiki were entertaining them all with a drag show and they seemed satisfied that a gang of fags weren't about to cause any trouble. We went over to speak to the leader of the refugees, Marcionílio de Mattos. For us, he was a bit of folklore, a real spectacle in this shithole of a town, because for us the fellow held the charm of having once been an outlaw and ridden with Lampião. He was being interviewed by Samuel Fereszin, from the* Correio, *an old crony of ours.*

*We listened to him, as he spoke of famine ("My father told me how, back in the great drought of '87, two bank robbers were killed and eaten by the people of Jacaré dos Homens.")*

*of happiness ("That woman over there, her name is Lália, and she's happy now, thankful to have sold her fourteen-year-old daughter, on this last trek south, to a rancher in southern Bahia. At least the daughter has a place to eat and sleep now, which is more than we got.")*

*of rebellion ("When a big wind blows, the grass'll bend; but let that grass catch fire and it'll burn a whole damn countryside.")*

*of property ("Up there? Plenty of land, all right; not very many owners, that's all. When your landowner sees he don't have any rain and don't have no harvest neither, he just sends his workers packing. And is he wrong? He's right. What's wrong is for him to own so much land in the first place.")*

*of religion ("God? I never heard of one good thing he done, guaranteed to be his doing—except what maybe happened a long, long time ago.")*

*of courage ("I like to have my fears straight up, but if the going gets rough, I will mix a little courage in.")*

*of death ("You have those who die less and those who die more. The ones that die more, they disappear. The ones that die less, they remain an example.")*

### Editorial office of the *Correio de Minas Gerais*
### 11:31 P.M.

—How's it going, son? I'm about to take off.

—Wait, Haroldo, we're just about to close up ourselves. The only thing left is that paragraph on page one about the Northeasterners.

—Did *O Estado* give you all the material you needed?

—Yeah, with the usual fuss.

—Nothing from Samuel?

—Nothing. Strange, huh?

—I wonder if something could have happened to him? Just wait and see, it'll turn out the excuse we gave *O Estado* was the right one.

Ênio gives three little taps on the desk with his fingertips.

—You know? I'm getting a little worried about the boy. No, I am. I'm having Euclides go over there and take a look, once the paper goes to press. Then he can give us a call.

—Good idea. And you put the paper to bed, okay? I hate to be late to a party. Shit, no good women left.

### Inside a taxi
### 12:03 A.M.

so much to think about what am I to do but oh I don't know jorge I really don't whether I'm right in trying to make you be a lot less egotistical less self-involved a little more interested in other people in me than in yourself I wonder if you even have the capacity and maybe it's the only salvation because as it is I'm at the end of my rope and even now people only accept you on my account but I don't know how long how much I can take I'm already so tired of

*(Author's note:*

*What a waste to let this moment go by without trying to capture the sense of it, if only in outline, to be able to show someone: this is how it was, back then. This is how people destroyed themselves, how consciences slept, how people tiptoed between fear and responsibility, how writers tried to ignore things or never managed to write things.*

*Yes, I know this has to be the way, it has to shed some light, I'm right in what I'm saying. So what if some of my stories wait ten years to be written.)*

### Plaza Station
### 1:12 A.M.

Samuel gives up trying to look for help. He's thinking about the paper, about the story, as if they were the obligations of a stranger. And then there was the party, the new crowd he was supposed to meet that evening—but none of that moves him, committed now to something he must undertake himself, for all those refugees. He thinks about Carlos Bicalho, dependent now upon that fellow with his beautiful companion; thinks about Carlos's pregnant wife; then about Andrea. . . . Preoccupations of a stranger. . . .

The soldiers, meanwhile, exhausted by so much tension, have let their arms finally drop to their sides and are milling around, relaxing, talking among themselves, taking a break.

The refugees, also exhausted, are trying to get comfortable, sharing a smoke; the children asleep now, with stomachs a little calmer.

In the quiet plaza, nearly empty of the curious, a fellow in his early twenties, more handsome than ugly, more sensitive than shrewd, readies himself anxiously for what will have to be done, when the train is already loaded and the final moment is at hand.

### 488 rua Tupis, 15th floor
### 9:18 P.M.

*it's him it's him!* The bell. *lúcio!* It must be Lúcio, it has to be him. *let me antônio*

—Let me answer it, Antônio. *it's him he's here he's here* Will he be angry with me? *no of course not* Of course not, or he wouldn't come. *oh!?* Marcelo!

—Hello, Roberto.

—Hey, hey! How are you? Come in, come in. *and lúcio my lúcio?*

—Before anything else, a big hug, eh?

—Thanks, thanks. *where did he pick this one up* And this, this must be your girl, right?

—That's right, the one I told you about, remember? When I called you earlier today? Aurélia, this is Roberto.

—Nice to meet you.

*little miss typing pool*—Delighted, Aurélia. Roberto Miranda. Come in, come in. Know something, Marcelo?

—What?

—You're the first ones to arrive at my party.

—You're kidding. Are we too early?

—Don't be silly. Let's get some drinks and we'll kick off the celebration.

# AFTER THE CELEBRATION

A cross-index of the characters, in order of appearance or reference, with additional* information regarding the fate of those who were alive during the events of the night of March 30.

*necessary?
surprising?
useful?
corroborative?
unnecessary?
useless?

**A Northeasterner with dark complexion,
Marcionílio de Mattos.
Page 3**

De Mattos was imprisoned for sixty-eight days. Witnesses who were jailed with him say that it was late on the night of June 5, or early next morning, on the sixth, that he disappeared. Very little is known about him, beyond the material contained in his depositions. The declarations of a certain Viriato, also a refugee from the drought, to the effect that de Mattos was the devil, were not taken seriously by the police, despite their release of an otherwise fictional account of the prisoner.

De Mattos told his story various times to interrogators until the forty-second day of his incarceration; the press checked it all out by sending special dispatches to the Northeast; for the first twenty days he was the hero of visionaries, the outlaw of respectable citizens, front-page material. After forty-two days of depositions, he was officially charged with having been the principal instigator of the riot; he was to be held at the DOPS pending the outcome of the investigation. He was forgotten until the night of the sixty-eighth day, when he was awakened for additional interrogation.

The other prisoners, also interrogated that night and on the following morning, swore they had never heard de Mattos make the slightest reference to an assassination plot that was to be carried out in the Northeast, in the early days of June. Those same inmates claimed not to have even known that the president of the republic, General Emilio Garrastazu Médici, had planned to be there at that time to take a firsthand look at the effects of the drought. But did de Mattos know? None of them had heard him talk about it.


**Samuel Aparecido Fereszin, the reporter.
Page 3**

In the first week of April, the police already knew almost everything about Samuel Aparecido Fereszin, twenty-four, single, journalist, 333 rua Hermílio

Alves. They especially knew about his activities at Plaza Station on that night of March 30.

There were certain minor obscurities which still had to be cleared up, little things, although they would add nothing of consequence to the main fact: the disturbances of the thirtieth. For example: was he or was he not on intimate terms with Andrea de Almeida Laje, thirty-seven, single, journalist, 52 avenida Olegário Maciel, apartment 26? No, it is claimed. But then how did he know that she had a mole on the right side of her clitoris? Certain notebooks found in his room are explicit enough in this regard. However, his co-workers at the paper—not to mention the girl herself after a brief inquiry—insist that Samuel and Andrea hardly knew each other, that, yes, they occasionally saw each other at the office or at that little café on the corner. But apparently they barely even spoke upon such occasions. So then . . . so then how could he know of her preference for fellatio and cunnilingus, as is written there in black and white on the pages of his notebooks? Some reporters mention the enormous curiosity everyone at the office shared regarding this Andrea, and that, in this respect, Fereszin was no exception. The DOPS has therefore concluded that it would be beneficial to talk to Andrea again at headquarters, to finally clear up certain details once and for all.

The police also know: Samuel had always been a good boy, studious, excellent at grammar. He often bought huge quantities of books, and it appears that he read them. He had been working at the newspaper for the last eight months and done nothing improper, outside of an occasional distraction. He began to frequent the intellectual crowd in Belo Horizonte, and had lately become friends with Roberto J. Miranda, twenty-nine, single, an artist, 488 rua Tupis, 15th floor, the painter who gave the actual party, the suspect birthday celebration on March 30, and who was also in some manner involved with Andrea, the social columnist. Fereszin seemed to be at least superficially interested in politics.

As for his role in the violence at the station, there can be no further doubt, corroborative testimony has been conclusive in that respect. Ataíde Pimenta, twenty-eight, mulatto, married, house painter, 28 rua Januária, rear, record clean, testified that Fereszin had arrived at the plaza at approximately nine o'clock. He saw Fereszin conducting several interviews. He even helped him bring food back for the starving refugees. De Mattos, Natanel and Hildo Pessoa, refugees themselves, all agree on this: it was Fereszin's idea to set fire to the train. He arranged it with the Northeasterners: everyone should jump off the train in an apparent state of panic once the fire was raging; at that point a massive, threatening group of them should gradually coalesce to the left of the plaza and begin to disperse systematically throughout the city. He insisted that they must board the train peacefully and remain quiet until the moment the fire broke out.

It was he who went for the gasoline. Silvestre Brasil de Almeida, an employee at the nearby Shell Station, thirty-seven, mulatto, married, 1057 rua Herval, record clean, testified that the fellow in the photograph had indeed shown up, saying that his car had run out of gas somewhere nearby and would he sell him a gallon. Almeida also remembered how calm the fellow had seemed and how surprised he had acted about his gas gauge being broken. Police also ascertained: Fereszin then made his way to the back of the railroad station carrying the gasoline, poured it on four of the coaches, and ignited the blaze.

And still later there he was again, awaiting the group he was determined to lead across the city, dispersing them in small bands of three or four at a time, block by block as planned; while police, taken by surprise and busy with the fire, with saving the train, would effectively remain unable to regroup themselves for a time. The plan itself: everyone would scatter across the city, find slums, cellars, construction sites, markets, anywhere to hide, to disappear.

Samuel Aparecido Fereszin was busy leading a group of some three hundred of these refugees in the direction of the Santa Teresa Viaduct, when eight or nine soldiers appeared. There was a struggle, some shots, and he was left lying on the street, at Avenida dos Andraclas, dead.


## Carlos Bicalho, the student.
## Page 9

Carlos, sentenced to one year in prison (Article no.   , §   , under the National Security Code), is now on his way back home. His plans: to study, work hard, make a life for himself and his family, attempt to recover two lost years. His fears: will he be allowed to reenter college?, will he be able to get a job with a prison record?, how will he be able to make a life for himself and his family—a wife and child—if he cannot resolve the first two problems?

Carlos, on his way back home, on the train from Juiz de Fora to Belo Horizonte, has the same fears every ex-convict carries out of prison.

## The Brazilian military
## Page 10

On April 1, 1964, they staged a coup d'etat, successfully overthrowing the duly-elected government of President João Goulart. The plan, engineered by a group of generals, was orchestrated with the help of the United States Navy, under the Johnson administration, in an operation known as "Brother Sam," a fact which was heatedly denied in the late '60s, quietly publicized in the early '70s, and totally forgotten by 1984.

## Commissioner Humberto Levita of the DOPS.
## Page 13

He died of laughter, literally, in 1982. The strange illness—certainly of neurotic origin, at the very least psychological—manifested itself for the first time in 1978. After laughing for three years and six months, after passing through the greatest psychiatric clinics in the country (from the deep rest of sleep therapy emerged a thin smile that *Mona Lisa*fied his whole physiognomy), he died sapped of all his strength, emaciated because he kept on laughing at macaroni, rice, rare roast beef, beans, purees, soup—but especially macaroni—and never managed to swallow anything. He passed away weakly laughing his grim cackle.

## Candinho, the husband of Juliana.
## Page 23

Tuesday, 3/24/71—Episode of Queen Midas.
It was a night of solitude, sadness, and humiliation. I could have foreseen how it was going to end up that way. Come on, you old bastard, enough of this deceiving yourself. Old age is what corrupts one. I understood that look of hers and could easily have left. But sometimes a man feels so alone. So in need of beauty, of youth, of firm breasts—if only to touch! Then that odd way of calling me Daddy. Take off your clothes, Daddy. What about you? You first, Daddy. Let's do it together then. Don't be such a dope, Daddy. That was the second mistake: taking my clothes off in front of that scornful smile of hers, in front of that debauched little child. An old man of fifty-two doing a striptease in front of a girl of twenty. Maybe if I hadn't hesitated so much. . . . Why so quiet, Daddy?

Looks like my little daddy doesn't give a hoot about me. And the whole time I wanted to prove she was no better than I was. But it went all wrong. She was laughing at me, as if it were my first time, as if I were struggling (crossed out) was laughing perhaps at my effort to hide my belly. Can an old fart who can't answer for his paunch hope for any respect in this world? A naked old fart? What does any naked old man do in a bedroom with a girl who has her clothes on? Another mistake: to get into bed so quickly. What, Daddy's not gonna help me take off my little bitty clothes? A naked old man, walking across a bedroom, over to a girl with her clothes on, a girl who's laughing at him. Do I have to say all of this, describe it all? Oh, how all alone I feel. No, none of that. You've got no right to complain, you've chosen this old age. Anything but tears, not now, not anymore. Let's go, you old bastard, out with all of it. When I had her clothes off, it was all loveliness. My, my, Daddy, it's so taut, just like a little boy's. My excitement tickled her in her nudity, and she yanked me along by my sex: come on, beddy-bye, Daddy. She pulled me along like a bull by the nose ring, as if to say: just look at what I'm doing with your hard-on, you old fart. The effect for me—the one being humiliated—was disastrous, but no surprise to her: what's this, Daddy?, doesn't Daddy want his mommy anymore? She mixed a bit of a laugh into the question. Then, in bed. My kissing—not on the lips, Daddy—only seemed to give her tickles, my beard probably, and she kept giggling like a child at play. Yet so distant from me, from the affectionate and respectable man I wanted to be, feeling so excited because of those breasts! But she wouldn't have any of that, once more rejecting my aroused member, shoving my face downward to her breasts, and then offering her belly, serious now, with eyes almost closed, offering herself—I could have guessed, right from the beginning, from that first look of hers, and now even lying there together I could have guessed it, even before she whispered: that's for you, Daddy, kiss me there. Old farts are only good for that. With humiliation and desperation I buried my head between those thighs and drank her with hatred. And afterwards had to accept her exhaustion and my frustration: not now, Daddy, Momma's completely bushed now. Never again, no, Momma; never again!

I know I shouldn't go back there. Every day I think of the humiliation, but I know I'll end up wearing out that feeling the way I did my rejection of old age, or my love of Juliana. A strange masochism. Yes, I'll actually go back there . . . because to touch the gold of her youthfulness will compensate for all the humiliation, the sadness, the solitude of that night.

**God.**
**Page 23**

His Most Holy Divine Spirit, Creator of Heaven and Earth.


**Juliana's old girlfriend.**
**Page 27**

This one discovered her own husband masturbating over her as he spied on her morning shower. The woman was so flattered that she stopped sleeping with other men and fell passionately in love with her husband again. Through the steam covering the stall of the shower she could vaguely make him out, busily tending to his febrile occupation like some furtive hunter. And so the hunted one anxiously exposed her breast to his fearful arrow.


**Juliana.**
**Page 31**

Her confession to a young man:
—I have to think about that, actually: if I didn't like it better the way it was. Perhaps that madness of his, those little traps to try and kill us, perhaps they were a kind of love. Because . . . think of it: what does he do now? He simply goes out by himself every night, following young girls like an old lecher. I can't believe that the police haven't picked him up by now. Anyway, he actually looks rather happy. But I play no part in it, you see? Before, when . . . when he wanted to kill me, at least then we had a bond between us. You understand what I'm saying? It's just, well, I think he loved me then, because he actually still wanted to die with me. He didn't want to see me become a useless old bag, picking up my department store playboys. I was still included in his plan. But not anymore. . . . Now it's every man for himself, isn't that what you people say? Getting old is just that, isn't it? Well, he's gotten past his menopause; the crisis is over. But you see, he's cut himself off from me as well; he's left me, left me to myself; and now I'm alone, with no idea what is to happen.
—Now comes your own menopause, said the young man smiling.

**Carlos, the young man sleeping with Juliana.**
**Page 31**

—Your only chance to be readmitted is to make a public declaration in which you renounce communism. The rector has no wish to prevent you from recommencing your studies. But you have to understand: what he does not want is for you to present a bad example to the other students.

—How am I to renounce something I never was? That would be to admit to something that I've denied from the very beginning.

—That is your image, however. And the declaration simply pertains to your image.

—But sir, do you really believe they'd let me study in this place after I made such a declaration? Do you really believe my fellow students would accept me after I did such a thing?

—Why not?

—Sir, you know what the students are like.

—Well, it's in your hands.

—I don't need any permission from the rector. I'll take it to court. Then, if I still don't get readmitted, I'll take the entrance exams all over again and start out as a freshman.

—Come, come, Bicalho, lose four years? Besides the two you've given up already?

—Only if I don't win in court.

—Look, my boy, I'll be frank with you: it's not going to work. The rector has the means . . . you understand . . . at any moment he can take the appropriate action, in the interests of the university community.


**Juliana's cook.**
**Page 31**

Lady (pronounced *LAH-djee*, from that old-fashioned brand of facial powder once used by genteel ladies), the cook, dialed the Poison Control Center as soon as she saw Missuh Candinho and Missa Juliana writhing on the dining room floor shortly after dinner, gasping together. What has I done, Holy Mother 'a God!—she kept repeating with desperation, thinking it must have been something in the food she had prepared.

They remained on the critical list for two days, there at the hospital, while all the tears and desperation of poor, poor Lady did nothing to allay the suspicions of the police, who regarded her as a prime suspect. Arsenic had been found in the wheat flour. Should her employers die, she would certainly be tried for murder one, the police admonished her severely.

— Dear God in heaven!—cried Lady: black, thirty-eight years old, ugly, no man in her life.

**Andrea, the social columnist.**
**Page 41**

The police clerk asked for some identification, slipped the sheet of paper into the typewriter and began to record the proceedings. Andrea, the best part of those proceedings, was appropriately dressed for the occasion: a very short skirt, the longest she had in her wardrobe, white and pleated; a violet blouse, of sheer cotton, with the top button open; underneath, a slip, but no brassiere. Five men were reflecting upon her legs.

—Civil status?

The five men looked up at her face. (Why are they smiling?)

—Single.

—How long have you known Samuel Aparecido Fereszin?

The five men approved of the question, faces intent upon her reply.

—Well, I . . . I don't know, exactly. About five months, I suppose. . . .

The five men liked her response and looked at one another. (Approvingly?) The police clerk insisted:

—Five months.

The men stared at her, intently. (A little tensely?)

—Yes . . . more or less . . . five months. I just know him at the paper.

The five men continued to stare at her. (Disappointed?)

—Were you having, or have you ever had intimate relations with him?

Two of the men turned to the police clerk. (Surprised?)

—What do you mean?

The two men now turned to her. (Comprehending her shock?) Their eyes seemed curious, prying. (Wanting me!)

—Sexual relations.

Four men smiled, one of them who was seated proceeded to rub his hands together between his legs. She took a little while to answer, surprised, and the

other one also seated now chuckled under his breath. The police clerk repri-
manded him with a quick glance.

—No, never.

(Why this type of questioning?) The men were waiting for the clerk's next
move. (Disappointed?)

—Are you a communist?

—No.

—Did you know about his political activities?

—No.

(Were these men unbiased?)

—Did you know if he was a communist?

—No.

—You mean to say you had no intimacy at all with him?

All five paid strict attention.

—No.

The police clerk slowly looked to one side and the man seated on the right
nodded his head, authorizing something. (Or encouraging it?) The clerk took a
notebook out of the drawer.

—Were you aware of the existence of this document?

She shrugged her shoulders, as if to say no, she was not. The clerk opened
the notebook to a particular page and presented her with it:

—Read that.

She heard several audible gasps. Which one of them just clapped his hands
together? Another had cleared his throat. She read to herself: "especially in
risky situations. When Andrea took out my penis and put it in her mouth, there
on the terrace atop the Acaiaca Building, I knew she was going to . . ." She
stopped reading, tremulous, blushing.

—Go on.

She looked at the men, seeking help but discovering faces like people watching a film.

—No, I won't.

—Please do so.

(They can't make me. Why didn't I come with a lawyer?)

—No. Why should I read it?

The men were staring intently at her. (At the notebook? At my legs?) She
shifted in her chair, trying to pull her skirt down. The police clerk held out his
hand to her.

145

— I can read it for you, miss. We have to determine once and for all, miss, whether you recognize the document or not.

(A perverted old man?) She quickly shook her head no.

—No, I'll read it.

The men seemed pleased with the police clerk's decisiveness, and her own state of shock. They didn't seem to mind that she would read it to herself. (Have they already had a look at it?) She pretended to be reading, covering the opening of her blouse with the left hand, now that she sensed the shadows looming down upon her. Her eyes skimmed over the words in the notebook, words her mind refused to accept: "small breas— . . . the entire city down be . . . anybody could come right . . . feverishly, her breathing almost asthmatic, as she gobbled my . . ."—one of the men who had been standing came over to sit on the edge of the desk, to accompany her in her reading, twisting his neck to do so. She turned the page —"tongue . . . rhythm . . . coming to me . . . an odor, hers or the flowers' . . . psychological, I think . . . time . . ."—she turned the page—"closet boozer, poor thing . . . not really her faul— . . . to pose nude, I painted her all over instead of . . . living canvas . . . savage rainbow of color sucking . . ." She stopped reading, continuing to stare at the page to gain time. The police clerk doubted she had finished it.

—Do you recognize the handwriting?

She looked up at the clerk. The five men stared at her body, quickening the rhythm of their breathing.

—No. I never saw it before.

—This isn't a narrative of his intimacies with you?

—No.

—Are you familiar with Fereszin's handwriting?

—No.

The men seemed to be losing interest in the dialogue.

— We have two more notebooks like this in our possession.

(No, for the love of God!) The man seated on the edge of the desk was still straining his neck to get a look down the front of her blouse.

—We have to clarify certain details in order to establish the exact nature of the fellow's relations with you.

—But I never had anything to do with him!

The man twisted his neck a little bit more. She put her hand once more over the front of her blouse. (Should I?)

The man seated in the chair beside the police clerk chuckled quietly. The clerk smiled. (Solicitous? An attempt to be charming?)

—The things mentioned in this notebook, when did they occur?

(Did they?) The men were excited now.

—I already said I had nothing at all to do with him. This is an outrage, you're trying to force me . . . I had nothing to do with him, I hardly even knew him.

She spoke in a loud voice, protesting. The men enjoyed her reaction. (Excited?) The man on the table swung his left leg, his right foot resting on the floor.

—We have means of finding out the truth.

The police clerk, in saying so, barely moved his lips, while breathing peculiarly. (Threatening me now?) The others stiffened, tensely. The man's leg stopped swinging. (They wouldn't beat me!?)

—I swear it's the truth. I never had anything to do with him.

They perceived the fear in her voice. No one breathed.

—All right, miss. If that's the way you want it.

The police clerk said this while rummaging in the drawer once more. (For a revolver?) He took out a notebook similar to the one she had in her hand. She wanted to put the one she held down on the desk, but withdrew, afraid to brush against the leg of the man sitting on the edge of the desk: The man had slid forward on his buttocks. (Wanting to lean against me?) The clerk found a particular page, pointed to a part of it and:

—It says here that you have a mole on the right side of your clitoris.

She stared at all of them, her eyes indignant, searching for any sign of sympathy. Her blood had already rushed to her face and reddened her whole neck. The notebook in her hand trembled. She quickly tried to tear it up, with hatred. The man seated on the table reached out with both hands to stop her.

—Don't do that.

He grabbed her by the wrists, preventing her from moving to tear it any further. He kept her left hand very close to his fly. (Drawing it closer?) She opened her hands, dropping the notebook, violently pulling back her left hand.

—Let her go.

The man let her go at the same instant. (Who ordered him to?) He picked up the notebook and sat back on the edge of the desk again.

—Is it true or isn't it?

The police clerk had asked the question with something of a smile (Licentiously?), as if there were some intimacy between the two of them. She lowered her head and didn't answer.

—Mmm? The business about the mole, is it true or not?

She lifted her eyes, still trying to defy them. But she was in tears.

—That's got nothing to do with all this. *Nothing!*

She screamed it. The police clerk, calm, but once more speaking with his jaw set closed:

—Very well. We'll have to put you through an examination.

A few of the men laughed excitedly, others shifted in their chairs, one put his left hand in his pocket, the one seated on the desk slid forward a little on his haunches. She was crying, truly frightened now.

—No, for the love of God. It's true, yes!

She surrendered, beaten, obedient.

—And how could Samuel know about such a thing, without likewise having examined you?

—I don't know.

She was still crying.

—Is it a known fact?

—I don't know.

Still crying.

—The side he said, is it correct? Is it the right side?

—Yes.

Vanquished.

—Yours, or whoever's penetrating?

Laughter, rustling of clothes.

—My right, mine.

—And all that filthy business there in the notebooks, you did that with him?

—No.

—Do you give blow jobs? Well, do you? That's what it says here! Have you? Answer me!

—Yes.

—And sixty-nine?

—Yes.

—Do you like it?

—For the love of . . .

— I said did you like it? Did you!

—I liked it, yes.

—And how does he know that?

—I don't know.

—Answer me!

—I don't know. I tell you I don't know!

—And the filthy things in this notebook, they didn't happen?
She nodded yes.
—Then how?
—With other people. It was with other people.
—That would explain things. But is it true?
—Yes.
—The truth, now . . . and what about this, read here . . .
—It's true, yes.
She kept crying, barely making out the shadows around her.
—You did all that? Do you always do it? Do you?
—Please.
—Do you, *bitch?*
—It depends . . . please!
Humiliated, vanquished, open.
—On the length, or the thickness?
Laughter. She kept crying. She heard a slight moan, nearby.
—Who have you done it with? Tell us who they are.
—A fellow at work.
—At the paper? Who?
—It was a long time ago.
—I want his name!
—Haroldo.
—What's his position?
—He's the managing editor now.
Someone lit a cigarette.
—And the lousy creep told the other fellow?
—Yes, that must be it.
—What a bastard, eh?
There was no more severity in the clerk's tone of voice.
—Who else?
—My fiancé. *Ex*-fiancé.
—And how would Fereszin have heard about that?
—I don't know.
—Was he friends with the two of them?
—Lately he'd become friends with Roberto, my fiancé.
—The guy who gave that party the other day?
—Right.

—But isn't he a homo?

More laughter. And three more men lit cigarettes, inhaling deeply. (Tired of it all?)

—I don't know. That's his affair.

The police clerk began to type.

—They were friends, this Haroldo and Samuel Fereszin?

—I don't think so. I don't know for certain.

—What do you mean by that? Why not?

—I don't have very much to do with him anymore. With Haroldo. That was all a long time ago.

The police clerk kept typing. The men continued smoking, relaxing. Her crying had diminished, only a few tears and a handkerchief to wipe her eyes. They even offered her a smoke; compassionate with her. One of them quickly produced a lighter. She didn't want to smoke, though. They understood. The clerk stopped typing, pulled the sheet out, read it, handed it over to her.

—Read this and sign it, please.

Below the heading, date, name, identification number, and so forth, were written only some five lines, which she barely read: "merely knew him superficially . . . doesn't know how to explain . . . having nothing further . . ." She signed it.

—Thank you, miss. You're free to go now. Do you want someone to drive you home?

She was searching for something in her purse. She found it: a pair of dark sunglasses.

—No thank you. I can go now?

—Of course, of course. See the girl out, Zé.

She put on the dark glasses. The man who was seated on the edge of the desk got up, solicitously. The one seated to the right of the police clerk also stood up, patted the clerk on the shoulder, smiling. Andrea walked behind the man they called Zé and paused at the door: locked. The one who had complimented the police clerk now spoke:

—You were perfect, Maranhao. You only made one mistake.

Zé unlocked the door for Andrea.

—What was that?

She walked out.

—It's not cli*to*ris, it's *cli*toris.

And disappeared.

150

**Andrea's father.**
**Page 41**

The family decided that he must be insane, doing what he was doing: sleeping with the maids, abusing friendships, throwing away money, drinking like a fish, disappearing without a word for days at a time, even beating his wife from time to time. Then that terrible matter of embezzlement some years ago, back in Rio. That must have been the start of it all, they thought—the first sign of his insanity.

In April, he had overheard a conversation at the bar of the Alpine Restaurant: this Andrea somebody-or-other had committed the most obscene sort of perversities with the journalist who was killed at Plaza Station. The guy apparently kept a diary—unbelievable things. No mistake: a social columnist at the *Correio;* it was her, all right. The old man proceeded to smash the bar, bellowing incoherently. Taken home, he remained shut up in his room for the rest of the day, throwing things at whoever tried to peek in the door.

The only place for a madman is the hospital. Wrestled to the floor, bellowing "whore" and "sons of bitches," off he went. His wife spent the next few days indoors, too humiliated to face her neighbors. After two months of treatment, the madman seemed a bit calmer but had a queer look in his eyes. In late June—it was on St. Peter's Day—he sauntered out of the hospital without anyone's paying attention and was never heard of again.

Then five years later in '75, the family heard a story about some strange old coot who lived on a deserted island in the Araguaia River and was cohabiting with a mestiza woman and another couple. The story had appeared in a hunting and fishing journal and his wife had a premonition: it's him. Blue eyes, it's got to be him.

The psychiatrist took a strange position: if he's as happy as the hunter claims in that article—if it's not just another one of some hunter's tall tales—let him be. Andrea wired from Rio: Mother, if he wants to stay there, let him stay there. Stop. But the mother refused: it's immoral and ungodly.

So the mother set out with her brother-in-law, brother to the madman. It was him, all right, the madman himself; they found him after nine days of travel. The brother-in-law thought the island exquisite, a perfect place for a farm. The old man took them to see the rapids and swam in the nude—the wife ashamed, in the presence of her brother-in-law. The mestiza woman never showed herself; a simple trail of smoke billowing from a chimney. When the time came to ask what had to be asked, the old man said no, he wasn't coming back. He was happy there, he wanted to die there. He asked about the children, the sons, the daughters. Assis? A journalist in Rio, doing quite well these days. Ana? Fine, with two boys of her own. Andrea? In Rio again, I think she's about to be married to Murilão, a professional soccer player with the Fluminenses. What makes you think she's about to? She wrote and told me. Are they still talking about her in Belo Horizonte? Only the society pages . . . full of praise. The old fellow explained once more to the wife that it was here that he wanted to die. The brother thought: why not? And the old woman assented, with tears.

She went on to cry for many, many years; she missed him so, the crazy old coot.

### The young playboy.
### Page 44

The young playboy was busy doing what playboys tend to do on early April mornings, when they phoned him to say that Andrea had been arrested; where, and how? He dressed quickly, while the woman complained: how am I supposed to get home? He answered fucking get up and go. Leaving the door wide open and a whore busy cursing in his bed, he ran off to the DOPS.

—Which one do you mean, the, what-you-call-it-gossip columnist? We let her go . . . yesterday.

He ran to her house. Yesterday? Christ! How come they didn't tell me? The mother and sister sat wrenching in agony: she's still at the DOPS, she went there this morning, she's been gone for over two hours, now! He raced back to the DOPS. The bastard!

—The columnist? She just left.

—I want to talk to the commissioner.

—Commissioner Levita isn't in.

—Listen, man. My uncle is a general in ID-4. How would you like to lose your ass!

The officer hesitated. It must be true, the kid's too sure of himself.

—Go ahead and look. Ask anyone. She's probably home by now, you want to call her?

A finger up his nose.

—Look, I'm going there. If I get there and you're lying, I'll have your ass. Where's that cretin I talked to before?

—How do I know?

—Darkish looking, a skinny mustache? You can tell him for me—he's dug himself a nice fat hole in the ground.

Andrea was at home, crying. She hugged him gratefully.

—Did they do anything to you? Did anyone lay a hand on you?

—No . . . only . . . I was so afraid! They're horrible. . . .

—Tell me. If anyone so much as—I'll go right to my uncle.

—No, I promise. It was just that place, those people . . . everything about it was simply horrible!

—What did they ask you?

—If I knew Samuel. The one who died at the plaza.

—That's all?

—Yes, that's all. They wanted to know if there was any liaison between us.

—Was there?

—No, of course not.

—So why did they pick you up, then?

—I think he must have been in love with me.

**Haroldo, Andrea's second lover.**
**Page 48**

Questioned by an investigator known as Catfish, the managing editor of the *Correio de Minas Gerais* offered him a bourbon, spoke about the paper and the drudgery of running the thing, discussed the reporter Samuel Aparecido Fereszin who had worked for him, and then—in a jovial frame of mind— explained to Catfish that he'd often recounted his exploits with Andrea to the kid because

—I'm one of those types who like it twice: when I fuck the cat and when I chew the fat!

They laughed and laughed. Then Catfish completed the other's thought:

—And the kid probably took it all in the ear, whatever he could hear!

They laughed and laughed.

**The young painter, Roberto J. Miranda.**
**Page 50**

On the day following the party, Roberto woke up at four-thirty in the afternoon and found the house miraculously in order. Looking more closely: almost in order. Actually: oh, my God! And finally: an unmitigated disaster! The burgundy velvet sofa, stained with grease, an enormous oval blot! On the arm of the love seat, a cigarette hole! Cigarette burns in the carpet. The porcelain Marie Antoinette, nineteenth-century, decapitated! Paté all over the records!

Anxiously he searched for a book on the shelf, took it down, opened it and felt a bit less tragic. Removed one of the packets carefully hidden in the binding. Picked up a paper knife and a sheet of white paper. Poured out a little of the powder from the packet onto the paper. Carefully crushed the powder with the paper knife. Ground it into a very, very fine consistency. Folded an edge of the sheet of paper and cut it off with the paper knife. Cut the piece of paper in half. Rolled up one of the halves into a thin tube. Slipped the tip of the tube into one nostril, with the opposite end over the powder, and snorted.

**A lesbian.**
**Page 53**

After that kiss at the party, Cora Adélia pursued Andrea in every night spot and newspaper office in the city, sending her flowers, calling her up on the phone. She even tried to get hold of a copy of that famous diary, written by the terrorist, revealing what things he did with Andrea. She actually attempted to buy it at the DOPS. An investigator nearly beat her black and blue, shoving her around a lot. But one day the same investigator showed up at her apartment to sell her a copy for five-hundred cruzeiros. In 1972, Cora Adélia finally grew a mustache.

**Lenice, the mother.**
**Page 57**

Lenice told Colonel Bolivar of the military police, a minor hero of the '64 revolution, that what the DOPS were trying to do was absurd, trying to involve her son in that free-for-all at Plaza Station. The colonel, her lover since 1948, was cautious and protective:

—The staff of the DOPS is passing through a difficult moment, Lenice. If your Roberto knew this Samuel Fereszin, and if this fellow really was on his way to Roberto's apartment, the police must investigate the fact, my love. It's obvious they're not going to do anything to Roberto, because I've already vouched for him and explained to Levita that his involvement is purely circumstantial, that he was simply acquainted with some of the individuals involved. But Levita's staff does have to investigate the communist infiltration at that birthday party. There are some higher-ups who even suspect that the actual orders for the uprising originated at Roberto's party, that the instructions were given directly from there by phone. Just consider all the coincidences involved and see if the case doesn't demand a thorough investigation. Look: the student, Carlos, leader of the first phase of the rebellion by the refugees, had been invited to the party. A group of leftist intellectuals were there at the plaza before the riot; they talked with Fereszin and with the refugee leader de Mattos; and then later they show up at the party also. That's already been meticulously confirmed. Two hours go by and this Fereszin sets fire to the train: the uprising begins. The intellectuals may have been the contacts, isn't that obvious? The assistant from the Department of Labor, Otávio Ernâni, despite his being in the government—or despite his having been, because he was kicked out. Anyway, he was in the government at the time, and had definite leftist leanings. Well, he was there at the party too. And the whole business about the refugees was being handled by his department. It's at least enough to make you suspicious, isn't it? And there's more: Ernâni was the one who had arranged the job in his department for that student Carlos to begin with. And then in Fereszin's notes, whose phone number do you think they found? That's right, Ernâni's—as well as Roberto's. You begin to see just how many coincidences there are. This girl Andrea, for instance, his columnist friend. It turns out she hangs around with those same intellectuals who were at the plaza, and it seems that a diary kept by that Fereszin fellow was also found, and it has things in it—things, my love, that you wouldn't believe could go on between two people. And there she was: at the party. You can start to see how so many coincidences begin to add up, can't you? Well, this is precisely what has to be investigated, thoroughly investigated. I know Roberto has nothing to do with all this, I've explained everything to Levita. And Levita understands, so don't you worry that pretty little head of yours. . . .

**The son, Roberto J. Miranda.**
**Page 57**

After sniffing the white powder, on the afternoon following the celebration of his twenty-ninth birthday, Roberto checked the condition of the bathroom, the kitchen, the Greek Room and, my Lord!—it's a couple sixty-nining on the floor of the Blue Room! It was nearly five o'clock.

**God.**
**Page 66**

Not the same god as on Page 23. A different, terrifying one who frightened little children and whom Roberto, at twelve years of age, managed to destroy.

**Jorge Paulo de Fernandes.**
**Page 71**

The things De Fernandes told the police:
a) there were drugs in the house: marijuana and cocaine;
b) Roberto J. Miranda was a cocaine addict;
c) the crowd from the literary supplement was at Plaza Station prior to the celebration;
d) among the same crowd, Luis, the cripple, was addicted to marijuana and often beat up his own father;
e) Jacob, Rodolfo and Fúlvio were communists, or at least fellow travelers.
f) Yan corresponded with someone in China, a poet it seems, who visited Belo Horizonte with the acrobatic troop from the People's Republic of China;
g) Cláudia, a sociologist and women's libber had worked for a whole day as a prostitute just to find out what it was like;
h) Flávio went around saying that the revolution of '64 had suffocated Brazilian culture, that living here was like living in Burundi, Africa;
i) Andrea was in love with Roberto Miranda, and not with Samuel Aparecido Fereszin as has been claimed;
j) Samuel was one of those invited to the party.
k) Mônica was a personal friend, and he could vouch for her politics.

l) Otávio Ernâni was summoned to the phone two or three times during the party, always to deal with the problem of the Northeasterners and the imprisonment of Carlos Bicalho, a student;

m) he, the deponent, had actually been solicited by someone to act as defense lawyer for Carlos—someone he didn't know, just a voice on the phone;

n) in the Greek Room, a transvestite did a striptease;

o) he, the deponent, was superficially acquainted with the same Carlos, who was friendly with the staff of the supplement, but somebody that he could guarantee had clearly communist tendencies;

p) the writers and intellectuals from the supplement had all heard about Carlos's arrest, not at the station through Fereszin, but there at the party;

q) the reaction of those at the party was generally one of fear; fear and worry over what might happen to themselves now;

r) Otávio Ernâni drank too much;

s) Roberto Miranda had two lovers at the party: Andrea and a fellow named Lúcio something-or-other;

t) the party was more like an orgy;

u) to be honest, no one at the party seemed very preoccupied with what was happening at Plaza Station, unless some of them were discussing it in secret;

v) whoever wanted to kiss Andrea—I mean really kiss her—she let them;

w) a certain Aurélia got so smashed by the end of the party that she was making it with three different guys and couldn't tell them apart: "Which one are you," she kept asking;

x) Samuel Fereszin was barely known by anyone from that crowd, he was more a friend of Roberto Miranda's—perhaps because of Andrea, perhaps because Roberto actually wanted to seduce him;

y) the food was reasonably good;

z) the whiskey, national.

**Maria, Jorge's maid.**
**Page 71**

Maria worked for Jorge until the day she began to have visions of Our Lady. On that day, not dated exactly, but definitely in 1971, the Mother of God called upon her for something special, confiding a terrible secret to her concerning the end of the world, and charged her with the task of saving as many souls as possible, until the day of the inevitable. Maria stopped working, managed to collect a group of pious women—including the mother of Mônica—and left on a crusade. (Mônica occasionally received letters from the interior regarding the advent of possible miracles; cryptic messages such as the following: "Look at the sun today at noon; on the sun, a Sign will appear." An indignant Mônica perniciously refused Grace.)


## Filinto Müller.
### Page 73

The young republic was still astounded by the putrid corpse of Antônio Conselheiro when the son of Mr. Júlio Müller was born, back in the first year of our century; in the seventy-third year, when he died, the flight to Paris by jet was only ten hours long.

Filinto Müller had witnessed just about everything a man could in those seventy-three years.

What gods did he hear talk of, this child born in Cuiabá, in the state of Matto Grosso? (Many years later he would call himself an agnostic, and claim to appreciate the works of St. Paul far more than the life of Christ.)

What games did he play as a young boy, sitting on the dirt road and prospecting for rock crystals to sell to his father like real gold? (Gold!—the republic was still enchanted with the marvels of the former Empire; in every family there were stories of grandfathers who overnight had struck it rich!)

What remarkable facts did he hear in history class, with so much of history still ahead?

What was this little boy learning while the peasants of Santa Catarina and Paraná waged their "War of Impunity" against the landowners, against the immigrants (some of them his own relatives!), and against the government itself for four long years from 1912 to 1916?

And in 1914, what was he doing, what was he thinking, what mysteries moved his spirit when the world launched into its first modern war, while in the town of Juazeiro up in Ceará, Father Cicero and Congressman Floro Bartolomeu began their own great (though scarcely modern) war—using their outlaws, cowhands, and hired gunmen—against the state governor, at the instigation of the federal government?

Who were his heroes? What cowboys from out of the Far West galloped through the imagination of this strapping youth, this young man about to enter the Realengo Military Academy back in 1917 just as Virgulino Ferreira da Silva was preparing to leave Vila Bela (now known as Serra Talhada) and head for the badlands to eventually become the legendary Lampião?

What Napoleons molded him into the lieutenant that he was in 1922? Second Lieutenant Müller was billeted in the Vila Militar when First Lieutenant Eduardo Gomes, that same year, turned himself into a national hero at the Fortress of Copacabana, while at the Municipal Theater in São Paulo a gang of crazy-minded avant-gardists pioneered a revolution in the arts called Modernism. He was one of those lieutenants who stoutly opposed Artur Bernardes, the new president, the one defamed by apocryphal letters ridiculing the military, the one first dubbed the Oligarch and then the Iron Fist!

He was there and saw it all back in '24 when the military of São Paulo (re)initiated the revolution: he set out from Quitaúna with his batallion of artillerymen and joined the cause; he survived the defeat at Catanduvas and, together with his São Paulists, embraced the famous Column of Captain Luis Carlos Prestes, the transportable revolution that was advancing from the South. The two men fought side by side until the brief exile of the Column in Paraguay—he was there, he fought, he saw men die, he fraternized with his future enemy, Prestes, whom he still didn't recognize as an outlaw, whom he still regarded as a revolutionary soldier very much like himself, First Lieutenant Filinto Müller. And why did he finally choose not to return to Brazil along with the Column, and wage their guerrilla warfare, but instead to remain in exile, working as a taxi driver, odd-jobbing (ah, Filinto, the tearful memories of home while off in Paraguay)?

Two years later, he did return—with the iron-fisted Bernardes no longer in office; without the Column; without a uniform—to the government of Bernardes's successor, Washington Luís. Arrested, he defended himself there in the courtroom, and Justice applauded his revolutionary effort by granting him his freedom. He went to work for the Mesbla Corporation until the next revolution came, the one with the red scarves on everyone's neck tied in a knot that would hang the Liberal Alliance. It was 1930.

Now, here was a proper revolution for a reintegrated Captain Müller: secretary to the appointed Governor of São Paulo in 1932; director of the Civil Guard the same year in Rio; commissioner of the DOPS in '33; chief of police by 1937. For ten years, he played Cerberus to the Vargas Inferno. He witnessed, there in the prisons: the men with no testicles, the women slit open. He saw the terror on the faces of people picked up in their own homes and dragged away to be interrogated; the terror of the frightened communists, of the frightened Green Shirts, of the frightened liberals, and all the rest who simply didn't happen to agree. He saw historical truths being inculcated with 110-volt currents. What scenes must have passed through his mind while reminiscing—an interview for Veja magazine in 1972?: "They were ten years of intense effort and unlimited dedication." (Ah, Filinto, Filinto, how much better it would have been to have had certain limits.) The old senator, at seventy-two, takes a certain pride in his career even with respect to those years, well, look, those years . . . "Of course there were cases of torture. What can I tell you? That I was just following orders? No, that would be disloyal. That they represented arbitrary exceptions? No, that would be simple cowardice. I accept complete responsibility and refuse to shift that to anyone, whether above or below."

In '45, when Vargas was overthrown (Vargas the dictator! Vargas the god of the workers!), Colonel Müller, wise old owl, was campaigning off in Matto Grosso, initiating his longest-lived career, that of senator. During the twenty-six years he would hold that office he served as majority leader (Social Democratic Party) from 1956 to '64; whereupon, agreeing to the overthrow of President João Goulart "on behalf of the nation's salvation," he was destined to become, by 1968, the leader of another majority and serve as president of the Council for the Defense of the Rights of Humanity (cry, oh Muse), president of the Alliance for National Renovation, president of the Congress (my Lord, my Lord!). Yet in those twenty-six years he seldom spoke, discreet old fox, and only broke his silence in '72, self-critically: "The evil of all dictatorships is that they are incapable of limiting themselves in time. And what is worse: there slowly gathers around them a vast lobby of purely self-interested parties solely intent upon their self-perpetuation, hoping only to preserve the status quo at any cost. And these self-interested parties as a rule will isolate the chief of state and thereby keep him out of touch with the changing reality of the nation. And such dictatorships, which generally have been instituted with the very best of intentions and have produced materially beneficent results in a relatively short period of time, suffer a change, begin to lose their character, and concentrate almost exclusively upon remaining in power."

Ah, the old senator was there all right, he witnessed the countless popular revolts, saw the countless victims of the great droughts, actually met with Lampião, accompanied the revolution in the arts, endured the coffee crisis, survived the two world wars, the revolutions, the coups: '22, '24, '30, '32, '35, '38, '45, '55, '64—was a rebel, an exile, police chief, inquisitor, Nazi sympathizer, retired general, retired senator, good husband and father. Filinto Müller witnessed the tears and laughter of Brazil and then died very quietly, poisoned by lethal gas in tourist class of a Varig Airlines Boeing 707 on his seventy-third birthday.

### Verinha Nabuco, socialite and philanthropist.
### Page 74

Let no one take pity on Verinha Nabuco: she deserves this suffering, this anguish, this rejoicing of the second of April 1970. Will her Rudi Gernreich dress be perfect, absolutely perfect? Will the income from the benefit for the Home for Unwed Mothers be just moderately fantastic or absolutely so? Will the artists invited, for a 25 percent cut of the gross receipts from the benefit for unwed mothers, remain committed—absolutely committed—to appearing? Will the governor from the state of Guanabara actually put in an appearance as he promised to do? Will the catering be perfect, absolutely-nothing-out-of-place perfect? Oh my God, check and see if that pot-smoking waiter from last year's benefit isn't back among the staff again this year. And her daughter, her sweet little daughter, is she really a junkie? Will she come to the benefit and keep her promise to Mother? Unwed mothers are so desperately needy: they get little if any help from their families; it's not unheard of for them to smother their infants; so much misery, dear God! One simply must do something to help the poor and needy in Rio, the aged and the sick, the young artists, the slum dwellers, the destitute and tubercular, the unwed mother, the homeless child—so much wretchedness, dear God! Verinha Nabuco suffers annually for the poor of Brazil. But let no one pity her on this day of anguished martyrdom. It's also her moment of glory!

### Rodolfo, who can't stand Jorge.
### Page 74

They threatened to crack Rodolfo's spine if he didn't reveal exactly who gave the orders, at Roberto J. Miranda's home, for the subversive operations at Plaza Station. Who commanded the whole operation?—they punched him in

the spine. Who was fucking whom?—more punches in the spine. He was interrogated three times over a period of sixteen days and then freed without explanation.

## Mônica.
## Page 75

Mônica was killed with two shots in the back from a revolver fired by her
husband, Jorge Paulo de Fernandes, on the twenty-eighth of February 1971,
almost seven months after their marriage. A neighbor in the adjoining apartment had overheard the quarrel and—distinctly—the words *slut!* and (a different voice) *informer!* followed by three loud reports—and she called the police.
De Fernandes was caught red-handed, leaving by way of the garage.

## Ruiter.
## Page 77

Mr. Ruiter, the attorney for the defense in the upcoming trial of Jorge Paulo
de Fernandes, made frontpage headlines when he announced that the crime
was related to those events at Plaza Station of nearly a year ago—"a diabolical
plot" whose machinations he would finally reveal at the time of the trial.

## Carlos, the student.
## Page 80

Carlos Bicalho began to sell books. He was followed by an investigator
known as Peg Leg the Pirate from the moment he left the house every morning—no longer an apartment in Carmo among the modestly-well-situated, but
rather a hole-in-the-wall among the down-and-out over in Cachoeirinha. Carlos
carried a suitcase loaded down with the best-selling books of all time and
every genre, a hodgepodge of classics he purchased wholesale directly from
the publishers and sold from door to door at discount prices.

While awaiting the judicial decision to allow him to reenter college—his
case, from appeal to appeal, eventually reached the Federal Superior Court—he
had tried his luck at a number of jobs, experienced occasional hopes, and slowly

came to realize his true situation, even to the point of carrying the suitcase around to offices, institutions, editorial rooms, anywhere. His efforts to obtain more favorable employment—the competitive applications, the interviews—all ran into the brick wall of his criminal record involving the DOPS, and companies turned him down to protect their beloved sons from the taint of his corruption.

He worked from nine in the morning until ten in the evening. After two months at it, he was beginning to stoop a bit to one side as he walked even when he wasn't carrying his suitcase. His wife also took a job. Without training, the best she could manage was a nighttime position as a telephone operator. When Carlos got home, Ana departed, and they alternated at caring for Neusinha, their little girl. Once in a great while they engaged in exhausted intercourse, without much affection. They who had married to fuck a lot.

**God.**
**Page 81**

The Holy Spirit.

**Ataíde.**
**Page 85**

When they released Ataíde, a month and ten days after the events at Plaza Station, he spent seven and a half hours without the courage to return home. He kept walking, stopping at corners, hesitating, sitting on benches—suffering discreetly, looking like a man enjoying the sun. He had four fears: a) to learn whatever misfortunes had undoubtedly befallen his Cremilda; b) his crushed hand, useless for work anymore; c) his future—with such a hand—at the side of his lovely, sweet Cremilda; d) the hatred he felt.

Hunger finally led him home. His wife went pale and then blushed deeply at the sight of him. "My Taíde!" she screamed in pain and hugged him a long, long time while she cried. At once he knew how it was going to be: he would forever hear the voice of—never blot out the face of—Cockroach, saying "We were there at your place, the two of us. I had her in the front, he had her rear."

She cooked for him, crying, doctored his broken hand, weeping and hugging him, asking questions and being told: later, I'll tell you later, not now. She washed him, combed his hair, shaved him, brushed his teeth, kissed him, dressed him, put him to bed, waited for him to slowly relinquish his suffering and fall off to sleep (the voices hounding him: You won't talk, eh? How would you like us to go back there and have another fuck with your wife? Maybe we should bring her here and fuck her right in front of you?), for his sleep to grow peaceful and then fall asleep also, exhausted by her emotions.

## Cremilda So-and-So.
## Page 85

Toward the end of the first week of Ataíde's disappearance, two men arrived who wanted to know crazy things about him: where were his guns, his books, and who were their friends; what did she do, did he go out a lot, whom did they see together? Her shock and her unhesitating answers convinced the men that she didn't know anything. They wouldn't tell her anything about his whereabouts.

They returned two days later asking the same questions, to which she didn't know the answers. Even so, they shoved her around a bit and called her a little whore.

They disappeared for three days, then appeared again together, told her they had been following her to see whether she was telling the truth or not. Told her she should stop looking for her husband; if not, it would be that much the worse for him. And for you too, said one of them, who was partly turned away from her and when he turned around to face her he had his thing out, half limp. They laughed a lot at their little joke, at her shock, and left.

They came back the next day. She wasn't there. They waited, went to her parents' home, forced her to accompany them for further interrogation, told her if she did that again Ataíde would pay for it dearly, that she'd better not leave her house again without their permission. That same one from the day before took out his thing, hard now, and said: have some. She didn't want to; they slapped her around a little, smacks in the rear and slaps in the face, for five minutes, keeping her mouth gagged, and then left hurriedly, saying: his time's running out.

They came back the next day, very satisfied with her obedience. They told her: if you're nice to us today, we won't beat him. Let's make a pact: we'll only give him a hard time on days you give us one. Want to have a try? We won't let anyone touch him here, see? But you have to come across for the both of us, one each day. Oh, there's one other thing: if we don't reach this agreement, I don't know, you might just wind up with your Ataíde *a capon*. She gave in.

When they returned the next day, however, she didn't want to do it. She cried, begged, said she wanted to see Ataíde, at least that, how could she be sure he was even with them, even alive? They smacked her around a little, gagging her mouth. They told her taking her by force wasn't any fun, but they'd be back, and she wasn't going to like it. And don't even think of running away.

The kidnappers returned with a tape recorder. Ataíde was screaming. They were telling him that they'd been with her, that they'd fucked her front and back. Silence and then screams, mechanical noises, more screams. She gave in. She yielded every day, without saying anything. When they were leaving, she begged them to free Ataíde, for the love of God. They said he was fine and would be released any day now, depending upon her behavior. They wanted new variations; she obeyed. They came some fifteen more times, then missed a day, two days; anxious, nearly out of her mind with worry for her Ataíde, even wanting them to come and shove it into every conceivable part of her body, but that Ataíde not suffer more. That's how she felt, in the anguish of the third day, when she heard a knock on the door and she went to answer and it was Ataíde.


### Celma, the mother of a college boy.
### Page 91

**Mother**—You frighten me, Ana. Has something happened to my poor Carlos?

**Ana**—No, nothing like that. I haven't even heard from him.

**Mother**—That doesn't mean anything, child. He was never one to write very much. Remember the time he was away in Juiz de Fora? He only sent me two letters that whole year. And the same with you.

**Ana**—No, Mama Celma. He wrote me eight letters. And why do keep saying in Juiz de Fora, instead of prison?—oh, never mind.

**Mother**—You seem nervous, Ana. What's the matter?

**Ana**—Mama Celma, you know I've always been very close with Carlos, always loved him. . . .

**Mother**—I know, child, it's true. And you've been like a daughter to me.

**Ana**—Let me finish. This whole time, with all of our trouble, I've never ceased caring for Neusinha. I've waited patiently at home. I've never had a problem with my job at the telephone company, or with anything else. Carlos wrote very little, but he did write.

**Mother**—Life hasn't been easy for him.

**Ana**—I know, but just let me finish, Mama Celma. Wait and hear what I have to say. Up until last year, I knew he was still trying to arrange something for us, looking for some kind of job so that Neusinha and I would be able to join him in São Paulo. He even sent a little money now and then, not much, but some. But it's been over a year now with no money and no letters. And back home at my father's there's just not enough room for all of us. You know that's true, don't you, Mama Celma?

**Mother**—I know, child, but with the help of God . . .

**Ana**—God hasn't helped very much at home, Mama Celma.

**Mother**—What's this you're saying, Ana? You must never talk like that!

**Ana**—But it's true, Mama Celma, it's true. If Father doesn't have very much, can you imagine what it's like for me, with that nothing of a salary the phone company pays? What I mean is it's a very hard situation for me.

**Mother**—You know how I live, child, but if necessary I can take in a little more typing and that should help us out.

**Ana**—It's not just a problem of money. I'm trying to explain how things are.

**Mother**—I know, I know, child. But if you need . . .

**Ana**—First let me finish with what I came here to say. Only this: Carlos has abandoned Neusinha and me.

**Mother**—That's not true, Ana!

**Ana**—No, it is true. It's been over a year since I've had any news from him, and not one penny. Even if he's been arrested again, he still can send a letter. If he's not in jail he should write and send Neusinha something. But he hasn't, and it's either because he doesn't want to have any more to do with us . . . or because he's dead.

**Mother**—God forbid! Don't speak that way, Ana, God forbid such a thing to happen. Dear Lord!

**Ana**—But what am I to think? Tell me, Mama Celma, what else should I think?

**Mother**—Obviously, something's happened.

**Ana**—Right, something must have happened, and it has nothing to do with either of us. It's him. And to tell you the truth, Mama Celma, as far as I'm concerned I'm fed up with the whole thing. I've suffered too much and cried too much over this whole business with Carlos, and enough is enough.

**Mother**—What are you trying to say, Ana? Think of what you're saying! At least try and find out what's happened to him.

**Ana**—I was the one who wrote the last letter, over a year ago. Remember? You think I'm a fool not to see? It's one or the other: he's dead or he's found another woman. And either way—excuse me for saying this, Mama Celma— but either way, to me he's dead.

**Mother**—Don't say such things, child!

**Ana**—He is dead, Mama Celma, *dead!* And I don't want to hear anything more about it, which is what I've been wanting to come and tell you for the last six months or more.

**Mother**—Dear child, think about it more calmly. Give him time. You can't do this to Carlos.

**Ana**—And can he do it to me? Can he? Excuse me, Mama, and I know how a daughter-in-law can never be right about this, but I'm a young woman. I'm twenty-six, Mama Celma. Neusinha is going to be seven and for two years she hasn't seen her father. Is that right? You tell me, Mama Celma, tell me if you think that's right.

**Mother**—No one can judge without knowing first what's happened.

**Ana**—Mmm, yes, what's happened . . . and can't you even tell when it's staring you right in the face?

**Mother**—The job of a wife is to wait. The wife of Ulysses waited for ten years.

**Ana**—What do I care about her problems? Ten years? Do I know her?

**Mother**—The wife of Ulysses . . . the Trojan War.

**Ana**—Well . . . whatever, it doesn't matter. I've already decided: I'm getting a divorce.

**Mother**—What insanity! Ana! Only death can separate a husband from a wife.

**Ana**—Death? What do you mean death? I have a whole life ahead of me, Mama Celma.

**Mother**—The worst disgrace that can come to a family is divorce. A wife without a husband, children without a father.

**Ana**—That's how it is already.

**Mother**—It's different, very different. Married, the world has respect for you. A divorced woman can do nothing the whole world doesn't talk about. Think of Neusinha!

**Ana**—I've been thinking for six long months. I only came here to let you know my decision, so you won't have to hear it from somebody else. I'm getting married again, Mama Celma.

**Mother**—Married! You're already married, child. Married to my son! A wife should protect her husband's name, respect her husband's absence. I don't know what has come over your generation: nothing is sacred anymore. You marry just . . . just to sleep with your lover; then afterwards goodbye. And the children are the ones who suffer; they pay the price of where your head takes you. I didn't want my Carlos to marry in the first place—not at that age, without a college education, no experience in life. Ay, dear God no, I certainly didn't want that. Of course, he couldn't appreciate a mother's true concern and accused me of not liking his fiancée, of being a hypocrite—a hypocrite, that's right—that we were just as poor as anyone. As if it ever mattered to me that your father was a shoemaker; my Lord, as if that were a reason to stand in the way. So I'm supposed to be just like that snotty Nonato who didn't want his Cristina engaged to my son simply because we were poor? Dear God, if I didn't want anything it's what's happening now! My Carlos disappeared, in some kind of trouble, and his wife out looking for another man. That's what I didn't want! I knew your marriage was only for that anyway—sex, that's all, sex!

**Ana**—Mama Celma, that's not true and you know it. Just look at the terrible situation I'm in.

**Mother**—I bet you've already picked out a new husband, haven't you . . . well, haven't you!

**Ana**—Yes, you're so right! I've found one. I've found one and I'm going to marry him and I just came to let you know. And I've done it, so goodbye!

**A police commissioner from the DOPS.**
**Page 95**

The same one as on Page 140.

**Flávio Le Coq.**
**Page 103**

It is absolutely impossible to trace, after his flight from the investigation and from the country, the life of this visionary, poet, madman, who tried being sociologist, playwright, filmmaker, autocratic bureaucrat, editor, journalist, and finally Egyptologist. It is only known (How? Who actually told this extraordinary story? Who can guarantee that his wife didn't murder him?) that he and his wife were at a bar facing the Pyramids of Giza. Suddenly, he got up and (cupping his ears with both hands as if listening to something) walked off with that orthopedically inviable walk of his; walked away without heed to her calls, walked into the desert and was never heard of again.


## The beautiful-looking woman, Cristina.
## Page 104

He watched as she fingered the icy moisture on the outside of her glass.

—I keep thinking of Carlos.

—Mmm-hmm.

—I was so crazy back in those days.

—And now?

—Gone from my mind. A total blank, gone.

He was paying close attention, because they were to be married the following day.

—Is it common?: a patient going berserk against her analyst?

—It can happen. Anything can happen.

—I wanted to shake you, fling you out of your coldness, or pull you on top of me, I don't know which.

—That, mixed with other things.

She thought he was speaking of love.

—Don't be so smart, I didn't even like you back then.

—No, I meant feelings of guilt, abandonment, rejection.

Exposed, with no crutch to fall back on, she lifted her glass and drank a little gin. She didn't like the taste.

—Ask the waiter to get me a beer. This gin tastes horrible.

He waited for the waiter to come by and then asked unhurriedly. He drank a little of her gin. Made a face.

—Ugh, horrible all right. How could you stand it?

—Bitter, isn't it? From the lemon.

She drifted back over the past, to 1970, and then suddenly returned:

—If you had liked me back then, I probably wouldn't have given you such a hard time.

— Who knows?

—Why wouldn't you have anything to do with me back then?

—Who knows? Maybe I thought you were too ugly.

She smiled, so very beautiful-looking. The beer came. She took a swallow, caressing the coolness of the glass and licking the little mustache of foam off with her tongue. 1970: the barracks at Juiz de Fora, food for the prisoner, vitamins, medicines, calcium; he needs lots of calcium and vitamins, powdered milk, condensed milk, fruits, chocolate, wheat germ, yogurt. Guilt at not having done what his pregnant wife had asked them to do that night: not having made the effort to get Carlos released from jail, because she was on her way to a party. Was that possible? What insanity. . . . Looking after the pregnant wife to heal the mistake of not having helped him at that crucial moment; the stillborn baby girl like a message: why not kill yourself? The insanity of it all: Eduardo losing control of the analysis, turning to drugs to destroy yourself out of guilt; and before, before all that, long before, as a little girl, the nun forbidding a little girl to sing in the school chorus, and a young woman, a virgin without the courage to, and Carlos, also virgin, threatening to try it with a, a, a whore if she wouldn't do it with him and, oh, god! how she suffered when he said he'd already done it, already lost that, forever, forever; and later, when they moved from Ponte Nova to Belo Horizonte when her daddy won the lottery, her daddy not wanting her to be engaged to such a boy anymore, what suffering she went through; and Carlos arrested in Belo, covered with cigarette burns, telling her it wasn't her fault, sad, lost, perplexed, and she wanting to embrace him, kiss him, carry him away from there; vitamins, medicines, calcium, condensed milk, powdered milk; and the need for men, for a child, the child that Carlos's wife had now lost forever, a father that she herself had lost forever; and that chaos so difficult to overcome, even with the help of a man who loved her or someday would; Eduardo, attentive, watchful, protecting her; and she threw herself headlong, agile trapezist, certain of landing safely.

—What insanity.

—What?

—I keep remembering. Remember all the insanity?

—Mmm-hmm.

—I must have been quite a pain.

—You were.

—I didn't like myself either, back then. I think I also pretended a little. Every crazy person pretends a little, right?

—Right, but then can't give it up . . . pretending, that is.

She was quiet, thoughtful, a little less beautiful-looking. He was remembering the careful policing he had imposed upon himself to keep from loving her too much. He had masked himself in technique, a fragile protection against that shattered beauty. He was enjoying her silence. He could even guess what she was probably thinking. Her expression changed once more to a smile, that characteristic manner of recollection. Then the expression grew more serious, she turned to him, face to face, decisive, beautiful:

—You know?: I always liked you. From the very beginning.

He smiled, slightly embarrassed, drank some of his beer, and thought about the perfection she had attained; after all that had happened.


## The man, handsome, in a kind of ugly-looking way, Eduardo Santoro. Page 104

The deposition of the famous psychiatrist Eduardo Santoro was not very helpful to the police. He had known of Carlos Bicalho through a client who was from the same hometown as Bicalho, Ponte Nova. Family friends for many years. He would not divulge the name of his client for reasons of professional ethics, but could vouch for her in any case. She had no interest in politics. On the night of all the turmoil, they had agreed to pick up Bicalho and go to the party together; actually, he himself was more or less a gate-crasher, having been invited only by his client. They arrived at Bicalho's home and found a reporter there, the one who was killed while trying to cover the story of Bicalho's arrest for his newspaper. They had tried to figure out some way to obtain Bicalho's release, but had no idea what he might have done wrong. They called a Professor Cândido, one of his teachers; then Jorge somebody, an attorney who was thought to run around with the same crowd as Bicalho; and, oh yes, one more, a Mr. Otávio Ernâni. That reporter fellow finally told us that he had to get over to Plaza Station and would leave the problem of Bicalho to us.

—Had to get there? He said that he *had* to get there?

That's what he said. I thought it must have had to do with his job at the paper, his profession. Neither one of us thought very highly of him at the time. A rather gruff fellow. I couldn't say whether Bicalho knew any other people who were going to the party, outside of—obviously—his boss, Mr. Ernâni.

— Did you know the reporter was also going to the party?

— Going there?!

—You see? There you were talking with him, trying to locate three people who could perhaps help your friend, and of the five—five, no, six—and of the six only Professor Cândido was not going to the party. Strange, isn't it? Very strange.

**Author.**
**Page 104**

—This book (confides the author, taking back the originals) is the result of a failure. It's what I've managed to salvage from a pretentious project I'd broadly outlined some ten or more years ago (subtextually revealing that what his friends and enemies had been saying about him was the truth) and on which I've worked only fitfully since then, hampered by a lack of time, by too much time, by laziness, by not even knowing whether it would be worth the time, and by being defeated every time I dipped my hands in the muck (modestly self-demeaning before a project which, after all, was his own, and how many architects around here are equally (in)famous for exactly such unrealized projects?).

—I know (says the friend). I understand what you're trying to say. The book can be considered unfinished (he saw that the author had noted that "unfinished" and understood that the subject would be subtly reintroduced) or finished, for that matter. You could infinitely extend the second part or leave it as it is. I understand.

—Yes and no. The failure I'm talking about is at the very center, which doesn't exist. The book was originally to have been divided into three separate works: "Before the Celebration," "The Celebration," and "After the Celebration." I guess you could say Hieronymus Bosch had something of a hand in all this. (He smiled, because he had invented that idea on the spot, and now it was going to seem as if Bosch had been the point of departure for the project—a lie, but maybe true in a way, if one took an objective look at the book right now.) "After the Celebration" was to have been the inferno of the triptych. But then, as I was saying: the celebration, the party itself is missing.

—I know I know. You're right (his friend considered), as a conception, it's more rounded out.

—I concluded, though, that the book exists without the middle section, but it doesn't prevent me from perceiving the gap in it. Of course, I'm not going to let the reader notice. But it still makes me uncomfortable.

—And what would that missing part have been (asked the friend, after he realized the author wanted to talk more about it), I mean "The Celebration"?

—Well, in that section I could have thrown all the characters together who had been presented before, and have added still others, many more, for the actual party. All the conflicts, agitation, intrigues, fun, games, stories, anxieties (What's happening with me?, I'm getting too caught up in this, the author was thinking and tried to moderate his enthusiasm)—everything that occurs during a celebration which is tied to the central plot of the book. My problem though is of a purely technical nature: there was to be no third-person narration. I wanted to show the whole party as an action, you see, not as a narration. (Getting up, now.) I have some sketches, I'll show you (opening the drawer, taking out a folder, selecting three pages, sitting back down again). Take a look (handing the pages to his friend).

He reads: like to finish with this party, send everybody home, even had the insolence to call me his girlfriend, the nerve! Oh, Lúcio, what was it I did?, go away people, go away, I can't endure any more of this
—**Antônio, bring me a gin.**
   —**Roberto!**
   —**Hmm?**
—**Where did you ever find that marvelous specimen of a boy?**
My God, my God, do I have to put up with this?
—**I had him made special order, Cora Adélia.** I can't bear these intimacies from a drunken lesbian.
   —**Beautiful. Any more of that precious stone left?**
Wonder if Andrea will ever stop dancing with that fellow?

   (—**Marry, really? With veil and tiara?**
   —**The veil is gone, but as for the tiara, we'll manage something.**
   —**And have you screwed one another yet?**
   —**Must you always be gross?**
   —**What's this, Andrea? With me of all people? Our old friendship? . . . You feel? How about that?**
   —**Don't lean on me that way, stop doing that.**)
—**Who's the one dancing with Andrea, Roberto?**
—**Haroldo. You don't know him?**
—**No.**
—**He runs the paper.**

—Careful, he might be stealing your bride away.

God, how am I going to get out of this. The old cunt is such a crashing bore. —Just a second, Cora Adélia, while I go change the record. Naughty: I'll pretend not to like what's going on between Andrea and Haroldo. —Put on some less suggestive music, right? Oof, finally. Wonder if everything's going smoothly in the kitchen? I've such a horror of irresponsible waiters. Obviously, it's not their birthday celebration. Only you can make all this world seem right, only you can make the darkness bright. Isn't that music a bit slow? Only you and you alone, can thrill me like you do and fill my—shit! Lúcio and that black woman. Aah, a TV singer. Little cunt, that's all she is. Lúcio, what did I do? Júlia looks sad, can't have that, no one's allowed to be sad in my house. —Need anything, Júlia?

—No thanks, Roberto. I'm fine.

I never seem to be able to communicate with Júlia. Too withdrawn, too uptight. Pain in butt, that's what she is. What do you do with someone that quiet. —Where's Aníbal?

—Dancing with Elêusis. Don't worry, Roberto, I'm fine. Aníbal's fine. Everything, everybody's fine. The recipe is excellent. Mix the ingredients, stir a few minutes, serve cold. I need an intelligent thought so I don't sit with a long face in the middle of this party. What kind of look is Aníbal giving me

(—Don't you think Júlia's looking a little depressed, Elêusis?

—She always does.

—It seems a little more . . . more intense , now.

—If she had something on her mind, she'd tell you, at least, right?

Would she?)

as if he were seeing me now for the first time in a long time. Do I smile at him? I'll smile.

—Who you smiling about?

—Not about, for.

—Who you smiling for, then?

—My husband, is that all right?

—Oh, that's amusing. Falling in love?

—Don't be annoying now, Flávio. How about getting me a drink? A whiskey.

—Oh, waiter. Waiter! Over here. Look, bring a whiskey here for the lady. With ice, isn't it, Júlia? With ice.

—Certainly. Excuse me, sir, would you happen to know which one is Mr. Ernâni? There's a phone call for him, urgent.

—I'll tell him. You bring the whiskey. It was over in the corner there, just a minute ago, that I saw Otávio. —Just a minute, Júlia, I'll go tell Otávio.

> (—So, this was what happened. When we arrived here I noticed the ambulance parked right downstairs. I thought something was up, all right. Then the doorman explained that a couple here in the building became violently ill after their dinner, sounded like it was a bad case of poisoning. Well, let me think, this must have been about, what, about two hours ago, wasn't it Marília?

*Entre les deux mon coeur balance.*

—Wasn't it, Marília?

—Wasn't what?

—That we saw the ambulance here, downstairs. About two hours ago, right?

—I don't know. I wasn't with you. It must have been someone else.

> Shit, it was Lena I arrived with. I better stop drinking or start drinking a lot more. Otávio)

—Otávio.

—Mmm. Saved.

—Telephone. It's urgent.

—Just a minute, folks. Saved by the gong. By the bell.

—It's (said the friend) interesting, all right. Have any more like this?

—There's more (said the author). But just fragments, lost time. The artifices that the idea imposed were the best aspect of the project, a real challenge, but on the other hand, they caused me problems that, little by little, I felt were unsolvable. First of all, the book could end up being enormous, because I wouldn't be able to arbitrarily make cuts in time the way one does in third-person narration (he suspected his friend was getting bored and decided to summarize quickly), a cut, for example, like: two hours passed, or: two hours

175

later—you see? And then I began to think it would be a crashing bore anyway, if it got so big, and I couldn't think of any way for it not to end up like that. So I stopped, and the book I put together is this one, but it's hollow inside, there's no center. (Lately he seemed to derive a certain pleasure, the author observed to himself, from disparaging more and more what he was trying to do—discovering new defense mechanisms?)

—The book really doesn't seem finished (said the friend, surprising the author a little by returning to the subject again), I have to admit. Of course, you could try extending the second part, picking up all the characters cited in the first part; you could really introduce that central core you keep talking about; you could also throw in two or three more stories at the beginning, as well. It's a book that can be a hundred pages or five hundred.

—Right. And the plot? I have to know what you thought, objectively, of the plot, of the stories.

—Plot? No. Plots, stories: that has no importance.

—Just don't start calling them syntagms and suprasyntagms.

—Let's just take the book by how it's divided, and call them episodes. Or segments.

—Okay (said the author, smiling, because both of them were trying now to avoid a discussion that had already grown a bit tiresome), episodes.

—Fine. The "Short Documentary" I don't think should be the first episode. The reader will think it's just a book about politics, and it isn't.

—It isn't, right.

—You should open with the old couple, the "Thirtieth Anniversary," which, besides, is the best story. On its own. . . .

—Exactly what I didn't want to touch was that first story—sorry, it just slipped out—first episode. It's important to the work's development to start with "A Short Documentary," important for any reader who has lived out our history. I open with documents, develop through reality, and close with a fable, when one of the protagonists becomes fused with the devil (said the author, delighted with the opportunity to explain that there was actually very little that was unintentional about the book).

—Right (muttered the friend), . . . I see what you mean. Another little problem, though, was in the episode about Andrea. I don't know, perhaps you have your reasons, but there's a lot of interference on your part, conceptualizing the character, explaining, or even more—explication what the reader would have discovered for himself if (a little delicate to say this) the story were better written.

—Perhaps you're right (said the author, disappointed at his frend's not having liked precisely that story), because with that episode I restricted myself to more or less a particular style, deliberately Fitzgeraldean, almost to homage to *poor Scott,* shall we say? (indicating that, even seeming to have been a failure, the intention was still sophisticated), and also because I wanted to show a protagonist seen through the prejudices of the society that had engulfed her. Hence, Fitzgerald: the third person, the commentary—as a technique. The author of that short story is actually one of the shallow, prejudiced members of the society which finally judges Andrea. He's also in there, the son of a bitch. It's as if the sheriff of *High Noon* had no right whatsoever to simply leave, despising the whole ton. But that's a problem without a solution, I think.

—And there's this business here (said the friend, picking up the manuscript, searching for a particular page, page 42, and, finding it, pointing to a phrase), right here; you can't get away with this. (Reading.) "She held onto her resentment, and a three-by-four photograph of him." That kind of enumeration went out with Machado de Assis: love lasted nine months and fifty-five-hundred cruzeiros.

—Cross it out. There. What else?

—You have this guy, the informer . . .

—I don't like that episode either (the author warned).

—It's not that. Just that the business of farting is in rather poor taste, don't you think? You could cut that.

—Now you're going to start talking to me about poor taste? But if I'm trying to show exactly the grossness, the egoism, the vanity that takes hold of the guy, once he's home alone—just where he doesn't have to police himself, or be such a hypocrite. That's when the guy relaxes, Christ, because to keep up that kind of pretense, twenty-four hours a day, that would be too much for anyone. So the fart, I think, comes in at the right moment there.

—I still think it's in bad taste (said the friend, who then paused for an interval, which began to seem rather long and soon would have become uncomfortable, but remembering at that point something he had left for later on—for now, perhaps—he muttered it while clearing his throat), I don't know, hrrghmmm (and picked up the conversation once more). Have you read *O Curral dos Crucificados,* by Rui Mourão?

—I knew it (said the author, smiling and not saying what *it* was).

—Well, there you are (said the friend, not needing to explain), I think, to a certain extent, there's a connection.

—Maybe so. They have what two straight lines of one angle have in common:

a point. In this case, the Northeasterners. While I was writing the book, my wife alerted me to the same thing. So I read Rui's book, saw it had nothing to do with mine, and continued. I even think it's interesting, the coincidence of the Northeasterners. It makes it seem like what happens is actually true. As for the rest, the intentions, directions, extensions, conceptions, generations, situations, actions, they're all different.

—Principally, the generations (said the friend).

—Principally, the situations (corrected the author). Nineteen-seventy with all its impossibilities. In 1970, my generation was no longer even a group as such. Carlos, Samuel, the author, the intellectuals are all, chronologically speaking, figures from another generation, the post-'64 generation, with a dramatic readiness that could still find no outlet.

—You wish to hide the fact that the author is you (said the friend, actually a little shocked)?

—No, it's just this: by age and social position, an Otávio, a Jorge, an Andrea, they would be my generation, people already well established, with good jobs and all that. The author, obviously, is me, but the way I think—today, in 1974—that the little intellectual of 1960 would have behaved in 1970 (said the author, insisting on that self-deprecation he'd been indulging in lately and smiling at this and thinking: what could it be that I have against what I was, or is it against what I am nowadays, or is it none of these things?). But the principal figures, the ones who really act, are of a much older generation, like Marcionílio, or a slightly younger one, like Samuel. Anyway, it's not a book about a specific generation, but about various generations who one day meet in the Brazil of 1970.

—But all of you, your group, are the group in the book, right?

—No (said the author, pausing perhaps a few too many seconds). Besides, all groups seem alike in Belo (speaking perhaps, who knows, for himself). At any rate, the group itself wasn't my real preoccupation. I wanted to talk specifically about certain people who were caught, with their own stories, in the events and climate of the year 1970.


**The pregnant girl.**
**Page 107**


Ana, the wife of Carlos Bicalho, gave birth in the radio patrol car to a baby girl, strangled by the umbilical cord. A man who happened to be passing by the house, alarmed by the cries for help and weeping of a child that seemed to be coming from somewhere inside, went and called the police, just as a precaution. The sergeant reluctantly agreed to drive the poor girl, already giving birth, to the nearest hospital.

## Mr. Ernâni.
### Page 107

On the thirty-first day of March 1970, the economist Otávio Ernâni woke up in disgrace and didn't know it.

He took Alka-Seltzer, Engov, a bath, Melhoral, and tried to remember whatever terrible thing it was that had happened to him at the party. He called various people, who were still asleep, noticed that he had turned down the bell on his phone, and left hurriedly for the department, two hours late and certain that something was definitely wrong. Whenever he drank it was like this: amnesia and a terrible headache.

Otávio suffered the first blow of that March 31 at precisely 11:30 A.M., when the minister informed him that the governor was demanding to know who was responsible for the disturbance of that morning. And since it was a matter for the Division of Migration, it would have to be he who would be held responsible. The word "disturbance" struck him as odd, but what seemed most important to him at the moment was:

"We're investigating the whole matter. As for my division, I assume all responsibility. Within an hour, I'll have a full report ready, sir."

As soon as he left the chamber he suffered the second blow: he found out through the papers, notably *A Tarde,* and from a number of fellow administrators, that Carlos Bicalho had been arrested. It seemed like a veritable revolution had been attempted by those Northeasterners, whom he had ordered to be returned by train. While a whole train went up in flames, and four people had died, and hundreds of drought people had scattered throughout the city, and dozens of wounded were being treated at hospitals, and agitators were being hunted down by police, he had been busy getting drunk at a scandalous party.

He called in an assistant and received the third blow: he couldn't speak to Carlos Bicalho at the DOPS because he was being held incommunicado; the head of Security had asked permission from the Minister of Labor to investigate all personnel in the Division of Migration; he, Otávio Ernâni, was actually suspected of being involved with the agitators who had organized the revolt; the minister had pledged his confidence in Otávio before the governor, despite the latter's suspicions that Otávio had fled the city this morning after the plot had miscarried.

—Holy shit. But are these people crazy?

At 12:30 P.M. he communicated to the Minister of Labor the fact that his division was now at the minister's disposal. No, there was no possible explanation for what had happened. No, he absolutely did not believe in any conspiracy. While those events were unfolding, he himself had been attending a birthday celebration. No, he had not been advised of the disturbances. No, he could not say anything about Carlos Bicalho without first being able to speak to the boy. Yes, he would release some explanations to the papers, assuming total responsibility in the area of his department. Certainly, a press conference at six o'clock.

The Minister of Security refused him any information. Otávio spoke personally with him, explained that he had already scheduled an interview with the press for six o'clock, and he needed to know what had happened plus whatever was going on at the moment. The irony of the response ("Come now, you're probably able to answer that better than I am.") further irritated him. But he put up with it, expediently.

At two o'clock he sent out for a hamburger, milk, and some antacid tablets for stomach relief. He had a suspicion that the routine work for the Division of Migration was not being passed on to him. Better anyway, for the moment.

He obtained authorization from the governor to get information from Security. Jacques telephoned to comment on the party, and he then got the fourth blow of the day: in a situation involving a genteel dispute between Lena and Marília—in which he was not exactly the object of the argument; the two were disputing who was the more invulnerable, who was less bothered by the presence of the other with regard to Otávio and/or observers—in that indiscreet and delicate situation, he, Otávio, completely plastered, had broken the crystal of convention by asking:

—Why don't we try out a ménage à trois?

—Holy Christ, Jacques.

The assistant from Security sent a memo asking what type of information he required. He wrote out a questionnaire, with a carbon copy for himself. Carlos Bicalho's wife arrived with her little daughter, two years of age, and a pregnant belly of eight months plus, wanting to know what her husband's situation was.

—I'm going to tell you frankly, I don't even know my own situation at this point. It seems everyone has gone crazy. Between now and tomorrow they could throw me out on the street or even arrest me. The least they'll probably do is throw me out.

At four o'clock, he left word he would be back at five-thirty and went out. He bought a shirt, underwear, a pair of socks, and walked over to the sauna at the Minas Tennis Club.

In the sauna he took heart, called Marília's home, and received the fifth blow of the day: she hadn't slept at home, wasn't she with you?, oh, my God, what could have happened to her, we called your residence and no one etc., etc.—It would be totally impossible for her to have been arrested. No need to worry about that, I assure you.

He arrived at the department at exactly five-thirty, smelling of eucalyptus, with no headache; read over twice whatever information had been forwarded by Security; made a few double-checks in Migration to complete the information; and relaxed while awaiting the hour of his meeting with reporters.

The press wanted to know how the whole business of those Northeasterners began in the first place.

—Yesterday morning, the assistant to the governor of Bahia had sent a message to our minister, informing him that a freight train loaded with some twelve-hundred drought people was headed for Belo Horizonte. The procedure we followed was quite normal: consultations with the governor on what steps to take, a final understanding between the governor and the ministers of Security and Labor and Social Services. Only at four in the morning was it actually decided for certain that the refugees should be shipped back. I myself, as general assistant to the minister of the department and as director of the Division of Manual Labor, to which that of Migration is subordinated, was personally charged with the task. We expedited the transfers and requested additional police reinforcements for the undertaking, all very much within normal procedure. By 6:00 P.M., police were already at Plaza Station. The refugees arrived at precisely six-twenty in the evening.

What was the role of Carlos Bicalho in these events?

—The young man had been working as a liaison in the department. As everyone knows, he's now been arrested. As he explained it to the police, he was just leaving work, a little past seven in the evening, when they themselves called for a representative of the Department of Labor, to resolve the problem of feeding the Northeasterners. According to what he told police, he went there to get some idea of the situation and then immediately tried to locate someone capable of settling the problem officially. For the rest of it, what happened there at the plaza between himself, the police, and the refugees, we still are unable to determine. The police are investigating.

Was anyone from the department aware of Carlos Bicalho's political activities?

—I was never aware of any sort of political activity on his part, and I still don't know of any, I haven't been able to talk with him personally as yet. If anyone else knows anything, I haven't been informed of it.

How long was he working in your department?

—A year and a half.

Who got him the job?

—I did. Officials in the department are normally exempted from competitive examination.

Why did the Northeasterners choose Belo Horizonte to emigrate to?

—It's impossible to determine a thing like that. The refugees don't choose, they go wherever they can. What they want is quite simply to leave where they are, to flee the drought. Minas, Rio, São Paulo, Paraná, Amazônia, it doesn't matter to them. What they want is to survive, that's all. And it seems to me a justifiable impulse.

Is it possible that someone may have plotted their coming to Belo Horizonte?

—I doubt it. Our labor market is incapable of absorbing unskilled manual laborers. No industry here would attract such laborers at the moment.

To speak more plainly, sir: isn't it possible, Mr. Ernâni, that Carlos Bicalho may have sent for them with political aims in mind, and using the department as a cover?

—I really don't think so. It doesn't make sense. What intention would he have, were that the case?

Political agitation, sir, of course.

—That makes no sense. Look, for a plan like that to work it would have had to rely on the collaboration of the governor of the state, who had already decided to ship back the refugees—because without reembarkation there would have been no problem. It would have had to rely on the collaboration of the police, who didn't even know how to direct, or had no means of controlling, the situation at the plaza. Not to mention counting on the potential for politicization—questionable at best—among a few poor drought migrants. All of which would certainly be expecting too much. It's an altogether absurd idea.

How many Northeasterners arrive annually in Belo Horizonte?

—We have no accurate way of answering that. They arrive in small droves, at random, and are swallowed up by the city. This year's census may be of some help in answering your question. The phenomenon of migrations from the Northeast, en masse, occurs only during the droughts. The Northeasterner likes his homeland, and about sixty percent of these migrants return home as soon as the rains begin again.

Setting aside the hypothesis of subversion, how would you explain the events of this morning?

—It's very simple: the well-behaved donkey suddenly gives a kick. And everyone is horrified: oh, but it was such a well-behaved donkey! Well, it happens that this well-behaved donkey has just traveled, with great hardship, all the way from the Northeast, undergoing twelve to fifteen days of total privation. He arrives here and finds nothing to eat, no jobs available, and they want to make him take the same road back without even stopping to have a drink of water. Naturally enough, he lets out with a kick. Poor donkey, now he's already sorry he kicked. It's the same well-behaved donkey as before, but no one trusts him anymore. They treat him like a wild ass.

## Esdras, the Hermetic.
## Page 107

This type of intellectual, who for certain periods of the year can be found in the southern and central portions of the country, is accustomed to go out late in the evening, but only during spring and summer. On winter nights, he never goes anywhere, being very sensitive to cold. And on autumn nights he generally writes, generally poetry, generally hermetic.

He's a disillusioned soul, intellectually rigorous (the book he writes and rewrites in secret never really satisfies him, never really reaches the desired level of perfection—and is never really born); a man with only one real friend; bitter toward women, because he's never figured out what to do with a breast other than to squeeze it. He doesn't believe that art has any value today, but it's still the only thing he prizes. He merely uses it at home anyway: like an old wrap; out of fashion.

When Esdras, the Hermetic, died in 1987, the only friend that he had collected his poems and published a posthumous volume. Some fifteen people read that heavy poetry—the only ones with the capacity to verify that he would someday become a landmark in poetry, along with Villon, Petrarch, Mallarmé. But for unknown reasons the only ones chose to remain silent. So the poetry of Esdras closed in upon itself: perfect.

## The neighbor.
## Page 110

The neighbor of Roberto J. Miranda told the police that, every March 30, without fail, there was a party in apartment 1501. The doorman confirmed the fact and said that the people were almost always the same. This discouraged Inspector Levita a little, for he was searching for some link between the party and the street disturbance. But he soon recuperated his spirits: the neighbor had been pro-Vargas and the doorman accepted bribes. Two more possible suspects!

## Luis. 1946-1972
## Page 111

This little story left the young collaborators of the supplement rather perplexed:

Luis and his father lived alone in an old house in the Floresta district behind the station. He was a brilliant youth, bitter, crippled in both legs from a congenital defect, incredible-looking face, erudite, cruel, emotionally unstable. He balanced himself on two gelatinous legs by some sort of miracle, and never managed to write a good play. His father was sad, fifty, a federal civil servant, grade 14, masochistic. Luis calculatingly destroyed him. The boys from the supplement got to know Luis during his alcoholic phase. They would help him home in the morning, tamed and stumbling; but before they had time to leave, they would hear him shouting, "Don't you dare complain! You're the one who made me like this!" He took a trip to Europe, and the father had to pay off the debts in installments. He became a homosexual in order to insult the old man by bringing other men in the house. He made the father give them the money whenever it was a paid trick. "Look at these legs, look at these legs! Look at what you did, you filthy bastard!" When marijuana came into vogue, around

'69, and those who needed to dreamed on it, he used it as a form of aggression. The same with cocaine, in '72: he prepared snorts in front of his father, staring at him, challenging him.

His father smothered him to death under a pillow and committed suicide with a bullet in the ear.


## Mr. de Fernandes. Jorge Paulo de Fernandes.
## Page 112

Was it Jorge's or his attorney Ruiter's idea to present Mônica's death as a consequence of the events at Plaza Station?

The defense was based upon two theses: a legitimate defense of his honor, arguing that the wife had been having extramarital relations with actual friends of the accused, and an irresistible compulsion, given the revelation made by the wife herself, that she was actually betraying him, ladies and gentlemen of the jury, in compliance with a plan of vengeance. And this upright man, here before you, this respecter of the traditions of his forebears and of the customs of this generous state of Minas Gerais, saw himself suddenly embroiled in a diabolical plot, a coercive net that could only have been manipulated by elements repudiating the Christian faith and the morality of the Brazilian family. These forces, together with the deceased, had planned the unworthy conduct of the latter with full premeditation, for the purpose of humiliating the defendant here before you, and punishing him for nothing less than his patriotic behavior during the police investigation of events linked to the disorder at Plaza Station, almost two years before. The defendant has testified, under oath, that he could not resist the terrible impulse to kill when the wife revealed that their very marriage was a sham, an act of revenge; that all had been carefully planned, to teach him not to denounce her friends; that even the men with whom she was having relations in order to humiliate him had been deliberately selected according to a previously arranged plan that was then coldly put into practice. Coldly, but not without a certain carnal pleasure, believe me. . . . Then quite cynically, she revealed to her husband the whole sordid plot the moment she had finished sleeping with the last man on the list, and was still carrying within her the hot sperm of her opprobrium. It's right there, ladies and gentlemen of the jury, right there in the findings of the medical examiner.

**Marília.**
**Page 113**

Caught in the same moment of surprise, they lifted their mouths at the same instant: she from his penis, he from her vagina. The door was quickly closed by the person who had just surprised them and who, in turn, also surprised, now withdrew. She hesitated a brief second, wiggled her bottom with excitement, and returned to his penis; he swiftly returned to her vagina.

**The beautiful-looking woman.**
**Page 113**

When she tried to find a psychiatrist in 1968, Cristina was failing apart. Patiently, Eduardo Santoro, thirty-four, single, trained in Switzerland, worked on that puzzle of eighteen hundred pieces, reassembling it piece by piece with absorbed fascination until he obtained the perfect woman whom he married five years later—three years after the celebration that had caused her to fall apart all over again.

**The man with a number of theories.**
**Page 113**

Patiently, Eduardo Santoro, thirty-four, single, trained in Switzerland, worked on that puzzle of eighteen hundred pieces, reassembling it piece by piece, until he obtained the perfect woman whom he married three years after the goddamn party that made her fall apart all over again. They had three children and all of them were happy or unhappy at the appropriate times.

**Aurélia.**
**Page 113**

Aurélia, abandoned by Marcelo at the party, stopped going out with rich boys, found a serious partner and got engaged. One night the fiancé was there in the living room, eating cornmeal bread with coffee, when he heard, on the TV, an emergency call from the Misericórdia Hospital for donors of type O-positive blood; he said goodbye to his fiancée and his future mother-in-law, gave blood, came down with an inexplicable case of tetanus, and died two days before the wedding. On Saturday, Aurélia began flitting about to the hairdresser, the seamstress, the manicurist, and finally her bath. The mother hardly paid attention to this or that request for help from her daughter, finding it strange that she should be interested in such petty diversions two days after the death of her fiancé; though of course Aurélia shouldn't just lock herself up in a room somewhere, dead to the world. So she suffered an incredible shock, fell into a chair, and began weeping softly to herself when the daughter emerged from her room, dressed as a bride, at four in the afternoon.

## Marcelo.
## Page 114

Caught in the same moment of surprise, they lifted their mouths at the same instant: he from her vagina, she from his penis. The door was quickly closed by the person who had just surprised them and who, in turn, also surprised, now withdrew. He swiftly returned to her vagina; she hesitated a brief second, wiggled her bottom with excitement, and returned to his penis.

## "The old bird's crazy." Professor Candinho.
## Page 114

—Absolutely impossible. Lady has our entire confidence.

—Professor, professor. Someone put arsenic in the flour tin. If it wasn't she, who was it? You? Your wife? It had to be the maid.

—But *cui prodest? Cui?* She knows we haven't any money. What she would end up with is no job. I think—I don't wish to interfere with your work, but I think what ought to be investigated is the source of the flour, the factory, all the flours in the city. And if someone else has eaten bread and been similarly poisoned.

—We went to the six factories that sell to that supermarket and found nothing. Zip, Professor; it's quite a fix.

(The detective known as Angelmaker has another hypothesis he intends to investigate on his own: someone from that party on the fifteenth floor was definitely interested in seeing the professor dead. Perhaps he knew something that could compromise the group, some conversation he might have overheard. . . .)

## Mr. de Fernandes.
### Page 114

Jorge Paulo de Fernandes was exonerated by a vote of 12 to 0. A bastion of familial honor for all the families of Minas to admire.

## Lúcio, 36 Plaza Negrão de Lima.
### Page 114

Lúcio realized that Roberto was afraid of being arrested, laughed at him about it, and began to ask for certain favors. In order not to tell the police what had happened at the party, he demanded (from April until August, when Roberto refused to put up with any further extortion and called upon the hated Colonel Bolivar):

500 *cruzeiros*
1 blue imported Swiss shirt
1 imported pair Levi's
1 alligator belt
1 pair shoes with high heels
150 more *cruzeiros*
1 necklace semiprecious stones from the Sahara
1 Cross brand ball-point pen
1 kick in the ass, while assuming the appropriate position (on all fours)
1 trip to Rio, alone
personal charge account at the Around-the-Clock Club
3 Italian print polo shirts
the right to slap him in the face, including in public
300 more *cruzeiros*
1 pair white linen slacks
1 stereo turntable
1 amplifier, imported

2 speakers

10 albums, besides the ones he took from Roberto's apartment

1 Yamaha 350 motorcycle

But Lúcio never got his bike. Two men showed up at his house, very respectful, calling his mother ma'am and asking to speak privately to her son, Lúcio, it wouldn't take long, right up in his room if you like, ma'am. In the bedroom, one of them took out a sheet of paper from a pocket and opened the dresser. Lúcio tried to protest, what's going on, hey, what do you think you're doing, and received a quick slap in the face, strong, sharp. He tried to yell, Mother, call the, another slap in the face. The other man kept looking back at the sheet of paper he had with him, searching through the dresser, ripping everything apart. Together, they tore the blue shirt, the Levi pants, the print polo shirts; they put the necklace in a pocket, took whatever money they could find, gathered the record albums up. They didn't say a word, merely additional slaps in the face.

—Take off the slacks and shoes.

A slight hesitation, a slap. He took them off without fear, understanding why. They ripped the slacks, burned the toe of one shoe with a lighter, cut the belt with a razor blade.

—And the pen?

Lúcio didn't understand at once, but soon enough, with another slap in the face. The men put the pen in a pocket; they carried out the hi-fi and records, with Lúcio helping in his underpants, and placed them all in the back of the C-14 van.

The mother, back inside making coffee for the visitors, came to the door, sorry they were leaving so quickly, but got indignant with her Lúcio:

—For shame, my God! Come in here and put on some clothes, Lúcio!

The two men forced Lúcio into the van, without his mother even noticing that they were, and decidedly so, but all the while excusing themselves:

—Don't worry, ma'am. He has his clothes in the van. It's just that we're in such a hurry. He'll be right back.

Lúcio was scared. He immediately thought of the Death Squad. His anxiousness lasted exactly thirteen minutes, from his house to the Around-the-Clock Club. The three of them went in together. The doorman would have barred Lúcio, if one of the men hadn't pushed him aside, delicately but meaningfully, with a hand on the chest: "Don't get into this." At the bar, they called the manager.

— This hotshot has no more account here.

Despite the darkness, many saw that the boy was actually in his underpants, and they recognized him. One of the men asked:

—How many slaps?

—Two left.

Slap. Slap. In the middle of the dance floor.

As they returned to Plaza Negrão de Lima, Lúcio even thought of God, thanking him. The mother, and with her a young girl, came running out of the house as soon as they heard the sound of the van. The men made Lúcio get out, consulted the list once more while whispering together, a bit constrained by the presence of the two women: the mother just beginning to recover from the shock; one of the men muttering, on all fours, little dog; the other forcing Lúcio to the ground; the girl asking, what's going on, Lúcio; one kick in the ass; the mother's screams, and then loudly, in his ear:

—Understand, hotshot?

—Answer!

—Yes.

—Understood everything?

—Yes.

—Then get lost, hear?

—Show up around here again and we have orders to take you apart, piece by piece.


**Otávio.**
**Page 115**

Otávio opened the door at nine in the evening and, caught with a look of surprise on his face and the pleasurable taste of fried egg in his mouth, he received Lena in an almost tactless manner. Marília arrived home to her parents at a little past six with the decision that she would leave home for good if there was a scene. Lena was put off by Otávio's hesitation and said immediately to shock him:

—Am I disturbing you? Is Marília here?

—No, honestly. I'm just in a terrible state of confusion. Come in, come in.

—You forgot?

—Forgot what, tell me? We made a date here for tonight, right? Right: I forgot. Today everything's taking me by surprise.

—Yes. So I read in the papers.

—Oh, fuck it all. The worst of it was getting so smashed last night.

—Yes. You really were highly insulting.

—And you? I don't remember anything.

—Well, to tell you the truth, so was I.

—Tell me about it later. You'd like to stay, right?

—Yes, I'd thought about it. (She smiled.) Mistakenly, obviously.

Marília's father wanted to know where she'd been till such an hour. Otávio grew tense over Lena's "Mistakenly, obviously," worried that Lena had decided: "Forget it." She turned to the sofa for help and sank into its peace until finally remarking:

—So you were dismissed.

—Yes. They made me resign.

—What a bore, eh? What will you do now?

—Hmmn, I don't know. Think I might go back to school. Who knows . . . (He smiled.)

—Fix me a whiskey? I'm tired of hating you.


## Marília.
## Page 118

Marília didn't know if that taste of penis was actually in her mouth or her memory. Otávio is serving the whiskey, without ice, the way Lena likes it.

—Hating me why?

—For having deceived me so. And because I was such a fool. But now it's all okay. When I actually blurt things out it's because I'm okay.

—Listen, Lena. You remember that phone call, yesterday? Remember?

—So?

—You must have realized I was sincere: I said right away I wanted you back; I didn't even think of Marília. Well, that was the truth: so give me a little time, that's all. Let me settle this mess first. And just forget the party; forget it.

Marília fought with her father, with her mother; packed her suitcase; swore she had had enough of those scenes; and left home, never to return again. That was around nine o'clock. A little before ten, she will arrive at Otávio's place seeking shelter, confounding the reunion between himself and his wife, and contributing definitively to the happiness of all three.

**Lena.**

**Page 119**

Lena drank it down in one gulp, the way she once saw a man do it at a bar.

—Your friend was also high yesterday.

—And you weren't?

—No. I watch myself at such times.

—Like now?

—Now? (She smiled.) You can pour me another.

Otávio served her another whiskey and himself a beer. Marília arrived with her suitcase; opened the front door with her key; found the glasses, purse, blouse, cigarette butts; heard suspect noises in the bedroom. She felt indignant, took her suitcase to leave again, went as far as the door, came back again, shut off the light, lay down on the sofa, and went to sleep; in order to recover finally from the six orgasms with Marcelo and the fights with her parents. Lena drank another like the man at the bar, while Otávio eyed her with patient desire.

—Know something, Lena, I've been sitting here thinking about this whole day, this whole mess. For me, it makes a certain sense: in a way it's a new opportunity, you know? Suppose we try and begin again—calm down, it's only a hypothesis—begin again with you, leave the department. Hell, I knew that returning those refugees wasn't going to solve the problem, but I still expedited the transfers, I still asked for police reinforcements. But that's over with now, for me.

—Someone else will do it in your place, that's all.

—I know, obviously they will. But not me. I'm actually going to be allowed to give my own opinion next time something like that occurs, or even write an article.

—Right. I'm sure you will.

Why the sarcasm, Otávio wondered? Marília didn't awaken when a nude Otávio turned on the living room light, leaned over to reach for his cigarettes on the arm of the sofa, and saw her and was terrified—and felt his new life was certainly about to be destroyed on the very first day. Lena asked him for another whiskey and warned him:

—Today, I'm going to get blasted, even if I didn't do it yesterday.

—And other things too that you didn't do yesterday?

Lena smiled, drank, got serious.

—She's a lot more beautiful than I am.

—Her body? No.

—Really?

—You're firmer.

Lena got up, decisively.

—Let's go to bed.


## Carlos Bicalho.
## Page 121

December 31, 1979.

—Beautiful?

—She had a lovely body. Must still be, even now. Shit, let's talk about something else.

A long pause.

—Remember the end of the '60's?

—Not much. What about it?

—Shit, up here in Recife . . . I was still a boy, in ROTC. Had a wild time of it, son of a bitch. For me, politics didn't even exist then.

—Certain things bothered me, the student type of thing. It was a heavy situation for some people in those days. Sabotage, war. Me, I didn't go in for that.

—Were you married already?

—Even had a kid, a little girl. And another one on the way.

—Two?

—She died, stillborn. I was in jail at the time, Juiz de Fora.

—That business of the refugees, wasn't it?

—Right.

The Mineiran, from Belo Horizonte, slowly felt out the possibility of a personal conversation, sentimental, nostalgic—not even caring if he ended up crying a little. That's why he took that long pause when he realized they were beginning to turn to politics. He kept thinking about his family, wanting the Pernambucan from right there in Recife to ask him: and your family? The Pernambucan sipped a little of his beer. The Mineiran understood that his family would end up rising out of the past to sit there at the table with him at that bar in Recife. So he continued:

—They talked about it here?

—Damn straight. All over the Northeast, I figure. I still remember; I was a young boy at the time but I still remember. It was one hell of a mess, wasn't it? A real federal case.

—That's right.

The Mineiran escaped again to the past. What must have happened to those people from back in 1970?

—I think I was the one who got fucked the most by that whole mess.

—What do you mean? Some people died, didn't they?

—The dead are dead. Getting fucked has to do with jail, school, family. I wanted to study economics back then, do research, get a doctorate. I fucked it all. Or it fucked me.

—Just you?

—In a way. I was the sacrificial lamb in the group. I mean, lots of them were involved in the investigations; they wound up in the can for two or three days; nothing was proven against them, and they let it go at that. My group—that is, our group—began to take shape around '67, and became a consolidated force in '68. A hell of a lot of confusion going on that year; when the whole fucking business first began anyway. Of those of us in the School of Economics I was the only one with a certain political commitment. I'm not saying I was a leader, an organizer; nothing like that. I just joined in; you know how it is with students; so I participated. Then in '68, I think I was in my second year, I got a month in the can for attending a Congress of the National Student Union in São Paulo, even though it was banned. So I already had a label in Belo Horizonte, which affected the way I was eventually treated by the police in '70.

—You were the only one from your group to go to that congress?

—Mmm. Today, I see it was actually my role in the group. People said: those kids working on the supplement staff have definite leftist leanings, when the truth was that those people working on the supplement had no leanings whatsoever, it was just because I'd been jailed in Ibiúna, at the congress, you see? The whole group was just incorporating my own political image in '68, in '70, and in the interval as well. So much so, that their whole literary output amounted to a couple of linguistical studies, lots of abstract bullshit, and not much else that I can see. To this day I don't think they've come up with any great shakes.

—And you?

—Me? I wrote some off-the-wall poetry that belonged way back in another generation. My own generation had established itself at the end of the '60s, and here I was busy imitating work that had been done in the '50s and even earlier. In that respect my time in the can was a good thing: it relieved the country of one more bad poet.

The Mineiran kept thinking about that poetry, how much he had liked to write it. Rhymes of artillery with liberty, hunger and warmonger, revolution and solution. He drank a little more of his beer, which was already getting kind of warm. Maybe he was talking too much, boring the Pernambucan sitting there with him. They ordered another round of beers. Almost midnight now: the passing of another decade, the fireworks, the disconcerting joy of other people's celebrations. The Pernambucan looked up:

—And what happened to those people?

—Don't really know. I lost all contact. They must be there though, still working. Who knows? As I say, I lost contact. When I got out of prison we had nothing left in common, so I didn't bother with them. Once in a while I still run into one or two of them; by chance, that's all. What the hell, it's been six years since I left Belo Horizonte.

—Ever finish your degree?

—They didn't let me. Decree 477. I couldn't even find a job. I went to court, naturally. It just sat at a complete standstill for two years, you know how the courts work. So, I went off to São Paulo. Couldn't study there either; they wouldn't let me transfer.

—Family and all?

—No, no way. I didn't even have a job. The family stayed in Minas with the in-laws, waiting for the situation to improve. I sold books, collections, encyclo-pedias, the same as I'd done in Belo Horizonte. I got to walking crooked from the weight of the suitcase, and my hands were all covered with calluses. Then I started drinking like a fish, became a lush, wandered around with no work, living like garbage. It was the worst period in that entire ten years, including jail. Finally, after almost five years, my wife got fed up with all the hassle I'd caused her. She went and got a divorce, found somebody else, and that was that.

He cut it short because he had ended up a little weepy-eyed after all.

—I was just about a total loss there in São Paulo, when I met up with some old friends from my student days and began to get myself together again, began to understand some things a little better, setting aside my personal hang-ups, analyzing my situation a little more closely, politicizing myself. Well, they fi-nally arranged some work for me. And so now, here I am: almost five long years in this political struggle.

—I think you'll like the Northeast.

—Yes, I think I might. But even if I don't . . .

—Right, a job is a job.

They began to hear them setting off the first of the fireworks. The Mineiran lifted his glass, the Pernambucan lifted his, they touched.

—Shit, been a long time since I saw my daughter, a long time. . . .

The Mineiran was melancholic, with his eyes a little moist.


## The editor in chief, Haroldo.
## Page 124

Who spread the story of Samuel's diary about Andrea? How was it that a fact known only to the police, to a woman interested in keeping it a secret, and to a dead reporter could become a subject for barroom conversations, for offices, teas, and masturbations? How can pusillanimity come to be envied? Yet, to the extent that the story became known, Haroldo—the man who had discovered the mole on the right side of Andrea's clitoris—was alternately envied, hated, sought after, and even seduced by frustrated ladies in heated telephone conversations.


## The man, a mulatto. Ataíde.
## Page 125

Ataíde shed the first of his four fears the day following his return from prison. Cremilda denied everything, that any investigator had ever touched her; no, it must have been some trick of theirs. Because, as she explained, she'd spent those forty days desperately searching here and there, trying to find out where he might have been imprisoned, but not even that much information would they have the decency to provide her with. So she went to the morgue, the first-aid stations, all the hospitals, all the police stations, the DOPS (he interrupted: what they told you there? She: that you weren't there; that you had probably just split; that lots of women's husbands leave them; and then who do the wives come running to?—all sorts of things like that), army posts; she said she went everywhere, wherever they were holding any of the wounded or arrested picked up in the disturbance at the station.

The second fear took a lot longer for Ataíde to conquer. The doctors told him his hand would no longer be of any use, with the ligaments torn, the bones smashed and already reset in that position; nothing could be done. The fear of being unable to work was ultimately vanquished only when Ataíde learned to paint left-handed. At first he was desperate; he fumed with hatred, kicked the roller; but finally managed to paint almost as quickly, almost as carefully, almost as finely as with his right hand.

The third fear, his intimacies as a cripple with his lovely Cremilda, he never overcame. Because they never got used to it, either one of them—to that cold hand. He avoided touching Cremilda with that hand. He even discovered a trick: he wrapped the hand under the sheet when he was on top of it. But the beginning of any intimacy at all remained difficult: embracing each other, helping her take off her underwear—he had always liked to help; enjoyed so much seeing the hairs begin to appear. But he lost all pleasure. Before, they used to have sex as much as five times a week. Now: twice, once . . .

Hatred, his fourth fear, led him to plan the following crime with the utmost care: advise all his friends and neighbors that he and his wife were moving to São Paulo; sell the furniture, the TV, everything, and make the trip; return several months later, secretly, with his wife, on the bus that normally arrives at seven in the morning; check advertisements for houses to let; and Cremilda would ask for the key, to see if the place might possibly work out for them (it shouldn't be furnished, or they would demand some identification before handing over the key); then Cremilda would lure the investigator known as the Cockroach to the house, where Ataíde would already be hidden, just waiting; waiting for them to take off their clothes and scatter them around the house; waiting for him to leave his revolver somewhere; waiting for her to lie with him on the floor in the bedroom, as if to fornicate; then tiptoe closer, in his bare feet, and put a revolver to his head; let him see who was going to kill him; hand the revolver to his wife, Cremilda, and drive the knife into his body as many times as was needed; wipe away all the fingerprints, leaving only the panties; make it look like a crime of passion; take the bus back to São Paulo, get there by morning, work like every other day, try to forget it all.

Perfect. But why did Cremilda want to be the one to use the knife?

It was almost a year later when Roberto cleared up the mystery of the pornographic diary that belonged to Samuel—Samuel: taken in '71 as a one-time subversive (by the police); as a sexual pervert (by mothers of susceptible daughters); and as a troublesome hero, an accusation, a symbol—a lesson lost which left them silent for many years, humiliated (by all the young intellectuals who had once known him and treated him, in those days, with condescension).

The truth had not surfaced before that because, as everybody already knows, Roberto did not figure in the actual investigation. So on the eve of yet another party, this time his thirtieth birthday, Roberto felt tenderhearted—he was tanked—and talkative, unable to resist the temptation to finally tattle:

—It was a novel. I read a few sections, they were good. Samuel was trying to extend the methodology of *cinema verité* and the experience of Truman Capote with *In Cold Blood*. It was to have been a documentary novel. He said he was aiming at a blend of straightforward reportage with the specificity of a Michel Butor, even incorporating certain techniques of the *école du regard*. In his case, I think it was more the technique *du voyeur*—no malevolence intended, hmm, people? He wanted to capture the total life of the person: details, appearances, intimacies, illusions, facts, lies—the whole truth. He chose Andrea for a protagonist—a marvelous choice, of course. Only *I* could have been better. Any information about Andrea was immediately noted, checked out, investigated, verified. If he hadn't been killed, I think he would have gone mad. He even paid the doorman from her building to provide reports on her. And he followed her in the street, without being seen, of course. I related quite a few things myself to him, even certain intimacies. I did a biography of her for him that would have made a marvelous story. Marvelous. . . . He annotated everything, all the clothes she used, how she coordinated her outfits during the week, her jewelry. Such and such a necklace she only used with such and such a blouse, such and such a skirt on the days she wore her hair up—things like that, minutiae. That's why I said *voyeur*, it really was without malevolence. Each detail he would uncover, of course, expanded the project: he wanted to exhaust Andrea. She really does possess something in the way of literary character, there's an aura of the silver screen about her, I don't know. . . . I really pine for her, you know? I even got up the courage to phone her in Rio, to invite her to the party. She wouldn't get on the phone, but I left her the message. Well, anyway, getting back to the story. It was at this point that Haroldo from the *Correio de Minas* also enters the picture, another Mr. Protagonist. And a royal bastard, to boot. The part of the novel that the police got hold of is the part related by Haroldo Protagonist to Samuel the Author, in the first person. I think that's where the confusion arose. Now: I don't know why it was that he actually told all those things to Samuel, or if perhaps he didn't even realize that it was a novel the other was writing. Right: I know people who have already asked him that, if he knew what Samuel planned to do with the material, and he said no. Personally, I think the S.O.B. probably talked about it to make the kid envious. Sick! Now: I don't know if the intimate details in the story are true, that business of the mole on her box, for instance. If it was a lie, it was Haroldo's, because Samuel refused to invent anything, and he was doing an incredibly rigorous job with the whole project. Only, the work began to bog down somewhat, just before he died, because he'd reached a point where the collaboration of Andrea was indispensable, and Samuel didn't have the nerve to approach her. I think at that point he was also in love with her. . . .

**The refugee, Viriato.**
**Page 129**

After the year 1970, which became known as the year of "Misfortune," and much better known by that than by its real name—1970—the inhabitants of Curralin'u, in the backlands of Alagoas, emigrated no more to the South. Seventeen families from Curralin'u had made the trip, in March of that year Misfortune, all the way to Belo Horizonte or, in the opinion of most, Belerizonte. Only seven families returned that following August with Viriato: ten entire families were lost, plus another thirteen people from the families that did make it back including the wife of Viriato—the one who would eventually tell the story of their diaspora, misfortune, and return. Of the thirteen missing, nine were children, one was an old woman of thirty, one a young boy, and two more were heads of families.

The story told by Viriato, repeated over the years, became the single, incomprehensible truth of Curralin'u. Some ten to fifteen years later, the story was incomprehensible even for Viriato, who kept adding stray words here and there, picked up perhaps from other members of the long migration who wouldn't dare or hadn't the gift for good narration.

If one were to try and put together what Viriato would be narrating in Curralin'u, by 1985, the story would sound more or less like this:

"God had ceased helping the backlander and Beelzebub had come up from Hell to take advantage of the fact, and dry with his mighty heat the lands he spat with fire. After two years of living in Satan's domain, seventeen families from Curralin'u had decided to vacate the premises, no questions asked. For several days they walked, and everywhere they went they came across the mark of the Infernal Unmentionable: No trespassing!—he owned everything in sight. In Cabrobó they met up with thirty-two families who were going to join a man named Marcionílio in Juazeiro. From there, they would likely head south. That made forty-nine families. In Juazeiro, they met up with the so-called Marcionílio, with his employment permit for pickers needed in Minas Gerais. No one as yet comprehended the fact that the man was Beelzebub himself. Could be that sometimes the Devil stepped out of him, for relaxation, and then God took charge, because he made meat and flour come out of empty knapsacks, made milk appear in water bottles, made a dying child walk. Or maybe Beelzebub too knows how to work miracles, and Marcionílio was Him the whole time without resting.

"Everyone believed they knew where it was this Asmodeus was leading the great exodus: Belerizonte. But how is it that the journey took close to a month, till near the end of March? Anybody knows that from Juazeiro to Belerizonte is no more than three days; with stopping . . . maybe a week? Trains and trucks were purposefully stalled along the way, with two hundred families, so a city identical to Belerizonte could be built in some foreign land. What took the most trouble was making the Park, but for that Lucifer himself rose out of Marcionílio, went there to resolve the matter and returned, without losing his place.

"No sooner arrived, their misfortune began. They were rounded up and beaten by Marcionílio's henchmen, soldiers of Satan with helmets known as MP's. And so there they sat, locked up for three entire days, no food, waiting for the train to come and carry them, still living flesh, straight down to Hell. Strangers come from many leagues around the city to have a look at the Northeasterner Brazilians, corralled like pigs at a circus. The strangers spoke the Brazilian tongue, as if they had spent many years practicing, but the trick could still be ascertained in certain of their words and the curious pronunciation. Police called *dopses.* And soon, children and grandparents died there, trapped like cattle. There were cries and lamentations, prayers and curses— such a terrible sound that the people of the city could no longer sleep and covered their heads with pillows; at ten leagues could be heard the wailings of consternation. Then the government, with its ears aching, ordered an end to the Devil's purpose and permitted the families to return to the backlands. But now the Satan within Marcionílio raged so hot with hatred that he burned the bench where he sat and the floors where he stood, so the train went up in flames. A terrible fire! The families fled the train; the shots; the horses, trucks, and sirens. Many deaths! . . . From Curralin'u, five families who had huddled together for protection got locked away in the *dopses.* Finally it was proven that Marcionílio was the communist Asmodeus and the *dopses* hunted down all his accomplices among the prisoners. Many were beaten, because these *dopses* are identical to the police themselves, and some of those caught even vanished, but there was food for everybody—two times a day they could eat there! In among the prisoners collected day after day were two more families from Curralin'u which finally and all together managed to get to return to the backlands. In the month of June, missing thirteen people from seven families, everybody alive was taken to a farm the property of the government down there in Minas, and told to pick potatoes and cut wheat while the government watched you with their guns and ammunition. That was how you paid for all the meals you got in prison, and justly so. So all of us picked the harvest, way into the middle of August, until we got put on another train heading back up northeast— and were told in no uncertain terms never to come back south that way to Minas Gerais again. Marcionílio? They say he clean evaporated from the prison yard one day in a cloud of black smoke, like Beelzebub himself!"


**Andrea.**
**Page 131**

Andrea died of pneumonia in 1997, lamenting only not being able to realize the one great dream of her old age: to witness the passing of the century. In spite of the fact that epitaphs were completely out of fashion, her wishes were respected: "Forget us not, we of the XXth century"—says the inscription on her tomb.

**Marcionílio de Mattos.**
**Page 132**

*PEASANT LEADER KILLED*
*IN ESCAPE ATTEMPT*

*The peasant leader and ex-outlaw Marcionílio de Mattos was killed yesterday in a shoot-out with security agents after having attempted a spectacular prison break from the headquarters of the DOPS here.*

*De Mattos, the frustrated peasant leader who, three months ago, attempted to extend his campaign of rural subversion to the city—by leading a veritable regiment of migrants closely aligned with extremists here in the capital—yesterday seized a police officer's gun, immobilized a guard, fled from the DOPS headquarters, and ran down Avenida Afonso Pena while firing back at his pursuers. A shot from one of the agents who was chasing him struck the subversive in the head, whereupon he fell lifeless.*

This press note was distributed by the federal police to all the newspapers in the city and the branch offices of those in Rio and São Paulo on the sixth of June 1970 with the recommendation not to give it undue publicity in their papers. *O Estado de Minas Gerais* made a slight alteration at the beginning of the release, adding: "According to the information of security officers." And the *Correio de Minas Gerais* changed, in the last line, the expression "the subversive" to the name of de Mattos.

**Roberto.**
**Page 134**

A gang of thirty youths armed with long wooden sticks suddenly crashed Roberto's birthday party in 1971. The door opened with a splintering thud and the youths, with their hair cropped and wearing civilian clothes, entered on the run, yelling, beating, trampling. Excited by the panic they were producing they began to tear the clothes off the women present while shouting old-bag whore cunt. They broke into all the bathrooms, frightening one poor girl into a dead faint. Then proceeded to smash the hi-fi, TV, records, glasses, mirrors, sculptures, paintings, antiques, furniture, toilets, bidets, perfume bottles, liquor cabinets, knickknacks, plates, heads, stomachs, hands, feet. They tore up books, clothes, window curtains. Anyone who attempted to escape ran the human gauntlet blocking the doorway. Roberto himself was already bleeding profusely from the going-over inflicted with occasional rhetorical flourishes of: "Think you can just go right ahead and corrupt the whole city? Think you can get away with it! Eh, faggot? Do you! Do you!" Faggot commie whore cunt were the punitive cries of exultation. Then quite suddenly, when a whistle was blown, the invaders let go of their victims and exited immediately: orderly, swift, powerful. An end to the celebration.

# SELECTED DALKEY ARCHIVE PAPERBACKS

PIERRE ALBERT-BIROT, *Grabinoulor.*
YUZ ALESHKOVSKY, *Kangaroo.*
FELIPE ALFAU, *Chromos.*
  *Locos.*
  *Sentimental Songs.*
IVAN ÂNGELO, *The Celebration.*
ALAN ANSEN, *Contact Highs: Selected Poems 1957-1987.*
DAVID ANTIN, *Talking.*
DJUNA BARNES, *Ladies Almanack.*
  *Ryder.*
JOHN BARTH, *LETTERS.*
  *Sabbatical.*
ANDREI BITOV, *Pushkin House.*
LOUIS PAUL BOON, *Chapel Road.*
ROGER BOYLAN, *Killoyle.*
CHRISTINE BROOKE-ROSE, *Amalgamemnon.*
BRIGID BROPHY, *In Transit.*
GERALD L. BRUNS,
  *Modern Poetry and the Idea of Language.*
GABRIELLE BURTON, *Heartbreak Hotel.*
MICHEL BUTOR,
  *Portrait of the Artist as a Young Ape.*
JULIETA CAMPOS, *The Fear of Losing Eurydice.*
ANNE CARSON, *Eros the Bittersweet.*
CAMILO JOSÉ CELA, *The Hive.*
LOUIS-FERDINAND CÉLINE, *Castle to Castle.*
  *London Bridge.*
  *North.*
  *Rigadoon.*
HUGO CHARTERIS, *The Tide Is Right.*
JEROME CHARYN, *The Tar Baby.*
MARC CHOLODENKO, *Mordechai Schamz.*
EMILY HOLMES COLEMAN, *The Shutter of Snow.*
ROBERT COOVER, *A Night at the Movies.*
STANLEY CRAWFORD, *Some Instructions to My Wife.*
ROBERT CREELEY, *Collected Prose.*
RENÉ CREVEL, *Putting My Foot in It.*
RALPH CUSACK, *Cadenza.*
SUSAN DAITCH, *L.C.*
  *Storytown.*
NIGEL DENNIS, *Cards of Identity.*
PETER DIMOCK,
  *A Short Rhetoric for Leaving the Family.*
ARIEL DORFMAN, *Konfidenz.*
COLEMAN DOWELL, *The Houses of Children.*
  *Island People.*
  *Too Much Flesh and Jabez.*
RIKKI DUCORNET, *The Complete Butcher's Tales.*
  *The Fountains of Neptune.*
  *The Jade Cabinet.*
  *Phosphor in Dreamland.*
  *The Stain.*
WILLIAM EASTLAKE, *The Bamboo Bed.*
  *Castle Keep.*
  *Lyric of the Circle Heart.*
STANLEY ELKIN, *Boswell: A Modern Comedy.*
  *Criers and Kibitzers, Kibitzers and Criers.*
  *The Dick Gibson Show.*
  *The Franchiser.*

  *George Mills.*
  *The MacGuffin.*
  *The Magic Kingdom.*
  *Mrs. Ted Bliss.*
  *The Rabbi of Lud.*
  *Van Gogh's Room at Arles.*
ANNIE ERNAUX, *Cleaned Out.*
LAUREN FAIRBANKS, *Muzzle Thyself.*
  *Sister Carrie.*
LESLIE A. FIEDLER,
  *Love and Death in the American Novel.*
FORD MADOX FORD, *The March of Literature.*
CARLOS FUENTES, *Terra Nostra.*
JANICE GALLOWAY, *Foreign Parts.*
  *The Trick Is to Keep Breathing.*
WILLIAM H. GASS, *The Tunnel.*
  *Willie Masters' Lonesome Wife.*
ETIENNE GILSON, *The Arts of the Beautiful.*
  *Forms and Substances in the Arts.*
C. S. GISCOMBE, *Giscome Road.*
  *Here.*
DOUGLAS GLOVER, *Bad News of the Heart.*
KAREN ELIZABETH GORDON, *The Red Shoes.*
PATRICK GRAINVILLE, *The Cave of Heaven.*
HENRY GREEN, *Blindness.*
  *Concluding.*
  *Doting.*
  *Nothing.*
JIŘÍ GRUŠA, *The Questionnaire.*
JOHN HAWKES, *Whistlejacket.*
AIDAN HIGGINS, *Flotsam and Jetsam.*
ALDOUS HUXLEY, *Antic Hay.*
  *Crome Yellow.*
  *Point Counter Point.*
  *Those Barren Leaves.*
  *Time Must Have a Stop.*
GERT JONKE, *Geometric Regional Novel.*
DANILO KIŠ, *A Tomb for Boris Davidovich.*
TADEUSZ KONWICKI, *A Minor Apocalypse.*
  *The Polish Complex.*
ELAINE KRAF, *The Princess of 72nd Street.*
JIM KRUSOE, *Iceland.*
EWA KURYLUK, *Century 21.*
VIOLETTE LEDUC, *La Bâtarde.*
DEBORAH LEVY, *Billy and Girl.*
JOSÉ LEZAMA LIMA, *Paradiso.*
OSMAN LINS, *Avalovara.*
  *The Queen of the Prisons of Greece.*
ALF MAC LOCHLAINN, *The Corpus in the Library.*
  *Out of Focus.*
RON LOEWINSOHN, *Magnetic Field(s).*
D. KEITH MANO, *Take Five.*
BEN MARCUS, *The Age of Wire and String.*
WALLACE MARKFIELD, *Teitlebaum's Window.*
  *To an Early Grave.*
DAVID MARKSON, *Reader's Block.*
  *Springer's Progress.*
  *Wittgenstein's Mistress.*

# FOR A FULL LIST OF PUBLICATIONS, VISIT:
## www.dalkeyarchive.com

# SELECTED DALKEY ARCHIVE PAPERBACKS

CAROLE MASO, *AVA*.

LADISLAV MATEJKA AND KRYSTYNA POMORSKA, EDS.,
*Readings in Russian Poetics: Formalist and
Structuralist Views*.

HARRY MATHEWS, *Cigarettes*.
*The Conversions*.
*The Case of the Persevering Maltese: Collected Essays*.
*The Human Country: New and Collected Stories*.
*The Journalist*.
*Singular Pleasures*.
*The Sinking of the Odradek Stadium*.
*Tlooth*.
*20 Lines a Day*.

ROBERT L. MCLAUGHLIN, ED.,
*Innovations: An Anthology of Modern &
Contemporary Fiction*.

STEVEN MILLHAUSER, *The Barnum Museum*.
*In the Penny Arcade*.

RALPH J. MILLS, JR., *Essays on Poetry*.

OLIVE MOORE, *Spleen*.

NICHOLAS MOSLEY, *Accident*.
*Assassins*.
*Catastrophe Practice*.
*Children of Darkness and Light*.
*The Hesperides Tree*.
*Hopeful Monsters*.
*Imago Bird*.
*Impossible Object*.
*Inventing God*.
*Judith*.
*Natalie Natalia*.
*Serpent*.

WARREN F. MOTTE, JR.,
*Oulipo: A Primer of Potential Literature*.
*Fables of the Novel: French Fiction since 1990*.

YVES NAVARRE, *Our Share of Time*.

WILFRIDO D. NOLLEDO, *But for the Lovers*.

FLANN O'BRIEN, *At Swim-Two-Birds*.
*The Best of Myles*.
*The Dalkey Archive*.
*Further Cuttings*.
*The Hard Life*.
*The Poor Mouth*.
*The Third Policeman*.

CLAUDE OLLIER, *The Mise-en-Scène*.

FERNANDO DEL PASO, *Palinuro of Mexico*.

RAYMOND QUENEAU, *The Last Days*.
*Odile*.
*Pierrot Mon Ami*.
*Saint Glinglin*.

ANN QUIN, *Berg*.
*Passages*.
*Three*.
*Tripticks*.

ISHMAEL REED, *The Free-Lance Pallbearers*.
*The Last Days of Louisiana Red*.
*Reckless Eyeballing*.
*The Terrible Threes*.

*The Terrible Twos*.
*Yellow Back Radio Broke-Down*.

JULIÁN RÍOS, *Poundemonium*.

AUGUSTO ROA BASTOS, *I the Supreme*.

JACQUES ROUBAUD, *The Great Fire of London*.
*Hortense in Exile*.
*Hortense Is Abducted*.
*The Plurality of Worlds of Lewis*.
*The Princess Hoppy*.
*Some Thing Black*.

LEON S. ROUDIEZ, *French Fiction Revisited*.

LUIS RAFAEL SÁNCHEZ, *Macho Camacho's Beat*.

SEVERO SARDUY, *Cobra & Maitreya*.

ARNO SCHMIDT, *Collected Stories*.
*Nobodaddy's Children*.

CHRISTINE SCHUTT, *Nightwork*.

JUNE AKERS SEESE,
*Is This What Other Women Feel, Too?*
*What Waiting Really Means*.

AURELIE SHEEHAN, *Jack Kerouac Is Pregnant*.

VIKTOR SHKLOVSKY, *Theory of Prose*.
*Third Factory*.
*Zoo, or Letters Not about Love*.

JOSEF ŠKVORECKÝ,
*The Engineer of Human Souls*.

CLAUDE SIMON, *The Invitation*.

GILBERT SORRENTINO, *Aberration of Starlight*.
*Blue Pastoral*.
*Crystal Vision*.
*Imaginative Qualities of Actual Things*.
*Mulligan Stew*.
*Pack of Lies*.
*The Sky Changes*.
*Something Said*.
*Splendide-Hôtel*.
*Steelwork*.
*Under the Shadow*.

W. M. SPACKMAN, *The Complete Fiction*.

GERTRUDE STEIN, *Lucy Church Amiably*.
*The Making of Americans*.
*A Novel of Thank You*.

PIOTR SZEWC, *Annihilation*.

ESTHER TUSQUETS, *Stranded*.

LUISA VALENZUELA, *He Who Searches*.

PAUL WEST, *Words for a Deaf Daughter* and *Gala*.

CURTIS WHITE, *Memories of My Father Watching TV*.
*Monstrous Possibility*.
*Requiem*.

DIANE WILLIAMS, *Excitability: Selected Stories*.
*Romancer Erector*.

DOUGLAS WOOLF, *Wall to Wall*.
*Ya! & John-Juan*.

PHILIP WYLIE, *Generation of Vipers*.

MARGUERITE YOUNG, *Angel in the Forest*.
*Miss MacIntosh, My Darling*.

REYOUNG, *Unbabbling*.

LOUIS ZUKOFSKY, *Collected Fiction*.

SCOTT ZWIREN, *God Head*.

---

# FOR A FULL LIST OF PUBLICATIONS, VISIT:
# www.dalkeyarchive.com